THE MYSTERY OF THE DOWNS

THE MYSTERY OF THE DOWNS

BY

JOHN WATSON

AND

ARTHUR J. REES

CHAPTER I

THE storm had descended swiftly, sweeping in suddenly from the sea, driving across the downs to the hills at high speed, blotting out the faint rays of a crescent moon and hiding the country-side beneath a pall of blackness, which was forked at intervals by flashes of lightning.

The darkness was so impenetrable, and the fury of the storm so fierce, that Harry Marsland pulled his hat well over his eyes and bent over his horse's neck to shield his face from the driving rain, trusting to the animal's sagacity and sure-footedness to take him safely down the cliff road in the darkness, where a slip might plunge them into the breakers which he could hear roaring at the foot of the cliffs.

Hardly had Marsland done so when his horse swerved violently right across the road—fortunately to the side opposite the edge of the cliffs—slipped and almost fell, but recovered itself and then stood still, snorting and trembling with fear.

He patted and spoke to the horse, wondering what had frightened it. He had seen or heard nothing, but the darkness of the night and the roar of the gale would have prevented him, even if his face had not been almost buried in his horse's neck. However, the rain, beating with sharp persistence on his face and through his clothes, reminded him that he was some

7

miles from shelter on a lonely country road, with only a vague idea of his whereabouts. So, with a few more soothing words, he urged his horse onward again. The animal responded willingly enough, but as soon as it moved Marsland discovered to his dismay that it was lame in the off hind leg. The rider was quick to realize that it must have sprained itself in swerving.

He slipped out of the saddle and endeavoured to feel the extent of the horse's injury, but the animal had not entirely recovered from its fright, and snorted as his master touched it. Marsland desisted, and gently pulled at the bridle.

The horse struggled onwards a few paces, but it was badly lamed, and could not be ridden. It thrust a timid muzzle against its master's breast, as though seeking refuge from its fears and the fury of the storm. Marsland patted its head caressingly, and, facing the unpleasant fact that he was on an unknown lonely road with a lame horse in the worst storm he had ever seen, drew the bridle over his arm and started to walk forward.

He found it difficult to make progress in the teeth of the gale, but he realized that it would be useless to retrace his steps with the wind at his back, for only the bleak bare downs he had ridden over that afternoon lay behind, and the only house he had seen was a shepherd's cottage on the hill-side where he had stopped to inquire his way before the storm came on. There was nothing to be done but face the gale and go forward, following the cliff road which skirted the downs, or to seek shelter for himself and his horse at the way-side house until the fury of the storm had abated. Prudence and consideration for his horse dictated the latter course, but in the blackness of the night—which hung before him like a cloud—he was unable to discern a twinkle of light denoting human habitation.

The storm seemed to gather fresh force, rushing in from the sea with such fury that Marsland was compelled to stand still and seek shelter beside his horse. As he stood thus, waiting for it to abate, a vivid flash of lightning ran across the western sky, revealing lividly the storm clouds flying through the heavens, the mountainous yellow-crested sea, and the desolate, rain-beaten downs; but it revealed, also, a farm-house standing in the valley below, a little way back from the road which wound down towards it from where Marsland stood.

The lightning died away, the scene it had illumined disappeared, and a clap of thunder followed. Marsland heaved a sigh of relief. He judged that the house was less than half a mile down the hill, a large, gaunt, three-storied stone building, with steeply sloping roof, standing back from the road, with a barn beside it. Doubtless it was the home of a sheep-farmer of the downs, who would at any rate afford shelter to himself and his horse till the violence of the storm had passed.

The horse responded to an encouraging appeal as though it fully understood, and Marsland doggedly resumed his battle with the storm. The road slanted away slightly from the cliff when horse and rider had covered another hundred yards, and wound through a long cutting on the hill which afforded some protection from the gale, enabling them to make quicker progress. But still Marsland could not see a yard in front of him. Even if his eyes had become accustomed to the darkness, the heavy rain, beating almost horizontally on his face, would have prevented him seeing anything.

He had matches in his pocket, but it was useless to attempt to strike them in such a wind, and he reproached himself for having come away without his electric torch. Slowly and cautiously he made his way down the road, feeling his footsteps as he went, the tired horse following obediently. The cutting seemed a long one, but at length a sudden blast of wind, roaring in from the sea, told him that he had emerged into the open again. He counted off another hundred paces, then paused anxiously.

"The house ought to be somewhere on the left down there," he muttered, staring blindly into the dark.

He wondered in an irritated fashion why there were no lights showing from the farm-house, which he felt must be very close to where he stood. But he recollected that farmers kept early hours, and he realized that the occupants of the house might well be excused for going to bed on such a night even earlier than usual.

As though in answer to an unspoken wish, a flash of lightning played over the sky. It was faint and fitful, but it was sufficient to reveal the farm standing a little way ahead, about a hundred yards back from the road. He saw clearly the hedge which divided its meadows from the road, and noted that a gate leading into a wagon drive on the side of the meadow nearest him had been flung open by the force of the gale, and was swinging loosely on its hinges.

"They'll thank me for closing that gate if they've got any stock in the meadows," said Marsland.

The swinging white gate was faintly visible in the darkness when Marsland came close to it, and he turned into the open drive. He noticed as he walked along that the gale was not so severely felt inside as out on the road, and he came to the conclusion that the farm was in a more sheltered part of the downs—was probably shielded from the wind by the hill through which the cutting ran.

He reflected that it was a good idea to build in a sheltered spot when farming on low downs facing the English Channel. He was glad to be able to walk upright, with the wind behind him and the rain on his back instead of beating on his face. For one thing, he found he was able to make some use of his eyes in spite of the darkness, and soon he discerned the house looming bleakly ahead of him, with the barn alongside.

As Marsland passed the barn, his horse surprised him by whinnying sharply and plucking the loose bridle from his arm. He felt for his matchbox and hastily struck a match. The wind extinguished it, but not before its brief splutter of light showed him the horse disappearing through an open doorway.

He followed it and struck another match. It flared up steadily under cover, and he saw that he was in a small storehouse attached to the barn. Gardening tools were neatly piled in one corner, and in another were a stack of potatoes and some bags of grain. His horse was plucking ravenously at one of the bags. By the light of another match Marsland espied an old lantern hanging on a nail above the tools.

He took it from the nail, and found that it contained a short end of candle—a sight which filled him with pleasure.

He found a tin dish on top of the cornstack, opened one of the bags, poured a measure of oats into it, and set it before his horse. The animal eagerly thrust his nose into the dish and commenced to eat. Marsland patted its wet flank, and then examined the injured leg by the light of the lantern. His examination failed to reveal any specific injury beyond a slight swelling, though the horse winced restively as he touched it.

Marsland left the horse munching contentedly at its food, shut the door of the storehouse to prevent the animal wandering away, and set out for the house. The light of the lantern showed him a path branching off the drive. He followed it till the outline of the house loomed before him out of the darkness.

The path led across the front of the house, but Marsland looked in vain for a ray of light in the upper stories which would indicate that one of the inmates was awake. He walked on till the path turned abruptly into a large porch, and he knew he had reached the front door. Instead of knocking, he walked past the porch in order to see if there was any light visible on the far side of the house. It was with pleasure that he observed a light glimmering through the second window on the ground floor. Judging by the position of the window, it belonged to the room immediately behind the front room on the right side of the house.

Marsland returned to the porch and vigorously plied the knocker on the door, so that the sound should be heard above the storm. He listened anxiously for approaching footsteps of heavily-shod feet, but the first sound he heard was that of the bolt being drawn back.

"Where have you been?" exclaimed a feminine voice. "I have been wondering what could have happened to you."

The girl who had opened the door to him had a candle in her hand. As she spoke, she shielded the light with her other hand and lifted it to his face. She uttered a startled exclamation.

"I beg your pardon," said Marsland, in an ingratiating tone. "I have lost my way and my horse has gone lame. I have taken the liberty of putting him in the outbuildings before coming to ask you for shelter from the storm."

"To ask me?" she repeated. "Oh, of course. Please come in."

Marsland closed the door and followed her into the dark and silent hall. She led the way into the room where he had seen the light, placed the candle on the table, and retreated to a chair which was in the shadow. It occurred to him that she was anxious to study him without being exposed to his scrutiny. But he had noticed that she was wearing a hat and a dark cloak. These things suggested to him that she had been on the point of going out when the storm came on. The mistaken way in which she had greeted him on opening the door seemed to show that she had been waiting for some one who was to have accompanied her. Apparently she was alone in the house when he had knocked.

"I am sorry to have intruded on you in this unceremonious way," he said, reviving his apology with the object of enabling her to dismiss any fears at her own unprotected state. "I am completely lost, and when I saw this house I thought the best thing I could do was to seek shelter."

"You are not intruding upon me," she said coldly. "The house is not mine—I do not live here. I saw the storm coming on, and, like you, I thought it was a good idea to seek shelter."

It was apparent to him that her greeting had been intended for some one who had accompanied her to the house and had gone to one of the farm buildings for some purpose. He noted that her manner of speaking was that of a well-bred young lady rather than of a farmer's daughter.

The room in which they were sitting was evidently used as a parlour, and was sombrely furnished in an old-fashioned way. There was a horsehair suite, and in the middle of the room a large round table. Glancing about him into the dark corners of the room which the feeble light of the candle barely reached, Marsland noticed in one of them a large lamp standing on a small table.

"That will give us a better light," he said; "providing, of course, it has some oil in it."

He lifted the lamp to the centre table, and found it was nearly full of oil. He lit it, and it sent out a strong light, which was, however, confined to a radius of a few feet by a heavy lampshade. He glanced at the girl. She had extinguished her candle, and her face remained obstinately in shadow.

He sat down on one of the horsehair chairs; but his companion remained standing a little distance away.

They waited in silence thus for some minutes. Marsland tried to think of something to say, but there was a pensive aloofness about the girl's attitude which deterred him from attempting to open a conversation with a conventional remark about the violence of the storm. He listened for a knock at the front door which would tell him that her companion had returned, but to his surprise the minutes passed without any sign. He thought of asking her to sit down, but he reflected that such an invitation might savour of impertinence. He could dimly see the outline of her profile, and judged her to be young and pretty. Once he thought she glanced in his direction, but when he looked towards her she had her face still turned towards the door. Finally he made another effort to break down the barrier of silence between them.

"I suppose we must wait here until the storm has cleared away," he began. "It is a coincidence that both of us should have sought shelter in this empty house in the storm—I assume the house is empty for the time being or we would have heard from the inmates. My name is Marsland. I have been staying at Staveley, and I lost my way when out riding this afternoon—the downs seem endless. Perhaps you belong to the neighbourhood and know them thoroughly."

But instead of replying she made a swift step towards the door.

"Listen!" she cried. "What was that?"

He stood up also, and listened intently, but the only sounds that met his ears were the beating of the rain against the windows and the wind whistling mournfully round the old house.

"I hear nothing——" he commenced.

But she interrupted him imperatively.

"Hush!" she cried. "Listen!" Her face was still turned away from him, but she held out a hand in his direction as though to enjoin silence.

They stood in silence, both listening intently. Somewhere a board creaked, and Marsland could hear the wind blowing, but that was all.

"I do not think it was anything," he said reassuringly. "These old houses have a way of creaking and groaning in a gale. You have become nervous through sitting here by yourself."

"Perhaps that is so," she assented, in a friendlier tone than she had hitherto used. "But I thought— in fact, I felt—that somebody was moving about stealthily overhead."

"It was the wind sighing about the house," he said, sitting down again.

As he spoke, there was a loud crash in a room above—a noise as though china or glass had been broken. Marsland sprang to his feet.

"There *is* somebody in the house," he exclaimed.

"Who can it be?" she whispered.

"Probably some one who has more right here than we have," said Marsland soothingly. "He'll come downstairs and then we'll have to explain our presence here."

"The man who lives here is away," she replied, in a hushed tone of terror. "He lives here alone. If there is anybody in the house, it is some one who has no right here."

"If you are sure of that," said Marsland slowly, "I will go and see what has happened in the room above.

The wind may have knocked something over. Will you stay here until I return?"

"No, no!" she cried, "I am too frightened now. I will go with you!"

He felt her hand on his sleeve as she spoke.

"In that case we may as well take this lamp," he said. "It will give more light than this." He put down his lantern and picked up the lamp from the table. "Come along, and see what havoc the wind has been playing with the furniture upstairs."

He led the way out of the room, carefully carrying the lamp, and the girl followed. They turned up the hall to the staircase. As the light of the lamp fell on the staircase they saw a piece of paper lying on one of the lower stairs. Marsland picked it up and was so mystified at what he saw on it that he placed the lamp on a stair above in order to study it more closely.

"What can this extraordinary thing mean?" he said to his companion. He put his left hand in the top pocket of his waistcoat, and then exclaimed: "I have lost my glasses; I cannot make this out without them."

She came close to him and looked at the paper.

The sheet was yellow with age, and one side of it was covered with figures and writing. There was a row of letters at the top of the sheet, followed by a circle of numerals, with more numerals in the centre of the circle. Underneath the circle appeared several verses of Scripture written in a small, cramped, but regular handwriting. The ink which had been used in constructing the cryptogram was faded brown with age, but the figures and the writing were clear and legible, and the whole thing bore evidence of patient and careful construction.

C

"This is very strange," she said, in a frightened whisper.

Marsland thought she was referring to the diagrams on the paper.

"It is a mysterious sort of document, whoever owns it," he said. "I think I'll put it on the table in there and we will study it again when we come down after exploring the other parts of the house."

He picked up the lamp and went back to the room they had left. He deposited the sheet of paper on the table and placed the candlestick on it to keep it from being blown away by the wind.

"Now for the ghosts upstairs," he said cheerfully, as he returned.

He noted with a smile that his companion made a point of keeping behind him in all his movements. When they had climbed the first flight of stairs, they stood for a moment or two on the landing, listening, but could hear no sound.

"Let us try this room first," said Marsland, pointing to a door opposite the landing.

The door was closed but not shut, for it yielded to his touch and swung open, revealing a large bedroom with an old-fashioned fourposter in the corner furthest from the door. Marsland glanced round the room curiously. It was the typical "best bedroom" of an old English farm-house, built more than a hundred years before the present generation came to life, with their modern ideas of fresh air and light and sanitation. The ceiling was so low that Marsland almost touched it with his head as he walked, and the small narrow-paned windows, closely shuttered from with-

out, looked as though they had been hermetically sealed
for centuries.

The room contained furniture as ancient as its surroundings: quaint old chests of drawers, bureaux,
clothes-presses, and some old straight-backed oaken
chairs. On the walls were a few musty old books on
shelves, a stuffed pointer in a glass case, a cabinet of
stuffed birds, some dingy hunting prints. The combination of low ceiling, sealed windows, and stuffed
animals created such a vault-like atmosphere that
Marsland marvelled at the hardy constitution of that
dead and gone race of English yeomen who had suffered nightly internment in such chambers and yet
survived to a ripe old age. His eyes wandered to
the fourposter, and he smiled as he noticed that the
heavy curtains were drawn close, as though the last
sleeper in the chamber had dreaded and guarded
against the possibility of some stray shaft of fresh
air eluding the precautions of the builder and finding
its way into the room.

"Nothing here," he said, as he glanced round the
floor of the room for broken pieces of glass or china
ornaments that might have been knocked over by the
wind or by a cat. "Let us try the room opposite."

She was the first to reach the door of the opposite
room to which they turned. It occurred to Marsland
that her fears were wearing off. As he reached the
threshold, he lifted up the lamp above his head so
that its light should fall within.

The room was a bedroom also, deep and narrow
as though it had been squeezed into the house as an
afterthought, with a small, deep-set window high up
in the wall opposite the door. The room was fur-

nished in the old-fashioned style of the room opposite, though more sparsely. But Marsland and the girl were astonished to see a man sitting motionless in a large arm-chair at the far end of the room. His head had fallen forward on his breast as though in slumber, concealing the lower part of his face.

"By heavens, this is extraordinary," said Marsland, in a low hoarse voice. With a trembling hand he placed the lamp on the large table which occupied the centre of the room and stood looking at the man.

The girl crept close to Marsland and clutched his arm.

"It is Frank Lumsden," she whispered quickly. "Do you think there is anything wrong with him? Why doesn't he speak to us?"

"Because he is dead," he answered swiftly.

"Dead!" she exclaimed, in an hysterical tone. "What makes you think so? He may be only in a fit. Oh, what shall we do?"

Marsland pushed her aside and with a firm step walked to the chair on which the motionless figure sat. He touched with his fingers the left hand which rested on the arm of the chair, and turned quickly.

"He is quite dead," he said slowly. "He is beyond all help in this world."

"Dead?" she repeated, retreating to the far end of the table and clasping her trembling hands together. "What a dreadful lonely death."

He was deep in thought and did not respond to her words.

"As we have discovered the body we must inform the police," he said at length.

"I did not know he was ill," she said, in a soft whisper. "He must have died suddenly."

Marsland turned on her a searching questioning look. Her sympathy had conquered her vague fears of the presence of death, and she hesitatingly approached the body. Something on the table near the lamp attracted her attention. It was an open pocket-book and beside it were some papers which had evidently been removed from it.

"What does this mean?" she cried. "Some one has been here."

"It is extraordinary," said Marsland.

He stood between her and the arm-chair so as to hide the dead body from her. She stepped aside as if to seek in the appearance of the dead man an explanation of the rifled pocket-book.

"Don't!" he said quickly, as he grasped her by the arm. "Do not touch it."

His desire to save her from a shock awoke her feminine intuition.

"You mean he has been murdered?" she whispered, in a voice of dismay.

CHAPTER II

SHE hurried from the room in terror. Marsland remained a few minutes examining the papers that had been taken from the pocket-book.

With the lamp in his hand he was compelled to descend cautiously, and when he reached the foot of the staircase the girl had left the house. He extinguished the lamp he was carrying, relit the lantern, and stepped outside. The lantern showed him the girl waiting for him some distance down the path.

"Oh, let us leave this dreadful house," she cried as he approached. "Please take me out of it. I am not frightened of the storm—now."

"I will take you wherever you wish to go," he said gently. "Will you tell me where you live? I will accompany you home."

"You are very good," she said gratefully. "I live at Ashlingsea."

"That is the little fishing village at the end of the cliff road, is it not?" he said inquiringly. "I am staying at Staveley, but I have not been there long. Come, I will take you home, and then I will inform the police about—this tragic discovery."

"There is a police station at Ashlingsea," she said, in a low voice.

He explained to her that he wanted to look after the comfort of his horse before he accompanied her home, as it would be necessary to leave the animal at the farm until the following day. She murmured a faint acquiescence, and when they reached the storehouse she took the lantern from him without speaking, and held it up to give him light while he made his horse comfortable for the night.

They then set out for Ashlingsea. The violence of the storm had passed, but the wind occasionally blew in great gusts from the sea, compelling them to halt in order to stand up against it. The night was still very black, but at intervals a late moon managed to send a watery beam through the scudding storm clouds, revealing the pathway of the winding cliff road, and the turbulent frothing waste of water dashing on the rocks below. Rain continued to fall in heavy frequent showers, but the minds of Marsland and his companion were so occupied with what they had seen in the old farm-house that they were scarcely conscious of the discomfort of getting wet.

The girl was so unnerved by the discovery of the dead body that she was glad to avail herself of the protection and support of Marsland's arm. Several times as she thought she saw a human form in the darkness of the road, she uttered a cry of alarm and clung to his arm with both hands. At every step she expected to encounter a maniac who had the blood of one human creature on his hands and was still swayed by the impulse to kill.

The reserve she had exhibited in the house had broken down, and she talked freely in her desire to shut out from her mental vision the spectacle of the murdered man sitting in the arm-chair.

On the other hand, the discovery of the body had made Marsland reserved and thoughtful.

He learned from her that her name was Maynard—Elsie Maynard—and that she lived with her widowed mother. Marsland was quick to gather from the cultivated accents of her voice that she was a refined and educated girl. He concluded that Mrs. Maynard must be a lady of some social standing in the district, and he judged from what he had seen of the girl's clothes that she was in good circumstances. She remarked that her mother would be anxious about her, but would doubtless assume she had sought shelter somewhere, as having lived in Ashlingsea for a long time she knew everybody in the district.

Marsland thought it strange that she made no reference to the companion who had accompanied her to the farm. If no one accompanied her, how was it that on opening the door to him she had greeted him as some one whom she had been expecting? She seemed unconscious of the need of enlightening him on this point. Her thoughts centred round the dead man to such an extent that her conversation related chiefly to him. Half-unconsciously she revealed that she knew him well, but her acquaintance with him seemed to be largely based on the circumstance that the dead man had been acquainted with a friend of her family: a soldier of the new army, who lived at Staveley.

She had told Marsland that the name of the murdered man was Frank Lumsden, but she did not mention the name of the soldier at Staveley. Lumsden had served in France as a private, but had returned wounded and had been invalided out of the army. He had been captured by the Germans during a night attack, had been shot through the palm of his right hand to prevent him using a rifle again, and had been left behind when the Germans were forced to retreat from the village they had captured. After being invalided out of the Army he had returned home to live in the old farm-house—Cliff Farm it was called—which had been left to him by his grandfather, who had died while the young man was in France. The old man had lived in a state of terror during the last few months of his life, as he was convinced that the Germans were going to invade England, destroy everything, and murder the population as they had done in Belgium. He ceased to farm his land, he dismissed his men, and shut himself up in his house.

His housekeeper, Mrs. Thorpe, who had been in his service for thirty years, refused to leave him, and insisted on remaining to look after him. When he died as the result of injuries received in falling downstairs, it was found that he had left most of his property to his grandson, Frank, but he had also left legacies to Mrs. Thorpe and two of the men who had been in his employ for a generation. But these legacies had not been paid because there was no money with which to pay them. Soon after the outbreak of the war the old man had drawn all his money out of the bank and had realized all his investments. It was thought that he had done this because of his fear of a German invasion.

What he had done with the money no one knew. Most people thought he had buried it for safety, intending to dig it up when the war was over. There was a rumour that he had buried it on the farm. Another rumour declared that he had buried it in the sands at the foot of the cliffs, for towards the end of his life he was often seen walking alone on the sands. In his younger days he had combined fishing with farming, and there was still a boat in the old boat-house near the cliffs. Several people tried digging in likely places in the sands after his death, but they did not find any trace of the money. Other people said that Frank Lumsden knew where the money was hidden—that his grandfather had left a plan explaining where he had buried it.

"What about the piece of paper with the mysterious plan on it which we found on the staircase?" said Marsland. "Do you think that had anything to do with the hidden money?"

"I never thought of that," she said. "Perhaps it had."

"We left it on the table in the room downstairs," he said. "I think we ought to go back for it, as it may have something to do with the murder."

"Don't go back," she said. "I could not bear to go back. The paper will be there when the police go. No one will go there in the meantime, so it will be quite safe."

"But you remember that his pocket-book had been rifled," he said, as he halted to discuss the question of returning. "May not that plan have been taken from his pocket-book after he was dead?"

"But in that case how did it come on the staircase?"

"It was dropped there by the man who stole it from the pocket-book."

"He will be too frightened to go back for it," she declared confidently. "He would be afraid of being caught."

"But he may have been in the house while we were there," he replied. "We did not solve the mystery of the crash we heard when we were in the room upstairs."

"You said at the time it was possibly caused by the wind upsetting something."

He was amused at the inconsequence of the line of reasoning she adopted in order to prevent him going back for the plan.

"At the time we did not know there was a dead body upstairs," he said.

"Do you think the murderer was in the house while we were there?" she asked.

"It is impossible to say definitely. My own impression now is that some one was in the house—that the crash we heard was not caused by the wind."

"Then he must have been there while I was sitting downstairs before you came," she said, with a shiver at the thought of the danger that was past.

"Yes," he answered. "The fact that you had a candle alight kept him upstairs. He was afraid of discovery. When we went upstairs to the first floor he must have retreated to the second floor—the top story."

She remained deep in thought for a few moments.

"I am glad he did not come down," she said at length. "I am glad I did not see who it was."

Again Marsland was reminded of the way in which she had greeted him at the door. Could it be that, instead of having gone to the farm for shelter with a companion, she had gone there to meet some one, and that unknown to her the person she was to meet had reached the house before her and had remained hidden upstairs?

"Did you close the front door when we left?" she asked.

"Yes. I slammed it and I heard the bolt catch. Why do you ask?"

"There is something I want to ask you," she said, at length.

"What is it?"

"I want you to promise if you can that you will not tell the police that I was at Cliff Farm to-night; I want you to promise that you will not tell any one."

"Do you think it—wise?" he asked, after a pause in which he gave consideration to the request.

"I do not want to be mixed up in it in any way," she explained. "The tragedy will give rise to a lot of talk in the place. I would not like my name to be mixed up in it."

"I quite appreciate that," he said. "And as far as it goes I would be willing to keep your name out of it. But have you considered what the effect would be if the police subsequently discovered that you had been there? That would give rise to greater talk—to talk of a still more objectionable kind."

"Yes; but how are they to discover that I was there unless you tell them?" she asked.

He laughed softly.

"They have to try to solve a more difficult problem than that without any one to tell them the solution," he said. "They have to try to find out who killed this man Lumsden—and why he was killed. There will be two or three detectives making all sorts of inquiries. One of them might alight accidentally on the fact that you, like myself, had taken shelter there in the storm."

She took refuge in the privilege of her sex to place a man in the wrong by misinterpreting his motives.

"Of course, if you do not wish to do it, there is no reason why you should." She removed her hand from his arm.

He pulled her up with a sharpness which left on her mind the impression that he was a man who knew his own mind.

"Please understand that I am anxious to do the best I can for you without being absurdly quixotic about it. I am quite willing to keep your name out of it in the way you ask, but I am anxious that you should first realize the danger of the course you suggest. It seems to me that, in order to avoid the unpleasantness of allowing it to be publicly known that you shared with me the discovery of this tragedy, you are courting the graver danger which would attach to the subsequent difficulty of offering a simple and satisfactory explanation to the police of why you wanted to keep your share in the discovery an absolute secret. And you must remember that your explanation to me of how you came to the farm is rather vague. It is true that you said you went there for shelter from the storm. But you have not explained how you got into the house, and from the way you spoke to me when you opened the door it is obvious that you expected to see some one else who was not a stranger."

She came to a halt in the road in order to put a direct question to him.

"Do you think that I had anything to do with this

dreadful murder? Do you think that is the reason I asked you to keep my name out of it?"

"I am quite sure that you had nothing whatever to do with the tragedy—that the discovery of the man's dead body was as great a surprise to you as it was to me."

"Thank you," she said. The emphasis of his declaration imparted a quiver to her expression of gratitude. "You are quite right about my expecting to see some one else when I opened the door," she said. "I expected to see Mr. Lumsden."

"Oh, I beg your pardon. I never thought of that." He flushed at the way in which her simple explanation had convicted him of having harboured unjust suspicions against her.

"I went to the farm to see him—I had a message for him," she continued, with seeming candour. "The storm came on just before I reached the house. I knocked, but no one came, and then I noticed the key was in the lock on the outside of the door. Naturally I thought Mr. Lumsden had left it there—that when he saw the storm he had gone to the stable or cowshed to attend to a horse or a cow. I went inside the house, expecting he would be back every moment. When I heard your knock I thought it was he."

"I am afraid you must think me a dreadful boor," he said. "I apologize most humbly."

She replied with a breadth of view that in its contrast with his ungenerous suspicions added to his embarrassment.

"No, you were quite right," she said. "As I asked you to keep my name out of it—as I virtually asked you to show blind trust in me—you were at least entitled to the fullest explanation of how I came to be there."

"And I hope you quite understand that I do trust you absolutely," he said. "I know as well as it is possible to know anything in this world that you were not connected in the remotest way with the death of this man."

Having been lifted out of the atmosphere of suspicion, she felt she could safely enter it again.

"I was not quite candid with you when I asked you to keep me out of the dreadful tragedy because of the way I would be talked about," she said, placing a penitent and appealing hand on his arm. "There are other reasons—one other reason at least—why I do not want it known I was at Cliff Farm to-night."

He was prepared to shield her if she was prepared to take the risk of being shielded.

"That alters the case," he said. "My reluctance to keep your name out of it arose from the fear that you did not realize the risk you would run."

"I realize it," she said. "And I wish to thank you for pointing it out so clearly. But it is a risk I must take."

"In that case you can rely on me."

"You will keep my name out of it?" she asked.

"I will tell no one," he replied.

CHAPTER III

"It seems to me as if the storm is abating," said Sir George Granville to his week-end guest.

He moved a piece on the chess-board and then got up from his chair and went to the window to listen to the rain on the glass.

His guest was so intent on the chess-board that he did not reply. Sir George Granville remained at the window, his attention divided between watching for his opponent's next move and listening to the storm.

Sir George's opponent was a young man; that is to say, he was under forty. He was evidently tall, and his well-cut clothes indicated that he possessed the well-built frame which is the natural heritage of most young Englishmen of good class. But his clear-cut, clean-shaven face suggested that its owner was a man of unusual personality and force of character. It was a remarkable face which would have puzzled the student in physiognomy. The upper portion was purely intellectual in type, the forehead broad, and the head well-shaped, but the dark eyes, with a touch of dreaminess and sadness in their depths, contrasted strangely with the energy and determination indicated by the firm mouth and heavy lower jaw.

The guest moved a piece and then looked at his host.

"You are not yourself to-night, Sir George," he said. "I think we had better finish this game some other time, or cancel it."

Sir George walked over to the table and looked at the position on the chess-board.

"Perhaps it would be better to cancel it," he said, "though it is generous on your part to offer to do so, with a piece to the good and the threatening development of your pawns on the queen's side. But I am off my game to-night. I am too worried about that nephew of mine to give you a good game."

"It is a bad night to be out," said the guest. "But surely he would find shelter somewhere in the downs."

"He may have met with an accident. He must have seen this storm coming. He should have been home hours ago in any case."

"Putting aside the possibility of an accident, the fact that he hasn't turned up in the storm indicates that he has found shelter," said the guest. "He is waiting until the storm is over."

"But on the downs there are so few places where one can obtain shelter except at a shepherd's cottage."

Sir George sat down in an arm-chair near the fire and invited his guest to take the chair on the other side. The room they were in was a large one, expensively furnished in black oak. The small chess-table with the chess-board and men had been placed near the large table in the centre of the room for the benefit of the light, but the autumn night was chilly, and the fire comfortable, and an open box of cigars and spirit-stand close by enhanced the appearance of indoor comfort. After his guest had declined a drink, Sir George mixed himself a whisky and soda and settled himself in an easy chair. His guest lit a cigar.

They had been seated in front of the fire but a few

minutes when the sound of the telephone bell was heard in the hall. Sir George jumped to his feet with an alacrity that was surprising in a man of his weighty figure.

"Perhaps that is Harry," he said to his guest as he hurried into the hall.

The guest lit another cigar and leaned back in his chair as he awaited the return of his host. The length of time Sir George was at the telephone would indicate to some extent the nature of the conversation. An absence of over a minute would suggest good news, and that his host was desirous of obtaining the full measure of it. To the surprise of the guest, five minutes elapsed without any sign of the return of his host. That the telephone conversation should have lasted so long seemed improbable.

The guest, with a delicate regard for what was due to a host, tried to keep his active mind from speculating on the nature of the news by telephone that was keeping Sir George away. He got up to examine the paintings on the wall, but found little in them to claim his attention. Nearly a quarter of an hour had elapsed since the telephone bell had rung. With a smile the guest returned to his chair. He had alighted on a solution of his host's long absence: Sir George had received good news and had gone upstairs to announce it to his wife.

Lady Granville was the second wife of Sir George, and was many years his junior. The baronet was sixty-four, and in spite of the fact that he was an experienced man of the world, whose wealth enabled him to get his own way, he was easily managed by his beautiful young wife.

Sir George, with a passion for chess and a predilection for a quiet life, had at the instance of his wife, taken a big house on the front at the fashionable resort of Staveley and had plunged into its social gaieties. That afternoon he had revolted to the extent of excusing himself from accompanying her to a garden fête in aid of the funds of the Red Cross by declaring that he must stay at home to welcome his guest, who was to motor down from London. Lady Granville had gone unaccompanied to the fête, and on her return home had adopted the wifely revenge of retiring to rest early, on the grounds that she had a severe headache.

When Sir George returned to his guest he was in a happy state of mind.

"It was he, Crewe," he exclaimed.

"And nothing wrong?" asked Crewe.

"No, nothing wrong with him," was the reply. "But he has had the most extraordinary adventure—gruesome, in fact."

"Gruesome?" The tone in which Crewe repeated the word showed that his interest had been aroused.

"Well, you might not call it gruesome, Crewe, as you have had so much to do with gruesome tragedies, but the fact of the matter is the boy seems to have discovered a murder."

"A murder?"

"That is how the police look at it, he says. Harry rang me up from the police station at Ashlingsea—a fishing village about twelve miles from here along the coast. His horse went lame and he was caught in the storm. He came across an old farm-house and went there for shelter, but he found the house was empty. He got in somehow, and on going upstairs found the dead body of a young man—the owner of the farm. Lumsden the owner's name is; quite a boy, that is to say, something under thirty. Cliff Farm is the name of the place. I know it well—I have often passed it while out motoring."

"How was he killed—did your nephew say?"

"Shot."

"The dead body was there and the house empty," said Crewe, in a meditative voice. "That looks as if the police will not have much difficulty in picking up the scent. The fact that he would be alone could not have been known to many people."

"I suppose not. I do not profess to be quite clear about everything Harry told me because I was so pleased to hear his voice and so astonished at his adventure. I went straight upstairs and told my wife. I know she was anxious about Harry though she said nothing before retiring—that is her way. Of course I only told her that Harry was safe. I said nothing about a murder because it would upset her. But, as I was saying, this young Lumsden, according to what Harry has learned from the police sergeant at Ashlingsea, lived alone. He didn't farm his land: he was a bit of a recluse."

"How far away is his farm?" asked Crewe.

"About nine or ten miles from here. What about motoring over in the morning?"

"Can we pick up your nephew? I should like to hear his account at first hand."

"We can go over to Ashlingsea first and bring him back to the farm with us. He is staying at an inn there, but I can get the Ashlingsea police station,

from where Harry rang up, to let him know that we
will be over for him in the car in the morning."

Crewe nodded. Sir George mixed himself another
whisky and soda, and lit a cigar. Crewe also lit a
cigar, and then they settled themselves in front of the
fire for a chat before retiring.

The tie between the great crime investigator and his
host was chess. Sir George Granville had been in
the front rank of English chess-players when Crewe
disappointed the chess world by suddenly retiring from
match chess, at the outset of a brilliant career, in order
to devote his wonderful gifts of intuition and insight
to crime detection. His intellect was too vigorous
and active to be satisfied with the sedate triumphs of
chess; his restless temperament and vital force needed
a wider and more vigorous scope.

But, despite the wide fame he had won as a crimi-
nologist, chess enthusiasts still shook their heads when
his name was mentioned, as people are wont to do
when they hear the name of a man of brilliant parts
who has not made the most of his life. It was nothing to them that Crewe had achieved fame in the rôle
he had chosen for himself; that the press frequently
praised him as a public benefactor who had brought
to justice many dangerous criminals who would have
escaped punishment but for his subtle skill. These
were vain triumphs for a man who had beaten Tur-
gieff and the young South American champion, and
had seemed destined to bring the world's champion-
ship to England.

The chess tie between Crewe and Sir George Granville had long ago strengthened into mutual regard.
Sir George liked and admired Crewe, though he did

not understand the depths of his character. Crewe
respected the baronet for the shrewd ability with
which he controlled his large interests, and the fact
that he had never allowed his career as a business
man to warp the kindliness of his nature or interfere
with the natural generosity of his disposition.

They talked of various things: of chess, at first, as
is inevitable with two chess-players. Sir George pulled
up the chess-table and reset the abandoned game in
order to see if there was not some defence to Black's
position at the stage when the game was abandoned—
the baronet had played with the black pieces. He
came to the conclusion that there wasn't, and con-
gratulated Crewe on his attack.

"Do you know, I cannot help regretting sometimes
that you have practically given up the game," he added,
as he placed the ivory chess-men one by one in the
box. "It is a long while since England has had a
really great chess-player."

"Oh, I don't know," replied Crewe. "There are
more things in life than chess."

"Some people do not think so," replied Sir George,
with a smile. "Your old opponent Merton was telling me at the club the other night that he would
consider his life had been well spent if he could but
find a sound answer to that new opening of Talsker's."

"That is proof that chess gets hold of one too
much," replied Crewe, with an answering smile.

"Still, you might have been champion of England,"
pursued Sir George meditatively.

Crewe shrugged his shoulders slightly.

"One cannot have it both ways," he said.

"You prefer crime investigation to chess?" continued Sir George inquiringly.

"In some ways—yes. Both have their fascination, but in chess the human element is lacking. It is true you have an opponent, but he is not like your hidden opponent in crime. When your hidden opponent has intelligence, then the game is wonderful—while it lasts. But intelligence in crime is as rare as it is in every other walk of life. Most crimes are like chess problems—once you find the key-move, the rest is easy. The really perfect crime mystery is as rare as a perfect chess problem. As a rule, the machinery of the human brain is not delicately adjusted enough, or sufficiently complex, to devise a problem both complex and subtle in crime—or in chess."

Sir George did not speak. It was so rarely that Crewe could be induced to speak of his experiences in crime investigation that he did not wish to check him by interrupting. But Crewe showed no sign of continuing. He sighed slightly, threw his half-smoked cigar into the fire, produced a large brierwood pipe with an amber mouthpiece, and slowly filled it, with his eyes fixed on the flames.

They remained thus for some moments in silence, though Sir George kept glancing from time to time at his companion. Several times the baronet was on the verge of speaking, but checked himself. At length Crewe, without looking away from the fire, said:

"You would like to ask me to go into this case your nephew has discovered to-night, but you do not think it would be quite courteous on your part to do so, because I am your guest."

"Well, yes, I *was* thinking that, though I don't know how you guessed it," said Sir George, in some surprise. "For more reasons than one I am worried about my nephew getting mixed up with this tragedy."

"Tell me why," said Crewe sympathetically, turning away from the fire and looking at his host.

It was past one o'clock when Crewe retired to his room. The object of his visit to Sir George Granville had been to obtain a rest after some weeks of investigation into the Malmesbury case, as the newspapers called it; his investigation having resulted in the capture of the elusive Malmesbury who had swindled the insurance companies out of £20,000 by arranging his own death and burial.

Crewe smiled to himself once or twice as he slowly undressed. Instead of entering into a quiet week-end he found that within a few hours of his arrival he was on the threshold of another investigation. He had not met his host's nephew, Harry Marsland, as the young man had left for his ride on the downs before Crewe reached the house. But from what Sir George had told him Crewe felt attracted to the young man. Marsland, who was the only son of Sir George's only sister, had purchased a junior partnership in a firm of consulting engineers shortly after attaining his majority, but as soon as the war broke out he offered his services and obtained a commission.

He had seen over six months' fighting before being wounded by a shell. The long strain of warfare, the shock of the explosion and the wounds he had received in the head from shell splinters made his recovery very slow. He had been in hospital for three months, and though now convalescent he would

never be fit for service again and had been invalided
out of the army. There had been a time in hospital
when his life hung by a thread. During days and
nights of delirium his mind had been haunted by the
scenes of horror he had witnessed at the front. He
had seen hundreds of men go through the agonies of
death from terrible wounds and gas torture; he had
seen human forms blown to pieces, and the men falling in hundreds from machine-gun fire as they charged
the German trenches.

The hospital doctors had hinted to Sir George of
the possibility of his nephew's reason being affected
by what he had gone through, but fortunately the
young man was spared this calamity. Sir George had
been warned not to let his nephew talk about the war
and to keep his mind occupied with more cheerful
subjects of conversation. In pursuance of these instructions no reference was made to the war in young
Marsland's presence, and his rank as captain was stu-
diously forgotten.

It was on the ground of his nephew's health and
the danger that lay in mental worry that Sir George
Granville begged Crewe, before he retired, to promise
to investigate the crime at Cliff Farm if it turned
out to be a case which was likely to baffle the police
and result in protracted worry to those innocently
brought into it. Crewe recognized the force of the
appeal and had promised to give some time to the
case if the circumstances seemed to demand it. He
reserved his final decision until after the visit to
Cliff Farm, which Sir George had arranged to make
in the morning.

Anxiety on his nephew's behalf got Sir George out

of bed early, and when Crewe reached the breakfast-room he found his host waiting for him. The heartiness with which he greeted Crewe seemed to embody some relief after a strain on patience.

"I rang up Ashlingsea police station half an hour ago and asked them to make some inquiries about Harry," said Sir George. "He doesn't seem to be much the worse for his night's experience. At all events, the landlady sent word back that he had gone out for a swim."

"I am very glad to hear that he is all right," said Crewe.

"They have given him our message," continued Sir George, "so he will be waiting for us."

"It ought not to take us much more than half an hour to run over. Is the road good?"

"Fairly good. We will get away as soon as we have finished breakfast. I told my wife not to expect us back until after lunch. That will give you time to look over the farm-house where the man was murdered."

Crewe smiled slightly at his host's idea that it would not take him long to reconstruct the crime.

"Are we to keep the object of our journey a secret from Lady Granville when we return?" he asked.

"Well, no. The fact of the matter is that I told her all about it this morning. It was best to do so. She will be of valuable assistance in looking after Harry if he has been upset by his experiences of last night."

They finished breakfast quickly, and Sir George got up from his chair.

"I told Harris to have the car ready," he said. "It will be waiting for us."

A few minutes later they were in the car and were going along the front at a good rate. When the houses became scattered, the road left the outline of the shore, made a detour round some sand dunes about a mile from Staveley, and then stretched like a white ribbon along the cliffs, between the downs and the sea, to the distant village of Ashlingsea. The road justified Sir George's description as fairly good, but there were places where it was very narrow, the width being scarcely sufficient to allow one vehicle to pass another. On the side where the road joined the downs there was a ditch, and in some places the water had collected and formed a pool.

"What is this?" exclaimed Sir George, as he pointed to an object at the side of the road some distance away.

The object was a motor-car, which had struck the ditch and overturned. Part of the car was lying on the downs. One of the front wheels had been wrenched out of position. To Crewe's surprise the chauffeur drove past without more than a sidelong glance at the wreck.

"Stop!" said Crewe. "We must have a look at this."

"Yes, we may as well have a look at it," said Sir George, as the car stopped. "But it is only one of Gosford's old cars. He has a garage at Staveley and has three or four old cars which he lets out on hire. They are always coming to grief. Quite a common thing to find them stuck up and refusing to budge. The occupants have to get out and walk."

Crewe got out of the car to inspect the wreck, but

Sir George did not follow him. He was content to look on. from his seat in the car. With some impatience he watched Crewe, as the detective examined the car first on one side and then the other. Crewe went back along the road for about forty yards and examined the track the wheels had made in running off the road and striking the ditch. Then he stood back a few yards, and, going down on his knees, examined the grass. He put his shoulder underneath the upturned side of the car to judge the weight of the vehicle.

"I believe we could turn it over," he called out to Sir George. "It is not very heavy."

"Get out, Harris, and see what you can do," said Sir George.

He sat and watched Crewe and Harris exerting their strength to lift the car. They were not successful in moving it.

"Do you mind, Sir George?" said Crewe persuasively.

Sir George did mind, but convention demanded that he should pretend to his guest that he did not.

"Gosford won't thank us," was the length of the protest he offered. "We may give the thing a bump that will bring it to pieces."

"I do not want to shove it right over," explained Crewe. "If we can get it on its side so that I can have a look at it inside I will be satisfied."

Sir George's contribution to the task turned the scale. Slowly the car was raised until it rested on its right side. Crewe bent down and inspected the inside of the car and the driver's seat.

"Thanks," he said. "I've got all I want."

"And what is it that you wanted?" demanded Sir George, in astonishment.

"Several things," said Crewe. "I wanted to get an idea of when the accident took place."

"How on earth could you expect to tell that?" asked Sir George.

"By the state of the car—outside and inside. The way the mud is splashed on the outside indicates that the car was out in last night's storm. The wet state of the cushions inside showed that rain had fallen on them—they must have got wet before the car capsized."

"Extremely interesting," said Sir George. "I'd never have thought of these things. Perhaps you can tell how many people were in the car at the time."

"No. All I can say is that one of them was injured, but not very seriously, as far as I can make out."

"And how do you make that out?" asked Sir George.

"By the blood-stains on the grass at the side of the car."

CHAPTER IV

POLICE-SERGEANT WESTAWAY sat in the sitting-room of Cliff Farm preparing an official report, with the assistance of his subordinate, Police-Constable Heather, whose help consisted in cordially agreeing with his superior on any point on which the sergeant condescended to ask his advice.

The constable was a short, florid-faced, bullet-headed young man, and he whistled cheerfully as he explored the old farm-house. His superior officer was elderly and sallow, with hollow dark eyes, a long black beard streaked with grey, and a saturnine expression, which was the outward manifestation of a pessimistic disposition and a disordered liver.

Sergeant Westaway looked like a man who found life a miserable business. A quarter of a century spent in a dull round of official duties in the fishing village of Ashlingsea, as guardian of the morals of its eight hundred inhabitants, had deepened his natural bent towards pessimism and dyspepsia. He felt himself qualified to adorn a much higher official post, but he forbore to air his grievance in public because he thought the people with whom his lot was cast were not worth wasting speech upon. By his aloofness and taciturnity he had acquired a local reputation for wisdom, which his mental gifts scarcely warranted.

"Heather," he said, pausing in his writing and glanc-

46

ing up irritably as his subordinate entered the room, "do not make that noise."

"What noise, sergeant?" asked Constable Heather, who gathered his impressions slowly.

"That whistling. It disturbs me. Besides, there is a dead man in the house."

"All right, sergeant, I forgot all about him." Constable Heather stopped in the middle of a lively stave, sat down on a chair, got up again, and went out of the room with a heavy tread.

Sergeant Westaway returned to his official report with a worried expression on his gaunt face. He was a country police officer with no previous experience of murders, and twenty-five years' official vegetation in Ashlingsea, with nothing more serious in the way of crime to handle than occasional outbreaks of drunkenness or an odd case of petty larceny, had made him rusty in official procedure, and fearful of violating the written and unwritten laws of departmental red tape. He wrote and erased and rewrote, occasionally laying down his pen to gaze out of the open window for inspiration.

It was a beautiful day in early autumn. The violent storm of the previous night had left but few traces of its visit. The sun was shining in a clear blue sky, and the notes of a skylark singing joyously high above the meadow in front of the farm floated in through the open window. The winding cliff road was white and clean after the heavy rain, and the sea was once more clear and green, with little white-flecked waves dancing and sparkling in the sunshine.

Sergeant Westaway, gloomily glancing out at this pleasing prospect, saw two men entering the farm from the road. They had been cycling, and were now pushing their machines up the gravel-path to the front door. One of them was in police uniform, and the other was a young man about thirty years of age, clad in cycling tweeds and knickerbockers, with a tweed cap on the back of his curly head. He had blue eyes and a snub nose, and a cigarette dangled from his lower lip. He was a stranger to Sergeant Westaway, but that acute official had no hesitation in placing him as a detective from Scotland Yard. To the eye of pessimism he looked like the sort of man that Scotland Yard would send to assist the country police. His companion in uniform was Detective-Inspector Payne, of the County police headquarters at Lewes, and was well known to Sergeant Westaway. The latter had no difficulty in arriving at the conclusion that the County Commissioner of Police, having several other mysterious crimes to occupy the limited number of detectives at his disposal, had asked for the assistance of Scotland Yard in unravelling the murder at Cliff Farm. Sergeant Westaway knew what this would mean to him. He would have a great deal to do in coaching the Scotland Yard man regarding local conditions, but would get none of the credit of sheeting home the crime to the murderer. The Scotland Yard man would see to that.

"How are you, Westaway?" exclaimed Inspector Payne, as he stood his bicycle against the wall of the house near the front door. "What do you mean by giving us a murder when we've got our hands full? We've burglaries in half a dozen towns, a murder at Denham, two unidentified bodies washed ashore in a boat at Hemsley, and the disappearance from Lewes of a well-known solicitor who is wanted for embezzling trust funds. Let me introduce you to Detective Gillett, of Scotland Yard. I'm turning the investigation of this murder of yours over to him. You will give him all the assistance he wants."

"Yes, sir," replied Sergeant Westaway.

"Glad to meet you, Westaway," said Detective Gillett, as he shook hands with the Sergeant.

Sergeant Westaway had come to the door to meet the new-comers, and he now led the way back to the room where he had been preparing his report.

Detective Gillett took up a position by the open window, and sniffed gratefully at the soft air.

"Fine view, here," he said, waving his hand in the direction of the cliff road and open bay. "Fine, bracin' air—sea—country—birds—and all that sort of thing. You chaps in the country have all the best of it—the simple life, and no hustle or bustle."

Sergeant Westaway looked darkly at the speaker as though he suspected him of a desire to rob him of the grievance he had brooded over in secret for twenty-five years.

"It's dull enough," he said ungraciously.

"But the air, man, the air!" said the London detective, inhaling great gulps of oxygen as he spoke. "It's exhilarating; it's glorious! Why, it should keep you going until you reach a hundred."

"Too salt," commented Sergeant Westaway curtly.

"The more salt in it the longer it will preserve you," said Gillett. "What a glorious day it is."

"The day is right enough," said Westaway. "But to-morrow will be different."

"Westaway doesn't like to be enthusiastic about

E

this locality for fear we will shift him somewhere else," said Inspector Payne. "However, let us get to business. I must be on my way back to Lewes in an hour."

Sergeant Westaway coughed in order to clear his throat, and then began his narrative in a loud official voice:

"At five minutes past nine last night a gentleman named Marsland came to the police station. I was in my office at the time, preparing a report. He told me that he had found the dead body of a man in this house."

"Who is this Marsland?" asked Inspector Payne. "Does he live in the district?"

"He does not," replied the sergeant. "He lives at Staveley. That is to say, he lives in London, but he is staying at Staveley. He is staying there with his uncle, Sir George Granville."

"I know Sir George," said the inspector. "And so this young gentleman who discovered the body is his nephew. How old is he?"

"About twenty-eight, I should say."

"What sort of young man is he? How did he impress you?"

"He impressed me as being an honest straightforward young gentleman. He gave me a very clear statement of who he was and how he came to call in at this farm last night. Nevertheless, I took the precaution of telephoning to Inspector Murchison at Staveley and asking him to have inquiries made. The inspector's report coincides with what Mr. Marsland told me. He has been in ill-health and came down from London to Staveley to recuperate. He has been there five days. Yesterday he left Staveley for a ride on the downs. He got lost and was caught in the storm which came up shortly after dusk. His horse went lame, and seeing this house he came here for shelter. The horse is in the stable now. There was no light in the house, and when he went to the front door to knock he found it open. He struck a match and lit a candle which was on the hallstand. He could see no one about. Then he lit a lamp in this room and sat down to wait until the storm was over. He was sitting here for some time listening to the rain when suddenly he heard a crash above. He took the lamp and made his way upstairs. In a sitting-room on the first floor he found the dead body of a man in an armchair. At first he thought the man had died a natural death, but on inspecting the body he found that the man had been shot through the body. As the storm was abating, Mr. Marsland made his way down to Ashlingsea and reported his discovery to me."

"And what did you do?" asked Inspector Payne, in an authoritative voice.

"I closed the station and in company with Mr. Marsland I knocked up Police-Constable Heather. Then the three of us came here. I found the body as Mr. Marsland had described. I identified the body as that of Frank Lumsden, the owner of this farm. Leaving Heather in charge of it, I returned to Ashlingsea accompanied by Mr. Marsland, and reported the matter by telephone to headquarters at Lewes, as you are aware, inspector. This morning I returned here to make a minute inspection of the scene of the crime and to prepare my report."

"Is the body upstairs now?" asked Detective Gillett.

"It has been left exactly as it was found. I gave Heather orders that he was not to touch it."

"What sort of a man was this Lumsden?" asked Inspector Payne. "Had he any enemies?"

"He may have," replied the cautious sergeant. "There are some who bore him no good will."

"Why was that?"

"Because they thought he hadn't acted rightly by them. He was the executor of his grandfather's will, but he didn't pay the legacies his grandfather left. He said there was no money. His grandfather drew all his money out of the bank when the war broke out, and no one was ever able to find where he hid it. But there are some who say Frank Lumsden found it and stuck to it all."

"This is interesting," said Detective Gillett. "We must go into it thoroughly later on."

"And what makes it more interesting is that a sort of plan showing where the money was hidden has disappeared," continued Sergeant Westaway. "It disappeared after Lumsden was murdered. Mr. Marsland told me that he found it when he was going upstairs to find out the cause of the crash he heard. It was lying on the second bottom stair. Mr. Marsland picked it up and put it on the table with the candle stuck on top of it. But when we came here this morning it was gone."

"That is strange," commented Inspector Payne. "What was the plan like? And how does Mr. Marsland know it had anything to do with the missing money?"

"Of course he doesn't know for certain. But when I happened to tell him about the murdered man's grandfather and the missing money he called to mind a strange-looking paper he had picked up. As he described it to me, it had some figures written in the shape of a circle on it, and some letters or writing above and below the circle of figures. He did not scrutinize it very closely when he first found it, for he intended to examine it later."

"And it disappeared after Mr. Marsland left the farm to go to the police station?" asked Detective Gillett.

"Showing, to my mind, that the murderer was actually in the house when Mr. Marsland left," added Sergeant Westaway, with impressive solemnity. "In all probability the murderer was hiding in the top floor at the time. I have ascertained that the crash Mr. Marsland heard was caused by a picture being knocked down and the glass broken. This picture I found on the stairs leading to the top floor. It used to hang on the wall near the top of the stairs. My theory is that the murderer, feeling his way in the dark while Mr. Marsland was in this room, accidentally knocked it down."

"I take it that Marsland did not go up to the top floor but left the house after examining the body," remarked Detective Gillett.

"That is so," replied the Sergeant. "He forgot about the crash when he found the body of a murdered man. His first thought was to communicate with the police."

"And the murderer, leaving the house after Marsland had gone, found this plan on the table and took it?" suggested Detective Gillett.

"That is my theory," replied Sergeant Westaway. "I forgot to say, however, that the plan was probably stolen in the first place from the murdered man's pocket-book—his pocket-book was found on the table near him. It had been opened and most of the papers it contained had been removed. The papers were scattered about the table. The way I see the crime is this: the murderer had killed his victim, had removed his pocket-book, and had obtained possession of the plan. He was making his way downstairs to escape when he saw Marsland in the doorway. In his alarm he dropped the plan on the stairs and then crept softly upstairs to the top of the house. After Mr. Marsland left the murderer came downstairs again, looked about for the plan, and after finding it then made off."

"A very ingenious reconstruction, sergeant," said Inspector Payne. "I shouldn't wonder if it proved to be correct. What do you say, Gillett?"

"Westaway is wasting his time down here," said the young detective. "We ought to have him at Scotland Yard."

CHAPTER V

Sergeant Westaway was flattered at the manner in which his theory of the murder had been received by men who were far more experienced than himself in investigating crime. His sallow cheeks flushed with pleasure and his pessimism waned a little. In his determination to place his hearers in possession of all the facts concerning the crime and the victim he gave them details regarding Lumsden's mode of life at Cliff Farm after his discharge from the army, and the gossip that was current in the district concerning him. While he was dealing with these matters they heard a motor-car approaching. It stopped outside the gates of the farmhouse, and the three police officials went to the door to see who had arrived.

"Why, it's Crewe!" exclaimed Detective Gillett, in a tone of surprise. "I wonder who has put him on to this?"

"That is Sir George Granville with him—the stout elderly man," said Inspector Payne.

"The other gentleman is Mr. Marsland," said Sergeant Westaway.

"Which is Crewe and which is Marsland?" asked Inspector Payne.

"The tall one on the left is Crewe," answered Detective Gillett.

As a police official, Inspector Payne was indignant at the idea of Crewe intruding into the case, but as a man he was delighted at the opportunity of meeting the famous private detective who had so often scored over Scotland Yard by unravelling mysteries which had baffled the experts of the London detective department. Crewe's fame had even penetrated to Ashlingsea, and Sergeant Westaway studied the private detective with awed interest as the three occupants of the motor-car walked up the drive.

Inspector Payne had pictured Crewe as a more striking personality than the tall young man in tweeds who was accompanying Sir George Granville and his nephew. The latter was talking earnestly, and Crewe was listening closely. Inspector Payne had an opportunity of noting the distinction and character which marked the detective's face in repose: the clear, clean-cut profile, the quick penetration and observation of his dark eyes as they took in the exterior of Cliff Farm. He concluded that Crewe was rather young for the fame he had achieved—certainly under forty: that he liked his face; that he looked like a gentleman; and that his tweed suit displayed a better cut than any provincial tailor had ever achieved.

His companion, Sir George Granville's nephew, was a young man of Saxon type, fair-haired, blue-eyed, with a clear skin which had been tanned brown as the result of his war campaigning in France. He was two or three inches shorter than Crewe, but was well set up and well-built, and although he did not wear khaki his recent connection with the army was indicated by his military carriage and bearing.

After the necessary introductions Crewe explained with an air of modesty that, Sir George Granville's nephew having had the misfortune to become asso-

ciated with the tragedy through the discovery of the
body, Sir George, as a public man, had conceived the
idea that he ought to do something towards discovering the author of the crime. That was how he himself came to be present. He hoped that he would
not be in the way of the police.

"Not at all; not at all," said Inspector Payne, answering for the County Police. "We'll be glad of your
help. And as for anything we can do for you, Mr.
Crewe, you have only to ask."

"That is very kind of you," said Crewe.

"You are just in time," continued Inspector Payne.
"Gillett and I have been here only a few minutes.
We were just going upstairs to look at the body when
you arrived."

On their way upstairs Gillett drew attention to some
marks on the margin of the stairs between the carpet
on the staircase and the wall. These marks were irregular in shape, and they looked as if they had been
made by wiping portions of the stairs with a dirty
wet cloth. Some of the stairs bore no mark.

"It seems to me that some one has been wiping up
spots of blood on the stairs," said Inspector Payne,
as he examined the marks closely.

On the linoleum covering the landing of the first
flight there were more traces of the kind, the last of
them being beside the door of the room in which the
body had been discovered.

The dead man was still in the arm-chair near the
window. There was such a resemblance to life in his
stooping posture that the men entering the room found
it difficult at first to realize they were confronted with
the corpse of a man who had been murdered. A ray

of sunlight fell through the narrow window on the
bent head, revealing the curly brown hair and the
youthful contour of the neck. The right arm was
slightly extended from the body towards the table near
the arm-chair in which the corpse was seated, as
though the murdered man had been about to pick
up the pocket-book which lay on the table. The pocket-book was open, and the papers which had been in
it were scattered about the table.

Payne, Gillett and Crewe inspected the body closely.
Sir George Granville and Marsland waited a little
distance away while the others conducted their examination. The dead man had been fully dressed when he
was shot. On the left side of his vest was the hole made
by the bullet, and around it was a discoloured patch
where the blood, oozing from the wound, had stained
the tweed. There were numerous blood-stains on the
floor near the dead man's feet, and also near the window at the side of the arm-chair.

"I see that the window is broken," said Inspector
Payne, pointing to one of the panes in the window
near the arm-chair.

"By a bullet," said Sergeant Westaway. He pulled
down the window blind and pointed to a hole in it
which had evidently been made by a bullet. "When
I came in the blind was down. I pulled it up in order
to let in some light. But the fact that there is a
hole in the window blind shows that the murder was
committed at night, when the blind was down. I
should say two shots were fired. The first went
through the window, and the other killed him."

"I think the bullet that killed him has gone through
him," said Crewe, who had moved the body in order

to examine the back of it. "It looks as if he was shot from behind, because the wound in the back is lower down than the one in front." He pointed to a hole in the back of the coat where the cloth showed a similar discoloured patch to the one in the vest.

"It must have been a powerful weapon if the bullet has gone through him," said Gillett. "That means we shall have no bullet to guide us as to the calibre of the weapon, unless we can find the one that went through the window."

"Perhaps there was only one shot fired after all," remarked Inspector Payne. "The victim may have been standing by the window when he was shot, and then have staggered to the chair. Otherwise if he were shot in the back while sitting in the chair the bullet should be embedded in the chair or wall. But I can see no sign of it."

"Not necessarily," said Gillett. "Look at the position on the arm-chair. It is possible that the bullet, after going through the man, went through the window. That would account for the broken pane of glass."

The pocket-book and the papers it contained were next examined. Inspector Payne asked Marsland concerning the mysterious plan he had picked up on the stairs. Marsland borrowed a sheet of paper from the inspector's large official note-book and drew a rough sketch of the plan as he remembered it. He explained that as he had lost his glasses while out in the storm he had not been able to make a close study of the plan. While he was engaged in reproducing the plan as far as he remembered it, Sergeant Westaway enlightened Crewe and Sir George Granville about the theory he had formed that the murderer was in the house when Marsland discovered the body, and that, after Marsland left, the murderer made his escape and took from the sitting-room downstairs the plan he had dropped on the stairs when he heard Marsland in the house.

"What do you make of this, Mr. Crewe?" asked Inspector Payne, as he took up the paper on which Marsland had sketched what he recalled of the plan. "Do you think this was meant to show where the old grandfather had his money?"

"That is very probable," said Crewe. "But it is not worth while trying to solve the riddle from a sketch drawn from memory. Get the murderer and you will probably get the original plan as well."

Sergeant Westaway, in pursuance of his duties as guide, took his visitors downstairs to the sitting-room for the purpose of showing them how the window had been forced in order to provide an entrance. He pointed to a mark on the sash which indicated that a knife had been used to force back the catch.

This was the room in which Miss Maynard had been sitting when Marsland had arrived to obtain shelter from the storm. Marsland noticed the chair beside which she had stood while they were in the room together before going upstairs to investigate the cause of the crash they had heard. He gave a start as he saw behind the chair a small tortoiseshell comb such as ladies sometimes wear to keep their hair up. He stooped quickly to pick it up, and as he did so he realized that he had blundered badly. In order to rectify the blunder he made a weak attempt to hide the comb, but he saw Detective Gillett's eye on him.

"What have we here?" asked the Scotland Yard man genially.

Marsland held out his hand with the comb resting in it.

"A woman in the case," commented Inspector Payne. "That ought to help to simplify matters."

Marsland bit his lips at the thought of how he had been false to his promise to Miss Maynard. He had kept her name out of the discovery of the crime, but he had unwittingly directed attention to the fact that a woman had only recently been in that room.

The comb was handed to Crewe for examination. It was about three inches long and was slightly convex in shape. On the outside was a thin strip of gold mounting. Crewe handed the comb back.

"You sat in this room before going upstairs, Marsland?" he asked, turning to Sir George's nephew.

"Yes; I was here about a quarter of an hour or twenty minutes."

"Was the window open when you came in? Did you close it?"

"I did not close it, but it must have been closed, as otherwise I would have noticed it open. It was raining and blowing hard while I was here." Marsland thought to himself that any information he could give about the window was useless in view of the fact that Miss Maynard had been in the room some time before he arrived.

"Was this the room in which you found the lamp that you took upstairs?" continued Crewe.

"Yes."

"I think you told me that there was no light in the house when you entered?"

"The place was in darkness. I found a candlestick on the hallstand. I lit that first and after coming in here I lit the lamp." He had decided to adhere in his statements to what Miss Maynard had told him she had done before he arrived.

"Did you notice when you lit the lamp whether the lamp chimney was hot, warm, or quite cold?" asked Crewe.

"I cannot be certain. I think it was cold, or otherwise I should have noticed."

"You lit the lamp before you heard the crash which startled you?"

"Yes. I lit it a few moments after I came into the room."

"Any foot-marks outside the window?" said Inspector Payne, thrusting his head out of the open window. "Yes, there they are, quite plainly, in the ground. Made by heavy hobnailed boots. We must get plaster impressions of those, Gillett. They are an important clue."

"I notice, inspector," said Crewe, "that there are no marks of any kind on the wall-paper beneath the window. One would expect that a man getting in through this window would touch the wall-paper with one foot while he was getting through the window, and as it was a wet night there ought to be some mark on it."

"Not necessarily," replied the inspector. "He may have jumped to the floor without touching the wall-paper."

"But there do not seem to be any impressions inside the house of these heavy nailed boots," returned Crewe. "Those impressions beneath the window show that they were made when the ground was soft from the rain. Wet muddy boots with nails in the soles ought to leave some traces on the carpet of this room and on the staircase."

"And what about those marks we saw on the staircase? They show that some one had been over the staircase with a wet rag."

"To wipe out the traces of those boots?" asked Crewe.

"Why not?"

"Why did the person wearing those boots walk on the uncarpeted part of the stairs near the wall instead of the carpeted part?"

"Because he knew that it would be easier for him to remove the traces of his footprints from the wood than from the carpet."

Crewe smiled at the ingenuity displayed by the inspector.

"One more doubt, inspector," he said. "Why did the man who wore those boots take such care to remove the traces of footprints inside the house and show so much indifference to the traces he left outside?"

"Because he thought the rain would wash out the footprints outside. And so it would have done if it had rained until morning. Let us go outside and have a good look at them."

They went out by the front door and made their way to the window, taking care to keep clear of the footprints.

"There you are, Mr. Crewe," said Inspector Payne. "There is evidence that the man got in through the window." He pointed to a spot beneath the window where a small piece of mortar between the brickwork had been broken off about fifteen inches above the ground. "And look at those parallel scratches on the mortar. It looks to me as if they were made by tha nails in a boot."

"Very true," assented Crewe, examining the marks closely.

"Now let us follow the footsteps to see where they start from," continued Inspector Payne.

It was no difficult matter to follow the marks of the heavy boots. In the soft soil, which had formerly been part of a flower-bed, they were quite distinct. Even on the grass beyond the flower-bed the impressions were visible, though not so distinctly. Eventually they reached the gravel-walk which skirted the front of the house, and here the traces were lost.

"I should say that the boots which made these marks are the ordinary heavy type worn by farm-hands and fishermen in this locality," said Crewe.

"No doubt," answered Inspector Payne. "But, though there are some hundreds of men in this locality who wear the same type of boot, the number of pairs of boots absolutely the same are small. That is particularly the case with these heavy nailed boots—the positions of some of the nails vary. A cast of three or four of the best of these impressions will narrow down the circle of our investigations. What do you say, Gillett?"

"It looks to me as if it is going to be a comparatively simple affair."

Inspector Payne turned to Marsland.

"I think you said you found the door open, Mr. Marsland. Do you mean wide open or partly closed?"

"I found it wide open," replied Marsland. "I thought at the time that it had not been properly closed and that the wind had blown it open."

"That means that the murderer got in through this window and left by the door," said Inspector Payne to Detective Gillett. "He left it open when he fled."

"But what about Westaway's theory that he was in the house when Mr. Marsland came here?" asked Gillett. "What about the crash Mr. Marsland heard when the picture fell down? What about the plan of the hidden money that disappeared after Mr. Marsland left?"

It was plain that Detective Gillett, who had to investigate the crime, was not in sympathy with Inspector Payne's method of solving difficult points by ignoring them.

Inspector Payne stroked his chin thoughtfully.

"There are a lot of interesting little points to be cleared up," he said cheerfully.

"Yes, there are," responded Detective Gillett, "and I've no doubt we will find more of them as we go along."

It was obvious to Marsland that in keeping silent about Miss Maynard's presence at Cliff Farm on the night of the storm, and the means by which she had entered the house, he was placing obstacles in the way of the elucidation of the tragedy.

CHAPTER VI

From the front gate of Cliff Farm the road wound up the hill steeply and sinuously, following the broken curves of the coastline till it disappeared in the cutting of the hill three hundred yards from the house, and reappeared on the other side. As far as could be seen from the house, the cutting through the hill was the only place where the road diverged from the cliff.

No other short cut on a large scale had been attempted by the makers of the road, which, for the most part, skirted the irregular outline of the bluff and rocky coast until it seemed a mere white thread in the distant green of the spacious downs which stretched for many miles to the waters of the Channel.

On the far side of the cutting the downs came fully into view, rolling back from the edge of the cliffs to a low range of distant wooded hills, and stretching ahead till they were merged in the town of Staveley, nearly ten miles away. Staveley's churchspires could be seen from the headland near Cliff Farm on a clear day, and the road in front of the farm ran to the town, skirting the edge of the cliffs for nearly the whole of the way.

Crewe and Marsland walked up the road from the house for some distance in silence. Sir George Granville had gone back to Staveley in his car, but his nephew and Crewe had arranged to stay behind and spend the night at Ashlingsea. Crewe desired to begin his investigations without delay, and Inspector Payne had asked Mr. Marsland to remain at Ashlingsea in case Detective Gillett wanted further light from him on incidental points. As they walked along, Crewe was thoughtful, and Marsland scrutinized the way-side closely, anxious to find the spot where his horse had swerved and stumbled on the previous night. Thus preoccupied, they reached the highest point of the cliff, a rocky headland which ran out from the hill-top on the other side of the cutting, forming a landmark well known to the fishermen of the district.

The headland, which was not more than a hundred yards across at the base, jutted sharply out into the sea. Immediately beyond it, on the Staveley side, the road ran along the edge of the cliffs for several hundred yards, with a light rail fence on the outside as some protection for traffic from the danger of going over the side to the rocks below. Where the grassy margin of the headland narrowed to this dangerous pass, an ancient and faded notice board on a post which had departed from its perpendicular position warned drivers that the next portion of the road was DAN-GEROUS, and a similar board was affixed to the other end of the protecting fence.

Marsland stopped opposite the point where the first notice-board confronted them from the narrowing margin of headline.

"It was somewhere about here that my horse took fright last night, I think," he said, examining the green bank on the side of the road farthest from the cliff. "Yes, here is where he slipped."

Crewe examined the deep indentation of hoofmarks with interest.

"It's lucky for you your horse shied in that direction," he said. "If he had sprung the other way you might have gone over the cliffs, in spite of the fence. Look here!"

Marsland followed him to the edge of the cliff and glanced over. The tide was out, and the cliffside fell almost perpendicularly to the jagged rocks nearly 300 feet below.

"They'd be covered at high tide," said Crewe, pointing downward to the rocks. "But even if one fell over at high tide there would not be much chance of escape. The breakers must come in with terrific force on this rocky coast."

"It's a horribly dangerous piece of road, especially at night-time," said Marsland. "I suppose there was some bad accident here at one time or another, which compelled the local authorities to put up that fence and the warning notices. Even now, it's far from safe. Somebody's had a narrow escape from going over: look at that notice-board leaning down on one side. Some passing motor-car has gone too close to the edge of the road—probably in the dark—and bumped it half over."

"I noticed it," said Crewe. "I agree with you: this piece of road is highly dangerous. There will be a shocking accident here some day unless the local authorities close this portion of the road and make a detour to that point lower down where those sheep are grazing. But local authorities never act wisely until they have had an accident. Still, I suppose the people of the country-side are so well used to this cliff road that they never think of the danger. Apparently it's the only road between Ashlingsea and Staveley."

Crewe slowly filled his large pipe, and lit it. He smoked thoughtfully, gazing round at the scene. The high headland on which they stood commanded an uninterrupted view of downs, sea, and coast. It was a clear day, and the distant city of Staveley, with its towering spires, was silhouetted against the sky like an etching in grey. To the left the fishing village of Ashlingsea nestled on the sands, its stone-grey houses gleaming in a silver setting, the sails of its fishing fleet flecked white on the sunlit blue of the sea.

On the Ashlingsea side the cliffs fell away quickly, and sloped down to a level beach less than a mile from the headland. About five hundred yards from the headland the cliff front was less precipitous, and a footpath showed a faint trail on its face, running down to a little stone landing place, where a fisherman could be seen mooring a boat. Crewe pointed out the path to Marsland.

"I should like to explore that path," he said. "I should say it is not very far from Cliff Farm. Do you think you could manage it?"

The question referred to the fact that Marsland was a wounded man. Crewe had taken a fancy to Marsland on account of his unaffected manner and manly bearing. It was evident to him that the young man had been a good officer, a staunch comrade, and that he had been extremely popular with the men under him. No word in reference to Marsland's military career had passed between Crewe and his companion.

Crewe was anxious to respect the medical advice which forbade Marsland to discuss the war or anything relating to his experience at the front. But in order to clear the way for candour and companionship Crewe thought it best to give an occasional indication that Sir George Granville had confided in him about his nephew's state of health and the cause of it. Crewe was somewhat amused at the pains taken to make Marsland forget his past connection with the Army, when in so many ways he betrayed to any keen observer the effects of military training and discipline.

"I can manage it quite easily," said Marsland with a smile, in reply to Crewe's question. "I am not such a wreck as you'd all like to make me out. Come along! I'll get to the bottom before you."

They walked along tó the cliff path. When they reached it they found it was not noticeable from the road, which at that point ran back three hundred yards or more from the cliff to enter the hill-cutting. Cliff Farm stood in the hollow less than a quarter of a mile away. The commencement of the path was screened from view by the furze which grew along the edge of the cliffs at this point. It took Crewe and Marsland some minutes before they could find the entrance to the path, but when they did they found the descent by it to the rocks below tolerably easy, the cliff at this point not being more than seventy feet high. The track ended abruptly about fifteen feet from the bottom, but the rocks afforded good foothold and handhold for the remaining distance.

The tide was out, and the coastline at the foot of the cliffs showed for miles towards Staveley in black rocky outline, with broken reefs running hundreds of yards out to sea.

"It's a bad piece of coast," said Marsland, eyeing the

reefs and the rocky foreshore. "If a ship had run ashore anywhere between here and Staveley in last night's storm she would not have had much chance."

Crewe did not reply; his keen eyes were fixed on a line of rocks on the right about a hundred yards from where they stood. He walked rapidly to the spot, and Marsland could see him stoop down by a pool in the rocks and pick up something. As he returned, Marsland saw that the detective was carrying a man's soft grey felt hat, stained and saturated with sea-water.

"I suppose somebody lost it from the cliffs last night," remarked Marsland.

Crewe wrung the hat as dry as he could with his hands, rolled it up, and placed it in an inside pocket of his coat before replying.

"I do not think it blew off from the headland," he said. "In fact, it couldn't have done so. There may be nothing in the find, but it's worth a few inquiries. But look at that fisherman, Marsland. He's a picturesque touch of colour."

The fisherman who had been mooring his boat had turned to come off the rough landing-stage. He stopped when he saw Crewe and Marsland, and stared suspiciously at them. He was an old man, but vigorous and upright, with a dark swarthy face, hooked nose, and flashing black eyes, which contrasted strikingly with a long snow-white beard. He wore a long red cloak fastened to his neck with clasps, and reaching nearly to his feet, which were bare.

He stood for a few moments looking at the two men, his red cloak making a bright splash of colour against the grey stones of the landing. Then, with a slight shrug of his shoulders, he walked quickly off the landing-place. Crewe nodded to him pleasantly as he approached, and asked him to where the path they had just descended led.

The old man, with a slight shake of his head, pointed to his lips and his ears, and then, accelerating his pace, walked rapidly away along the rocks towards the headland.

"Deaf and dumb, poor beggar!" said Marsland, watching his retreating figure until it turned the headland and was lost to view. "I say, Crewe, did you ever see such an odd fish on an English foreshore?"

"Italian, I should say," said Crewe. "But he looks as if he might have stepped out of a Biblical plate. He would make an admirable model for St. Peter, with his expressive eyes and hooked nose and patriarchal beard. We'll have a look at his boat."

They walked along the landing-place to the boat, which had been moored to an iron ring at the end. It was a halfdecked motor-boat about twenty feet long, empty except for a coil of rope thrown loosely in the bottom, and a small hand fishing-net. The boat was painted white, and the name *Zulietta* could be seen on the stern in black letters.

They turned away, and Crewe suggested to his companion that they should walk along the beach and back to Cliff Farm by the road instead of returning by the path they had just descended. He added that he wanted to have a good look at the approach to the farm from the village.

Marsland readily agreed, and they walked for some distance in silence. He glanced at Crewe expectantly from time to time, but the detective appeared to be wrapped in thought. When they had covered more than half the distance between the landing-place and the point where the cliffs sloped down to level ground, Marsland spoke.

"Have you reached any conclusions yet, Crewe?"

"About this murder?"

"Of course."

"I have not come to many definite conclusions so far," said Crewe meditatively. "But of one thing I am certain. The unravelling of this crime is not going to be quite such a simple matter as Inspector Payne seems to think."

"I gathered that you were doubtful about his theory that the man who killed Lumsden got in through the window."

"Doubtful about it?" echoed Crewe. "Doubtful is a mild word. I am absolutely certain that he didn't get in through the window."

"But the catch was forced."

"It was forced from the inside."

Marsland looked at him in amazement.

"How did you find out that?" he asked.

"By inspecting the sash. I had a good look at it from the inside and out. Apparently it hadn't been opened for some time before last night, and the marks of the knife which was used to force it were very distinct in the sash in consequence. But the marks were broader and more distinct at the top of the sash inside than at the bottom. Therefore the knife was inserted at the top, and that could be done only by a man inside the house."

"But why was the window forced if the man was inside?"

"In order to mislead us."

"But the footprints led up to the window."

"No," said Crewe. "They led away from it."

"Surely you are mistaken," said Marsland. "I don't like trying to put you right on a matter of this kind, but the marks of the boots were so distinct; they all pointed the one way—towards the window."

"Look behind you, at our own footprints in the sand," said Crewe.

They had left the rocks behind them some time previously and for five minutes had been walking on a strip of sand which skirted the cliff road—now level with the sea—and broadened into a beach nearer the village. Crewe pointed to the clear imprint of their footsteps in the firm wet sand behind them.

"We'll try a little experiment," he said. "Let us walk backwards for a few yards over the ground we have just covered."

He commenced to do so, and Marsland wonderingly followed suit. After covering about twenty yards in this fashion Crewe stopped.

"That will be sufficient for our purpose," he said. "Now let us compare the two sets of footprints—the ones we have just made, and the previous ones. Examine them for yourself, Marsland, and tell me if you can see any difference."

· Marsland did so. With the mystified air of a man performing a task he did not understand, he first scrutinized the footprints they had made while walking forwards, and then examined the backward ones.

"Find any difference in them?" asked Crewe.

Marsland stood up and straightened his back with the self-conscious look of an Englishman who feels he has been made to do something ridiculous.

"I cannot say that I do. They look very much alike to me."

"You are not very observant," said Crewe, with a smile. "Let me explain the difference. In ordinary walking a man puts down the heel of his boot first, and then, as he brings his body forward, he completes the impression of his foot. He lifts his heel first and springs off the ball of his foot for the next step. But in walking backwards a man puts down the ball of his foot first and makes but a very faint impression with his heel. If he walks very carefully because he is not sure of the ground, or because it is dark, he may take four or five steps without bringing his heel to the ground. If you compare the impressions your boots have made in the sand when we were walking forward with the others made by walking backward, you will find that few of the latter marks give the complete impression of your boot."

"Yes, I see now," said Marsland. "The difference is quite distinct."

"When I examined the window this afternoon, and came to the conclusion that it had been forced from the inside, I felt certain that a murderer who had adopted such a trick in order to mislead the police would carry it out in every detail," said Crewe. "After forcing the window he would get out of it in order to leave footprints underneath the window in the earth outside, and of course he would walk backwards from the window, in order to convey the impression that he had walked up to the window through the garden, forced it and then got into the house. As I expected, I found the footsteps leading away from the window were deep in the toe, with hardly any heel marks. It was as plain as daylight that the man who had made them had walked backwards from the window. But even if I had not been quite sure of this from the footprints themselves, there was additional confirmation. The backward footsteps led straight to a fruit tree about twenty feet from the window, and on examining that tree I found a small branch—a twig—had been broken and bent just where the footsteps were lost in the gravel-walk. The man who got out of the window had bumped into the tree. Walking backwards he could neither see nor feel where he was going."

"I see—I see," Marsland stood silent for a moment evidently pondering deeply over Crewe's chain of deductions. "It seems to me," he said at length, "that this man, clever as he was, owed a great deal to accident."

"In what respect?"

"Because the window where you found the footprints is the only window on that side of the house which has a bare patch of earth underneath. All the others have grass growing right up to the windows. I noticed that when I saw the footprints. If he had got out of any of them he would have left no footprints."

"On the contrary, he knew that and chose that window because he wanted to leave us some footprints. The fact that he selected in the dark the only window that would serve his purpose shows that he is a man who knows the place well. He is clever and resourceful, but that is no reason why we should not succeed in unmasking him."

"Doesn't the fact that he wore hobnailed boots indicate that he is a labouring man?"

"My dear Marsland, may he not have worn boots of that kind for the same reason that he walked backwards—to mislead us all?"

"I gathered that you do not agree with Inspector Payne that the marks on the stairs were caused by the intruder trying to obliterate with a wet cloth the marks he made by his muddy boots."

"Outside the house he does his best to leave footprints; and inside, according to Inspector Payne, he takes special pains to remove similar traces. It is hopeless trying to reconcile the two things," said Crewe.

"Well, what do you think were the original marks on the stairs that the intruder was so anxious to remove?"

"Blood-stains."

"But why should he go to the trouble of removing blood-stains on the stairs and yet leave so much blood about in the room in which the body was discovered?"

"I have asked myself that question," said Crewe. "At the present stage it is very difficult to answer."

"You think it adds to the mystery?"

"For the present it does. But it may prove to be a key which will open many closed doors in this investigation."

"Your mention of closed doors suggests another question," said Marsland. "Why did this man get out of the window and walk backwards? If he wanted to leave misleading clues it would have been just as easy for him to go out by the front door, walk up to the window from the path so as to leave footprints and then force the window from the outside."

"Just as easy," assented Crewe. "But it would have taken longer, because it is more difficult to force the catch of a window from the outside than the inside. I think that we must assume that he was pressed for time."

"But I understand that this man Lumsden lived alone. In that case there would be little danger of interruption."

"A man who has just committed a murder gets into a state of nervous alarm," was Crewe's reply. "He is naturally anxious to get away from the scene of the crime."

"But if this man knew the place well he must have known that Lumsden lived alone, and that the discovery of the crime would not take place immediately. But for the accident of my taking shelter there the body might have remained undiscovered for days."

"Quite true. But that does not affect my point that a murderer is always in a hurry to get away."

"Isn't the fact that he went to the trouble of washing out blood-stains on the stairs evidence that he was not in a hurry?"

"No," said Crewe emphatically. "I should be more inclined to accept it as evidence that he expected some one to call at the farm—that either he or Lumsden had an appointment with some one there."

Marsland looked very hard at Crewe as he recalled the greeting Miss Maynard had given him when she opened the door to his knock.

"I did not think of that," he said.

"That supposition gives us a probable explanation

why the blood-stains were wiped off the stairs, and not off the floor of the room in which you saw the body. The murderer was expecting a visitor by appointment. The suspicions of this visitor would be aroused if he saw blood-stains on the stairs. But as he was not expected to go upstairs the murderer did not trouble about the stains in the room. This is another indication of pressure of time."

Marsland felt that Crewe was on the track of discovering Miss Maynard's presence at the farm. He began to see in the light of Crewe's deductions that her chief object in having asked him to keep her name out of the affair was to shelter some one else. But having given his word he must keep it and stand by the consequences.

CHAPTER VII

DETECTIVE GILLETT made a journey to London in
order to visit Somerset House and inspect the will left
by James Lumsden, the grandfather of the man who
had been murdered. He had been able to ascertain,
from local sources of information at Ashlingsea, some
of the details of the will, but as an experienced detective he knew the value of exact details obtained
from official sources.

His perusal of the will showed him that Cliff Farm
and all the testator's investments and personal property had been left to his nephew Frank, with the ex-
ception of legacies to three old servants who had been
in his employ for over a quarter of a century.

Gillett had ascertained from previous inquiries that
Frank was at the front in France when his grandfather died. He had been brought up at the farm, but
as his inclinations did not tend to a farming life,
he had left his grandfather, and gone to London,
where he had earned a livelihood as a clerk prior to
enlisting in the Army. According to Ashlingsea gossip, old James Lumsden had been a man of considerable wealth; though local estimates of his fortune
varied considerably, ranging from £20,000 to five times
that amount. Gillett's inspection of the terms of the
will convinced him that the lower amount was somewhat nearer the correct figure; and an interview with
Messrs. Holding, Thomas & Holding, the London

solicitors who had drawn up the will, supported this view.

It was the elder Mr. Holding, the senior partner of the firm, who had transacted Mr. Lumsden's business and had taken the instructions for drawing up the will. The document had been executed seven years ago. Mr. Holden, senior, a white haired old gentleman whose benign appearance seemed out of harmony with the soulless profession he adorned, told Gillett that Mr. Lumsden had consulted him on several occasions about business matters, but the old man was extremely intelligent and capable, and kept his affairs so entirely in his own hands that he was not a very profitable client.

The solicitor did not even know the extent of the old farmer's investments, for his client, who hated to disclose much of his private affairs even to his solicitor, had taken care when the will was drawn up not to tell him much about the sources of his income. Mr. Holding had been consulted by Frank Lumsden after he had come into his grandfather's estate, and on his behalf had made some investigations concerning the time the old man had converted his securities into cash. Of course the grandfather had lost heavily in doing so, for the stock market was greatly depressed immediately after the war broke out. But he had probably realized between ten and fifteen thousand pounds in cash.

Where this money had gone was a mystery. All the ready money that Frank Lumsden had handled when he came into the property was the sum of eighty-five pounds, which had been standing to the old farmer's credit in the bank at Staveley. Most of this amount had been swallowed up by the funeral and legal expenses connected with the transfer of the deeds. The young man had naturally been eager to find some trace of the missing money. Mr Holding was inclined to the belief that the old man's mental balance had been disturbed by the war. He thought that fear of a German invasion had preyed on his mind to such an extent that he had buried his money, intending to dig it up after the war was over. Frank had sold some of the farming machinery in order to provide himself with ready money. In this way over £200 had been obtained.

Nothing had been paid to the three old servants who had been left legacies. The old farmer had fractured his skull through falling downstairs, and had died without recovering consciousness, and therefore without realizing the emptiness of the reward he had left to his faithful servants. To Mrs. Thorpe, his housekeeper, he intended to leave £200, and legacies of half that amount to two of his old farm-hands, Samuel Hockridge and Thomas Jauncey.

Mrs. Thorpe was a widow who had had charge of the domestic management of the house for thirty-seven years. Hockridge, who was over seventy years of age, had spent over thirty years with James Lumsden as shepherd, and Jauncey, another shepherd, had been twenty-eight years at Cliff Farm.

Detective Gillett had no difficulty in tracing each of these three old servants and interviewing them. Mrs Thorpe had gone to live with a married daughter at Woolwich. Gillett found her a comparatively cheerful old woman, and, though the loss of her legacy which her old master had intended to leave her was a sore memory, she had little complaint to make against him. She was full of hope that her master's money would ultimately be found and that she would get her legacy.

Hockridge had gone into the service of a neighbouring sheep-farmer on the Staveley Downs. It was true that his best days were over, but he had a profound practical knowledge of sheep, and as labour was scarce, owing to the war, the farmer had been glad to get him. When Gillett interviewed him in his new employment he found that the loss of his promised legacy from his old master had soured him. To the detective's optimistic view that the missing money would be found, he replied that it would be too late for him—he would be in his grave.

One hundred pounds was more than his year's earnings, and it represented wealth to him. He dwelt on the ease and comfort he would have been able to command with so much money. He could give no clue regarding the hiding-place of the old farmer's fortune. He was familiar with every foot of ground on the farm, but he knew of no place that suggested a hiding-place for a large sum of money. If it had been buried, his old master must have buried it himself, and therefore the garden was the most likely place. But the garden had been turned over by zealous searchers under the direction of Master Frank, and no trace of money had been found there.

It was evident to Detective Gillett that this feeble old man had not killed Frank Lumsden. Although he regarded the loss of the legacy as the greatest disappointment that could befall any man, he felt no active resentment. He accepted it as a staggering blow from fate which had dealt him many blows during a long life. The detective's inquiries showed that on the day of the murder, and for weeks before it, Hockridge performed his ordinary duties on the farm of his new employer, and therefore could not have been near Cliff Farm, which was ten miles away from the farm on which he was now employed.

Thomas Jauncey was an inmate of Staveley Infirmary, suffering from a severe attack of rheumatism which rendered him unable to get about except with the aid of two sticks. Gillett's inquiries established the fact that he was crippled in this way when Frank Lumsden was murdered. Nevertheless, he went over to Staveley to interview the old man. He found him sitting in a chair which had been wheeled into the yard to catch the weak rays of the autumn sunshine. He was a tall old man, with a large red weather-beaten face surrounded by a fringe of white whisker, and his two hands, which were crossed on a stick he held in front of him, were twisted and gnarled with the rheumatism that had come to him as the result of half a century's shepherding on the bleak downs. The mention of the legacy he had not received brought a spark of resentment to his dim eyes.

"Seems to me I ought to have been paid some'et of what belongs to me," he said to Detective Gillett, after that officer had engaged him in conversation about his late master. "Why didn't Master Frank sell the farm and pay his grandfather's debts according to what the will said? That's what ought to be done."

"Well, of course, he might have done that," said the

detective soothingly. "But there are different ways of looking at things."

"There is a right way and a wrong way," said the old shepherd, in a tone which ruled out the idea of compromise as weakness. "I ought to have been paid some'et. That's what my son says."

"Ah!" said Gillett, with sudden interest. "That is how your son looks at it, is it? And now I come to consider it, I think he's right. He's a man with ideas."

"No one can't say as he ain't always been a clever lad," said the withered parent, with a touch of pride in his offspring.

"I'd like to meet him," said the detective. "Where is he to be found?"

"He is gard'ner to Mrs. Maynard at Ashlingsea. Mrs. Maynard she thinks a heap of him."

"Ah, yes," said Gillett. "I remember Sergeant Westaway telling me that you had a son there. I'll look him up and have a talk with him about your legacy. We may be able to do something—he and I."

On returning to Ashlingsea, Detective Gillett made inquiries concerning the gardener at 'Beverley,' the house of Mrs Maynard. Sergeant Westaway was able to supply him with a great deal of information, as he had known young Tom Jauncey for over a score of years. Young Tom was only relatively young, for he was past forty, but he bore the odd title of Young Tom as a label to distinguish him from his father, who to the people of Ashlingsea was old Tom.

The information Gillett obtained was not of a nature which suggested that young Tom was the sort of man who might commit a murder. Mrs Maynard lived on her late husband's estate two miles south from Ashlingsea. The household consisted at present of herself, her daughter, a cook, a housemaid and young Tom, who was gardener, groom and handy man. Young Tom bore a reputation for being "a steady sort of chap." He liked his glass of ale, and was usually to be found at *The Black-Horned Sheep* for an hour or so of an evening, but no one had ever seen him the worse for liquor.

Detective Gillett took a stroll over to "Beverley" in order to interview young Tom. The house, an old stone building, stood in the midst of its grounds—well away from the sea—on a gentle eminence which commanded an extensive view of the rolling downs for many miles around, but the old stone building was sheltered from the fury of Channel gales by a plantation of elm-trees.

The detective found his man digging in the kitchen-garden and preparing the ground for the spring sowing. Young Tom was a thickset man of middle age with a large round face that he had inherited from his father. He was a man of slow thought, slow actions, and hard to move once he had made up his mind. According to Gillett's standards his appearance scarcely justified the parental description of him as a clever lad.

The detective was not an expert in gardening, his life having been spent in congested areas of London where the luxury of a plot of ground is unknown, but something in young Tom's method of digging attracted his attention. It was obvious that young Tom was not putting much energy into the operation.

The fact that his shirt-sleeves were not rolled up but were buttoned at the wrist seemed to bear out this opinion. With his heavy boot young Tom pressed down the spade vigorously, but he brought up only a thin spadeful of earth each time. Then with his spade in his right hand he twisted the blade among the earth so as to break it up.

Detective Gillett brought the conversation round from the weather and vegetable growing to his recent visit to young Tom's father. He spoke of the legacy and expressed regret that old Tom, who if he had his rights would be able to pay for proper care and nourishment, should have had to go to the infirmary. But, according to Detective Gillett, even adversity had its uses. The fact that old Tom was practically bed-ridden when the murder was committed prevented the idle gossip of the town from trying to connect him with the tragedy.

The detective had not expected to find in young Tom a fluent conversationalist, but after a few moments he came to the conclusion that he was a more than ordinarily hesitating one, even according to the slow standard of Ashlingsea. Apparently young Tom did not want to discuss the murder. Detective Gillett kept the conversation on that subject and soon arrived at the conclusion that young Tom was uneasy. It came to him suddenly that what was wrong with the man's method of digging was that to all practical purpose he was using only one arm. Young Tom was careful not to put any weight on his left arm.

"What is wrong with your arm?" exclaimed the detective in an imperative tone.

Tom stopped digging and looked at him.

"Nothing," he replied in a surly tone.

"Let me have a look," said the detective, stepping towards him.

"No, I won't," answered young Tom, stepping back slowly.

Gillett looked him over from head to foot as if measuring him. His eyes rested on the man's boots, and then turned to an impression made on the soft earth by one of the boots.

"I want you to come along to the police station with me," he said suddenly.

"What for?" asked Tom in a tone of defiance.

Gillett looked him over again as if to assure himself that he had made no mistake in his first measurements.

"I'll tell you when you get there," was the reply.

"I had nothing to do with it," said Tom.

It was plain to Gillett that the man was undergoing a mental strain.

"With what?" asked the detective.

"With what you want to ask me about."

For a clever lad young Tom seemed to be making a hash of things.

"I have not said what it is," said Gillett.

"But I know," said Tom.

If that was the extent of young Tom's cleverness it seemed to be leading him in the direction of the gallows.

"You think it is about this murder?" suggested Gillett.

There was a long silence. Gillett kept his eyes steadily on his man, determined not to help him out by substituting another question for the plain one that Tom found it so difficult to answer.

"I'll come with you to the police station," said Tom at length. "But you go first and I'll follow you behind."

It was obvious to Detective Gillett that Tom wanted to avoid giving the village cause for gossip by his being taken to the police station by a detective. The detective was not disposed to consider Tom's feelings, but he reflected that his main purpose was to get Tom to the station, and that since he was not prepared to arrest Tom at present it was desirable to get him there as quietly as possible.

"No," he said. "You go on ahead and I'll follow."

Tom accepted this plan and walked up the village street to the police station with the detective about forty yards behind. Constable Heather was in charge of the station, and when he saw Tom he greeted him affably. When Heather was made to realize by Tom's awkwardness that Detective Gillett was responsible for his visit, he whistled in a significant manner.

When Gillett entered the building Tom rolled up the sleeve of his left arm and displayed a bandage round the upper part.

"Do you want to see this?" he asked doggedly.

"I do," replied the detective with keen interest. He was anxious as to the nature of the wound, but he was too cautious to display a curiosity which would reveal his ignorance. He assisted at unwinding the bandage.

"Be careful," said Tom wincing, as the detective's hand touched his arm. "The bullet is in it."

"Is it?" said Gillett.

When the bandage was off he examined the wound carefully. It was a bullet wound through the fleshy upper part of the arm, dangerously inflamed and swollen from dirt and neglect.

"You had better get this attended to," said Gillett. "There is a risk of blood poisoning and the bullet must be removed. You'll be more comfortable without that bullet, and I want it."

"I had nothing to do with him," said Tom. He spoke in a loud excited voice. It was evident that he was feeling the strain of being under suspicion.

"But you were at Cliff Farm the night Frank Lumsden was murdered," said Gillett, eyeing him closely as he put the question.

Young Tom nodded a surly admission, but did not speak.

"What were you doing there? How did you get this?" Detective Gillett pointed to the wound. "Take my advice and make a clean breast of it. I'll give you five minutes to make up your mind." Gillett picked up a pair of handcuffs from the office table as he spoke, and jingled them together nonchalantly.

Young Tom's ruddy colour faded as he glanced at the handcuffs, and from them his eyes wandered to Police Constable Heather, as though seeking his counsel to help him out of the awkward position in which he found himself. But Police Constable Heather's chubby face was set in implacable lines, in which young Tom could recognize no trace of the old acquaintance who for years past had made one of the friendly evening circle in the tap-room of *The Black-Horned Sheep*. Young Tom turned his gaze to the floor and after remaining in silent cogitation for some moments spoke:

"I was in the garden. It was before the storm came on. I don't know who killed Frank Lumsden. I didn't see either of them. They were in the house before I got there. I saw a light in a room upstairs. Then a gun or something of the kind was fired and I felt that I was hit. I got up and ran."

"Do you mean that some one fired at you from the house?"

"That's what I mean."

"Whereabouts were you?"

"Just near the cherry-tree at the side of the house."

"Did you see who fired it at you?"

"No."

"Didn't anyone call out and ask you what you were doing there?"

"No."

"He just fired—whoever it was."

"I heard the gun go off and then I felt a pain in my arm. I touched it and saw it was bleeding. Then I ran and that is all I know."

"I want to know a lot more than that," said Gillett sternly. "Your story won't hold water. What were you doing there in the first place? Why did you go there?"

"I went there to look for the money. I thought there was no one at home and I meant to look for it in the garden round about."

"Did you take a spade with you?" asked Gillett.

"What would I want to do that for?" asked Tom.

"Well, you can't dig without a spade," said Gillett.

"There's spades enough in the barn," said Tom.

"You meant to dig for the money?"

"Yes."

"Where?"

"In the garden."

"Whereabouts in the garden? Don't you know that the garden has been turned over several times?"

"I've heard that, but I wanted to dig for myself."

"It would take one man a week to dig over the garden. No one knows that better than you."

"I was going to try just near the pear-tree. I count that's a likely place."

"And did you dig there?"

"No. Didn't I tell you there was lights in the house when I got there?"

"A likely story," sneered the detective. "You went there to dig in the garden, although you knew it had been turned over thoroughly. You didn't take a spade with you, and you didn't turn over as much as a single clod. But you came away with a bullet wound in the arm from a house in which the murdered body of the owner was subsequently found."

Dull as young Tom was, he seemed to realize that the detective had a gift of making things appear as black as they could be.

"I've told you the truth," he said obstinately.

"And I don't believe a word of your story," said Detective Gillett.

CHAPTER VIII

CREWE spent two days in making investigations at Cliff Farm and at Ashlingsea. He went over the farm very carefully in search of any trace of disturbed ground which might indicate where old James Lumsden had buried the money he had obtained from the sale of his investments. But he found nothing to support the theory that the money had been buried in the fields.

There were, of course, innumerable places where a few bags of money might be hidden, especially along the brook which ran through the farm, but though Crewe searched along both banks of the brook, as well as in the open fields, he found no trace of disturbed ground. The garden, he ascertained, had been thoroughly searched under the direction of Frank Lumsden.

Crewe realized that searching for the money without the assistance of the mysterious plan which Marsland had seen on the staircase was almost hopeless, and he was not affected by his failure.

His inquiries at Ashlingsea concerned the character and habits of the grandfather and the murdered man. In the course of his inquiries about the grandson he went up to London and called on the former employers of Frank Lumsden, and the firm of Messrs Tittering & Hemmings, wholesale leather merchants, gave Frank an excellent character. He had been a sober, industrious, and conscientious clerk, and they were greatly shocked at the fate that had befallen him. They could throw no light on the murder, for they knew of no one who had any enmity against Frank. Inquiries were also made by Crewe at the headquarters of the London Rifle Brigade, in which the young man had enlisted. His military record was good, and threw no light on his tragic fate.

Crewe returned to Staveley to continue his work on the case. Sir George Granville, in his anxiety to be helpful in solving the mystery, put forward many suggestions to his guest, but they were not of a practical kind. On points where Crewe did ask for his host's assistance, Sir George was unable to respond, in spite of his eagerness to play a part in the detective's investigations. For instance, Sir George was not able to give any information about the old boatman whom Crewe and Marsland had seen at the landing-place, at the foot of the cliffs near the scene of the tragedy.

Sir George had often seen the man in the scarlet cloak, and knew that he plied for hire on the front, but he had never been in the old man's boat, and did not know where he lived or anything about him beyond the fact that he was called Pedro by the Staveley boatmen, and was believed to be an Italian.

"I'll tell you what, Crewe," said Sir George, a bright idea occurring to him as the result of reactionary consciousness that he was not a mine of information in local matters. "You go up and see Inspector Murchison. He's a rare old gossip. He has been here for a generation and knows everybody and all about them. And mention my name—I'll give you my card. You will find he will do anything for me. I'd go along with you myself, only I have promised to make a call with Mildred. But Harry will go with you—Harry knows Murchison; I introduced him yesterday on the front."

After lunch, Crewe, accompanied by Marsland, walked up to the police station at Staveley to call on Inspector Murchison. The police station was a building of grey stone, standing back in a large garden. It would have been taken for a comfortable middle-class residence but for the official notices of undiscovered crime which were displayed on a black board erected in the centre flower-bed. A young policeman was sitting writing in a front room overlooking the garden, which had been turned into a general office.

Crewe, without disclosing his name or using Sir George's card, asked him if he could see the inspector in charge. The young policeman, requesting him to take a seat, said he would inquire if the inspector was disengaged, and disappeared into an inner office. He shortly returned to say that Inspector Murchison would see them, and ushered them into the inner office, where a police officer sat writing at a large desk.

Inspector Murchison of Staveley was in every way a contrast to Police-Sergeant Westaway of Ashlingsea. He was a large and portly man with a good-humoured smile, twinkling blue eyes, and a protecting official manner which ladies who had occasion to seek his advice found very soothing. He had been stationed at Staveley for nearly thirty years, but instead of souring under his circumscribed existence like Sergeant Westaway, he had expanded with the town, and become more genial and good-tempered as the years rolled on.

He was a popular and important figure in Staveley, taking a deep and all-embracing interest in the welfare of the town and its inhabitants. He was a leading spirit in every local movement for Staveley's advancement; he was an authority in its lore, traditions, vital statistics, and local government; he had even written a booklet in which the history of Staveley was set forth and its attractions as a health and pleasure resort were described in superlative terms. He was regarded by the residents as a capable mentor and safe guide in all affairs of life, and was the chosen receptacle of many domestic confidences of a delicate and important nature. Husbands consulted him about their wives' extravagance; wives besought him to warn husbands against the folly of prolonged visits to hotels on the front because there happened to be a new barmaid from London.

It was striking proof of Inspector Murchison's rectitude that, although he was the repository of as many domestic histories as a family physician or lawyer, none of the confidences given him had ever become common gossip. For all his kindly and talkative ways, he was as secret and safe as the grave, despite the fact that he had a wife and five grown-up daughters not less curious than the rest of their sex. He was an efficient police officer, carefully safeguarding the public morals and private property entrusted to his charge, and Staveley shopkeepers, as they responded to his smiling salutations when he walked abroad, felt that they could sleep in peace in their beds, safe from murder, arson, or robbery, while his portly imposing official personality guarded the town.

Inspector Murchison swung round on his office chair as Crewe and Marsland were brought in by the young policeman.

"What can I do for you, gentlemen?" he asked courteously.

"This is Mr Crewe," said Marsland. "Mr Crewe has been making inquiries about the murder at Cliff Farm."

"Glad to see you both," said Inspector Murchison, extending his hand. "If I can be of any assistance to Mr Crewe he has only to say so. Of course I've heard all about the murder at Cliff Farm. It was you who discovered the body, Mr Marsland. A terrible affair. Poor, inoffensive Frank Lumsden! I knew him well, and his grandfather too—a queer old stick. Buried his money where no one can find it. And that is what is at the back of this murder, Mr Crewe, I have no doubt."

"It certainly looks like it," said Crewe.

"What is your opinion, inspector, with regard to the money?" asked Marsland. "Do you think that young Lumsden found it and refused to pay the legacies, or that it has never been found?"

"It has never been found," said Inspector Murchison in a positive tone. "I'm quite certain of that. Why, it is scarcely more than a week ago that young Lumsden and his friend Brett came to ask me if I could throw any light on it. They had a mysterious looking cryptogram that young Lumsden had found among his grandfather's papers, and they were certain that it referred to the hidden money. They showed it to me, but I could not make head or tail of it. I recommended them to go and see a man named Grange who keeps a second-hand book shop in Curzon Street, off High Street. He's a bibliophile, and would be able to put them on the track of a book about cryptograms, even if he hadn't one in stock himself."

"What was the cryptogram like?" asked Marsland. "Was it like this?" He took up a pen from the table and attempted to reproduce a sketch of the mysterious document he had found on the stairs at Cliff Farm.

"Something like that," said the inspector. "How do you come to know about it?"

"I found it at the dead man's house before I discovered the body. I left it there, but it was stolen between the time I left the house and when I returned with Sergeant Westaway. At any rate it has not been seen since."

"Ah," said the inspector, "there you have the motive for the murder."

"You spoke just now of young Lumsden's friend, Brett," said Crewe. "Who is Brett?"

"He lives in Staveley—a young fellow with a little private means. He and Lumsden were close friends— I have often seen them together about the town. They served in the same regiment, were wounded together, taken prisoners together by the Germans, tortured together, and escaped together."

"Brett?" exclaimed Marsland in a tone which awakened Crewe's interest. "I know no one named Brett."

"No, of course you wouldn't know him, Mr Marsland," said the inspector genially. "You have not been so long in Staveley that you can expect to know all the residents. It's not a very large place, but it takes time to know all the people in it."

"I was thinking of something else," said Marsland.

"What sort of man was Brett to look at?" asked Crewe of the inspector.

"About the same age as Lumsden—just under thirty, I should say. A thin, slight, gentlemanly looking ,fellow. Rather a better class than poor Lumsden. I often wondered what they had in common."

Crewe, who was watching the effect of this description on Marsland, pressed for further particulars.

"Average height?" he asked.

"A little under," replied the inspector. "Dark complexion with a dark moustache—what there was of it."

"I think you said he had been wounded and captured by the Germans?" said Marsland.

"Tortured rather than wounded," replied the inspector. "The Germans are fiends, not men. Brett and Lumsden were captured while out in a listening patrol, and because they wouldn't give their captors any information they were tortured. But these brave lads refused to give the information the Germans wanted, and ultimately they succeeded in making their escape during an attack. I've listened to many of the experiences of our brave lads, but I don't think I've heard anything worse than the treatment of Brett and this poor fellow who has been murdered."

"Was it at Armentières this happened?" asked Marsland.

"I think it was," replied the inspector. "Then you've heard the story, too, Mr. Marsland?"

"No, I was thinking of something else," he answered.

"We must look up Brett," said Crewe. "Just write down his address, inspector—if you don't mind."

"He lives at No. 41 Whitethorn Gardens," said the police officer. "But I don't think you will find him there to-day. His landlady, Mrs. Penfield, promised to send me word as soon as he got back. When I heard of this murder I went down to see Brett to find out when he had last seen Lumsden, and to get a statement from him. But he had gone up to London or Liverpool the day before the murder. Mrs. Penfield expects him back early next week, but it is impossible to be certain about his return. The fact is, Mr Crewe, that he does some secret service work for the Foreign Office, and naturally doesn't talk much about his movements. He is an excellent linguist I'm told, knows French and Russian and German—speaks these languages like a native."

"There is no hurry about seeing him," said Crewe. "I'll look him up when he returns. In the meantime will you write down his address for me?"

Marsland, who was nearer the inspector, took the paper on which the police officer wrote Brett's address, and before handing it to Crewe looked at it carefully.

"And now can you tell me anything about an old boatman who wears a scarlet cloak?" asked Crewe.

"A tall old man, with a hooked nose and white beard?"

"That's old Pedro," replied Inspector Murchison. "He's well known on the front, although he's not been here very long, certainly not more than twelve months. But I hope you don't think Pedro had anything to do with the Cliff Farm murder, Mr. Crewe? We're rather proud of Pedro on the front, he's an attraction to the place, and very popular with the ladies."

"Marsland and I saw him in his boat at an old landing-place near the farm a few days ago," replied Crewe. "He's a man not easily forgotten—once seen. I'd like to find out what took him over in the direction of Ashlingsea."

"He's often over there," said the inspector. "That is his favourite trip for his patrons—across the bay and over to the cliff landing, as we call it. That is the landing at the foot of the cliffs near Cliff Farm —I daresay you noticed it, Mr Crewe?"

"Yes. They told me at Ashlingsea that the landing-place and boat-house belong to Cliff Farm—that they were put up by old James Lumsden."

"That is right," said the inspector. "The old man used to do a bit of fishing—that is ten or fifteen years ago when he was an active man, though getting on a bit—a strange thing to combine farming and fishing, wasn't it? But he was a queer sort in many ways, was James Lumsden."

"And where is this man with the scarlet cloak to be found when he is not on the front?" asked Crewe. "I'd like to have a little talk with him."

"You'll find that rather difficult," said the inspector with a laugh. "Old Pedro is deaf and dumb."

"Has he any friends here, or does he live alone?"

"He came here with his daughter and her husband and he lives with them. His daughter is a dwarf—a hunchback—and is supposed to be a bit of a clairvoyant or something of that kind. The husband is English, but not a very robust type of Englishman. They have a shop in Curzon Street off High Street—second-hand books."

"What is his name?" asked Crewe.

"Grange."

"And it was to this man you recommended young Lumsden to go for a book on cryptograms?"

"Yes; the same man," said the inspector. "I can tell you a queer thing about his wife. I've said she is a bit of a clairvoyant. Well, you know there is not much love lost between the police and clairvoyants; most of them are shallow frauds who play on the ignorant gullible public. But Mrs. Grange is different: she isn't in the business professionally. And, being a broad-minded man, I am ready to admit that there may be something in clairvoyance and spiritualism, in spite of the fact that they are usually associated with fraud. Well, one of my men, Constable Bell, lost a pendant from his watch-chain. It was not very valuable, but it had a sentimental value. He had no idea where he lost it, but he happened to mention it to Mrs. Grange—this dwarf woman—and she told him she might be able to help him in finding it.

"She took him into a sitting-room above the shop, and after getting his watch from him held it in her hands for a few moments. She told him to keep perfectly still, and concentrate his mind on the article he had lost. She closed her eyes and went into a sort of trance. Then in a strange far-away voice she said, 'I see water—pools of water among the rocks. I see a man and a woman walking near the rocks, arm in arm. I see the man take the woman in his arms to kiss her, and the pendant, caught by a button of her blouse, drops into the pool at their feet.' That was true about the kissing. Bell when off duty visited Horseley three miles from here, with his sweetheart, and he thought the dwarf must have seen them and was having a joke at his expense. However, he cycled over to Horseley when the tide was out next day, and much to his surprise he found the pendant in the water—just as the dwarf had told him. How do you account for a thing like that, Mr. Crewe?"

"It is very difficult to account for," said Crewe. "Does this dwarf hold spiritualistic séances?"

"Not that I am aware of," replied the inspector. "If she does, it is in a private capacity, and not as a business."

"Her acquaintance is worth cultivating. We will go and see her, Marsland."

Crewe cordially thanked Inspector Murchison for the information he had supplied, and set out with Marsland for Mr. Grange's shop in Curzon Street.

"A good man, Murchison; he has given us a lot of information," he said to his companion as they drove along.

"It seemed very scrappy and incomplete to me," was Marsland's reply.

"Gossipy is the right word—not scrappy. And there is nothing more valuable than gossipy information; it enables you to fill in so many blanks in your theory—if you have one."

"You have formed your theory of how this tragedy occurred?" said Marsland interrogatively.

"Part of one," replied Crewe.

Marsland accepted this reply as an intimation that the detective was not prepared to disclose his theory at that stage.

"That story about the pendant was remarkable," he said. "Do you believe it?"

"It is not outside the range of possibility," replied Crewe. "Some remarkable results have been achieved by psychists who possess what they call mediumistic powers."

"Do you really think it possible that, by surrendering herself to some occult influence, this woman was able to reproduce for herself the scene between Constable Bell and his sweetheart, and see the pendant drop?"

"That is the way in which psychists would explain it, but I think it can be accounted for in a much less improbable way. I know, from my own investigations into spiritualism and its claims, that some mediums are capable, under favourable conditions, of reading a little of another person's thoughts, provided the other person is sympathetic and tries to help. But even in this limited field failure is more frequent than success. But let us suppose that Constable Bell was an extremely sympathetic subject on this occasion. How was this woman, after getting Bell to concentrate his thoughts on the events of the day when he lost the pendant, able to discover it by reading Bell's thoughts?"

"Bell's thoughts would not be of much help to her, as he did not remember when or how he lost the pendant," said Marsland.

"The point I am aiming at is that sub-consciously Bell may have been aware of the conditions under which he lost the pendant, and yet not consciously aware of them. The human brain does not work as a uniform piece of machinery; it works in sections or in compartments. Suppose part of Bell's brain became aware that the pendant had become detached and tried to communicate the fact to that part of Bell's brain where he keeps toll of his personal belongings. That would be the normal procedure, and under normal conditions a connection between these two compartments of the brain would be established, and Bell would stoop down and pick up the pendant. But on this occasion Bell was intoxicating himself with kisses and had put his brain into an excitable state. Possibly that part which keeps toll of his personal possessions was particularly excited at the prospect of adding the lady to the list of Bell's belongings.

"Let us assume that it was too excited to hear the small warning voice which was crying out about the lost pendant. And when Bell's brain had become normal the small voice had become too weak to be heard. It was never able subsequently to establish a connection between that part of the brain to which it belonged and that part where Bell keeps toll of his property—perhaps it never tried again, being under the impression that its first attempts had succeeded. And so when Bell was asked by Mrs. Grange to concentrate his thoughts on the lost pendant he was able to reproduce the state in which his brain was at the time, and the medium was able to hear the warning in Bell's brain which Bell himself had never consciously heard."

Marsland looked hard at Crewe to see whether he was speaking jestingly or seriously, for he had been shrewd enough to discover that the detective had a habit at times of putting forth fanciful theories the more effectually to conceal his real thoughts. It was when Crewe talked most that he revealed least, Marsland thought. But as Crewe's face, as usual, did not reveal any clue to his mind, the young man murmured something about the explanation of the pendant being interesting, but unscientific.

"What science cannot explain, it derides," was Crewe's reply.

"Do you sympathize with the complaints of the spiritualists, that scientists adopt an attitude of negation and derision towards spiritualism, instead of an attitude of investigation?" continued Marsland inquiringly.

"I think there is some truth in that complaint, though as far as I am concerned I have not found much truth in spiritualism. However, Mrs. Grange may be able to convince me that she uses her powers to enlighten, and not to deceive. I am most anxious to see her."

CHAPTER IX

Staveley only differed from a hundred other English seaside resorts by having a sea front which was quite flat, the cliffs which skirted the coastline from Ashlingsea falling away and terminating in sand dunes about half a mile to the south of the town. At that point the cliff road, after following the coastline for nearly twelve miles, swept inland round the sand dunes, which had encroached on the downs more than half a mile from the sea, but turned back again near the southern outskirts of the town in a bold picturesque curve to the sea front.

From the sea front the town rambled back with characteristically English irregularity of architecture to the downs. There was the usual seaside mixture of old and new houses, the newest flaunting their red-tiled ugliness from the most beautiful slopes of the distant hills.

Crewe and Marsland drove slowly along to High Street by way of the front after leaving the police station. A long row of boarding-houses and hotels faced the sea; and there were pleasure boats, bathing-machines, a pier and a bandstand. The season was practically over, but a number of visitors still remained, making the most of the late October sunshine, decorously promenading for air and exercise. It was a typically English scene, except that the band was playing German music and the Kursaal still flaunted its German name.

The front was bisected about midway by the main business thoroughfare of the town, and there was a sharp distinction between the two halfs of the promenade which it divided. The upper half was the resort of fashion and the mode: the hotels were bigger and more expensive; the boarding-houses were designated private hotels. All the amusements were situated in this part of the front: the pleasure boats, the pier, the band, the goat carts, and the Bath chairs. The lower part of the front was practically deserted, its hotels and boarding-houses looked empty and neglected, and its whole aspect was that of a poor relation out of place in fashionable surroundings.

Although Marsland did not know much about Staveley he was able to guide Crewe to Curzon Street, and once in Curzon Street they had not much difficulty in finding the shop kept by Mr. Grange. It was a curious little white house standing back a few feet from the footpath, and trays of second-hand books were arranged on tables outside.

Crewe, after getting out of his car, began an inspection of the books on the trays outside the shop, and while engaged in this way he saw a young lady being shown out of the shop. She was a well dressed graceful girl, not much more than twenty. Behind her was the shopkeeper, a tall thin man past middle age, with a weak irresolute face disfigured by some cutaneous disorder, small ferrety grey eyes, and a straggling beard. As he opened the door to let the young lady out Crewe's quick ears heard him remark:

"Well, as I said, we didn't go because we saw the

storm coming up. I'm very glad now we didn't, as things turned out. It's a dreadful affair—dreadful."

To Crewe's surprise Marsland stepped forward when he saw the young lady, lifted his hat and put out his hand. Crewe thought she hesitated a little before responding.

"I am glad to see you, Miss Maynard," Marsland declared. "You are the very person I wanted to see. But this is quite an unexpected meeting."

"It is very kind of you," said the young lady with a smile.

To Crewe it was evident that she was more embarrassed than pleased at the meeting.

Marsland walked along the street a few paces with Miss Maynard and then came back to Crewe.

"Please excuse me for half an hour or so, Crewe. I have some things to talk over with this lady."

He rushed back to Miss Maynard's side without waiting for an answer. Crewe watched them for a moment and then he became aware that the shop-keeper standing at his doorway was watching them with a gaze of perplexity.

"Mr Grange, I believe?" said Crewe.

The shopkeeper produced a pair of spectacles from his pocket and put them on before replying. With the spectacles on his small grey eyes he peered at Crewe, and said:

"What can I do for you, sir?"

Crewe saw that the man was ill at ease, and he endeavoured to bring him back to his normal state.

"Have you a copy of a book called *Notitiæ Monastica?*" asked the detective. "It's a work on the early British religious establishments," he explained.

"No, sir: I don't think I've ever heard of the book. But perhaps I could get you one if you particularly want it."

"You might try and let me know. I'll leave you my address. Inspector Murchison told me that if anyone could help me you could."

"Inspector Murchison?" echoed Mr Grange peering again at Crewe.

"He was most enthusiastic about you," continued Crewe. "He said that if ever he wanted to know anything about rare books he would come to you. You have a good friend in the inspector, Mr Grange."

"I did not know—yes I think so—it was very good of him—very good indeed." Mr Grange was both relieved and pleased at being commended by the head of the local police, for he smiled at Crewe, blinked his eyes, and rubbed his hands together.

"And about Mrs Grange he was no less enthusiastic," continued Crewe. "He told me about her extraordinary psychic powers and the recovery of Constable Bell's watch-chain pendant. A most remarkable case. I take a great interest in occultism, Mr. Grange, and in all forms of psychic power—I have done so for years. Perhaps your wife would grant me the favour of an interview? I should so much like to meet her and talk to her."

"Certainly," exclaimed Mr. Grange, who was now delighted with his visitor. "I am sure she would like to meet a gentleman like yourself who is interested in—er—occultism. Excuse me while I run upstairs to her."

He left the shop by a side-door opening on the passage leading to the private apartments above the shop. A few minutes later he came back with an invitation to Crewe to follow him upstairs to the sitting-room. Crewe followed him into a room which overlooked the street. In an arm-chair beside one of the two windows sat Mrs. Grange. She rose to meet Crewe. She was about four feet in height but her deformed figure seemed to make her look smaller, Her skin was dark and coarse and her teeth were large. On her upper lip there was a slight growth of hair and her eyebrows were very thick and shaggy. She had deep black eyes, and after her bow to Crewe she gazed at him in a fixed penetrating way—the look of an animal on the watch.

Crewe took particular note of the way in which her black hair was dressed. He closed the door behind him and took a seat near it when the dwarf sat down in her arm-chair. Mr. Grange stood a few feet from his wife and again rubbed his hands together to express his satisfaction.

"It is very good of you to see me," said Crewe to the dwarf. "I was so much struck with the account Inspector Murchison gave me of your psychic powers that it occurred to me that you might be able to assist me in a somewhat similar way to that in which you assisted Constable Bell."

"I shall be pleased to try," said the dwarf slowly. "But success is not always possible." She spoke in a thin high pitched voice.

"So I understood," said Crewe. "But my case is, I think, less difficult than that of Constable Bell. I have not lost anything. On the contrary I have found something, which I want to restore to the owner.

If I gave you this thing I have found to hold, you could describe the owner to me could you not?"

"It is possible," said the dwarf.

Crewe produced from one of the pockets of his motor coat a brown paper parcel. He unwrapped the paper, keeping covert observation on the Granges as he did so, and displayed the old felt hat which he had found while making his way down the path from the top of the cliff.

"I am anxious to restore this to its owner," he said, as he held out the hat to the dwarf.

He intercepted the glance of angry reproach which she gave her husband. The latter had stopped rubbing his hands and now stood gazing alternately at the hat and at Crewe, with visible trepidation on his features. The dwarf gave the hat a quick glance, and then resolutely turned to Crewe.

"It is of no value," she said, in her high pitched voice, meeting his glance intently.

"Of very little value—from the monetary point of view," said Crewe. "But there are other reasons why the owner would like to have it restored to him. Do you think you could help me to find him?"

"No," she replied decisively. "I could not help you."

"Why?" asked Crewe.

"Because it does not interest me. I must feel an interest—I must feel in sympathy with the object on which I am asked to exert my powers. Without such sympathy I can do nothing, for when I close my eyes to see the vision I become as blind as those born without sight."

THE MYSTERY OF THE DOWNS   113

"And you have no interest in helping me to restore this hat to its owner?" asked Crewe.

"None," she replied.

"And you?" said Crewe, turning to her husband.

"I—I know nothing about it," he stammered. "It is not mine."

"This hat was lost over the cliffs near Ashlingsea. It was lost the night that the murdered body of the owner of the Cliff Farm was found. The owner was so anxious to secure possession of it that the morning after the murder he sent a boatman over to the scene to look for it. Is not that correct?" asked Crewe looking searchingly at Mr. Grange.

"I know nothing about it," was the reply.

"Perhaps you would like to try it on," said Crewe, picking up the hat and holding it out to the woman's husband.

"Me?" exclaimed the man, recoiling as he spoke. "Why should I? It is not mine."

"Come," said Crewe, "I will exchange the hat for a candid statement of what happened at Cliff Farm on that fateful night."

"It is not his," declared the dwarf. "We know nothing about Cliff Farm—we have never been there."

CHAPTER X

"WILL you come to some place where we can have a talk?"

"Yes. Where shall we go?"

Her eyes met his frankly, as she replied, and Marsland as he looked at her was impressed with her beauty and the self-possession of her manner. She was young, younger than he had thought on the night of the storm—not more than twenty-two or twenty-three at the most—and as she stood there, with the bright autumn sunshine revealing the fresh beauty of her face and the slim grace of her figure, she made a striking picture of dainty English girlhood, to whom the sordid and tragic sides of life ought to be a sealed book. But Marsland's mind, as he glanced at her, travelled back to his first meeting with her in the lonely farm-house where they had found the body of the murdered man on the night of the storm.

He led her to one of the numerous tea-rooms on the front, choosing one which was nearly empty, his object being to have a quiet talk with her. Since the eventful night on which he had walked home with her after they had discovered the dead body of the owner of Cliff Farm, several important points had arisen on which he desired to enlighten her, and others on which he desired to be enlightened by her.

"I thought of writing to you," he said after he had found seats for his companion and himself in a quiet corner of the large tea-room and had given an order to the waitress. "But I came to the conclusion that it was unwise—that you might not like it."

He found it difficult to strike a satisfactory balance in his attitude to her. On the one hand, it was impossible to be distant and formal in view of the fact that they were united in keeping from the police the secret of her presence at Cliff Farm on the night of the murder; on the other hand, he did not wish to adopt a tone of friendly familiarity based on his knowledge that she had something to hide. When he studied her from the young man's point of view as merely an attractive member of the opposite sex he felt that she was a charming girl whose affection any one might be proud to win, but his security against her charms was the feeling of distrust that any one so good-looking should have anything to hide. He had no sentimental illusion that she would confide her secret to him.

She waited for him to continue the conversation, and pretended to be engaged in glancing round the room, but from time to time she gave him a quick glance from beneath her long lashes.

"What I wanted to tell you most of all is that, when I went back to Cliff Farm the next day, the detective from Scotland Yard found a comb on the floor of the sitting-room downstairs where we sat after you let me in."

"A comb!" she cried. "What sort of a comb?"

"A tortoise-shell comb about three inches long, with a gold mounting."

"That is strange," she said. "It was found on the floor?"

"Close to the chair where you stood."

"Do they know whom it belongs to?"

"No, fortunately. But they are very anxious to find out. Naturally they think it points to the conclusion that there is a woman in the case."

"Of course they would think that," she said.

"Do you think any one in Ashlingsea could identify it as yours?" he asked. "Have you had it any length of time?"

"It was not mine," she declared. "I did not lose a comb."

"Not yours?" he exclaimed in astonishment.

"I am trying to think to whom it belonged," she said meditatively. "As far as I know, lady visitors at Cliff Farm were few. And yet it could not be Mrs. Bond—the woman who went there to tidy up the place once a week—you say it was gold mounted?"

"Rather an expensive looking comb, I thought," said the young man.

"Yes; it looks as if there was a woman in the case."

The arrival of the waitress with the tea-things brought about a lengthy pause in the conversation.

To Marsland it looked as if there must be two women in the case if the comb did not belong to Miss Maynard. But he was not altogether satisfied with her statement that it was not hers. It is difficult for a young man of impressionable age to regard a good-looking girl as untruthful, but Marsland recalled other things which indicated that she was not averse to seeking refuge in false statements. He remembered her greeting when he had knocked at the farm-house on the night of the storm. "Where have you been?" was the question she put to him, and then she had added,

"I have been wondering what could have happened to you."

They were not questions which might reasonably be directed to a chance visitor on such a night, and he remembered that there had been a note of impatience in her voice. This impatience harmonized with the start of surprise which she gave when he spoke to her. Obviously she had been expecting some one and had mistaken his knock for the arrival of the man for whom she had been waiting. And yet her subsequent story to Marsland in explanation of her presence at the farm was that she had been overtaken by the storm and had sought shelter there. She had made no reference to the man whom she had expected to see when she opened the door in response to Marsland's knock. When directly questioned on the matter she had declared that it was Frank Lumsden she had expected to see.

"Whom do the police suspect?" she asked, after the waitress had departed.

"I do not think they suspect any one in particular just yet," he replied.

"Have they no clue of any kind?"

"They have several clues of a kind. They have discovered some footprints outside the window of the room in which we sat. The window itself has been forced. And that reminds me of something else I wanted to tell you. The police have naturally questioned me in order to obtain any light I can throw on the mystery. One of the first things they asked me was how I got into the house. I told them that the door was open, and that as no one came when I knocked I walked in and sat down.   I think that was what you told me you did."

"Yes," she replied. "The door was open."

"You see, I forgot to fortify myself with a ready made story which would fit all these questions.   The theory of the police at present is that the murderer was in the house all the time we were there."

"Oh!" she exclaimed. It was obvious that she was deeply interested in that theory. "Because of the crash we heard?"

"Partly because of that, and partly because that strange looking document we found on the stairs has disappeared.   It was gone when I went back to the house with the police sergeant.   Their theory is that the murderer was in the house when I arrived—that is, when you arrived—but of course they didn't know about your being there.   As they reconstruct the tragedy, the murderer was making his way downstairs with the plan in his hand just as I—meaning you—arrived at the door.   In his alarm he dropped the plan and retreated upstairs.   The crash we heard was made by him knocking down a picture that hung on the wall near the top of the staircase—that is on the second floor.   After we left the house he came down, found the plan in the sitting-room and made off with it."

"To think of his being in the house all the time I was there alone!" she said. "It makes me shudder even now."

"The police are under the impression that they will not have much difficulty in getting hold of him, but on the other hand Mr. Crewe thinks there are some puzzling mysterious features which the police have overlooked."

"Mr. Crewe!" she exclaimed. "Do you mean the famous London detective?"

"Yes."

"How does he come into it?"

"My uncle, Sir George Granville, is responsible for that. Perhaps you know him?"

"I know him by sight," she said.

"I have been staying with him," continued the young man. "And when I rang him up from the police station at Ashlingsea, after leaving you, he was greatly excited about my discovery. He knows Crewe very well—they used to be interested in chess, and that brought them together. Crewe had come down to Staveley for the week-end as my uncle's guest, and they were sitting up for me when I telephoned from Ashlingsea."

"Was that Mr. Crewe who was with you this morning?" she asked.

"Yes. Rather a fine looking man, don't you think?"

She had other things to think of than the appeal of Mr. Crewe's appearance to her feminine judgment.

"What did he want at Grange's shop?" she asked.

It occurred to him that he would like to ask that question concerning her own visit there. What he said was:

"He wanted to make some inquiries there."

"Inquiries?" She looked at him steadily, but as he did not offer further information she had to put her anxiety into words. "About this comb?"

"As a matter of fact, I am not fully in his confidence," said Marsland with a constrained smile. "Crewe is a man who keeps his own counsel. He has to, in his line of business."

She was not quite sure that a rebuke was contained in this reply, but she gave herself the benefit of the doubt.

"Does Mr. Crewe know that I was at Cliff Farm that night?" she asked.

"No. I thought I made my promise on that point quite definite."

"You did," was her candid reply to his undoubted rebuke. "But I will release you from that promise if you think you ought to tell him."

"I am under no obligation to tell him anything more than I have told the police."

"I thought that perhaps the fact that your uncle has brought Mr. Crewe into the case might make a difference."

As he made no reply to that suggestion she branched off to something else that was in her mind:

"Do you think Mr. Crewe is as clever as people say he is?"

"There is no doubt that he is a very remarkable man. I have already had proof of his wonderfully quick observation."

"Then I suppose there is no doubt that he will find out who killed Frank Lumsden?"

He looked at her steadily as he replied:

"His appearance in the case lessens the guilty person's chance of escape. But Mr. Crewe does not claim to solve every mystery which is presented to him."

"Do you think he will solve this one?" she asked.

He knew that she had a secret reason for hoping that some aspect of it would prove insoluble, but this knowledge did not influence his reply.

"It may baffle him," he replied meditatively. "But I have been so deeply impressed with the keenness of his observations and his methods of deduction that I feel sure he will get very near to the truth."

CHAPTER XI

CREWE walked to the street known as Whitethorn Gardens, which he learned was situated in the older portion of the town, off the less fashionable end of the front. It was a narrow street, steep of ascent, full of old stone houses of deserted appearance, which faced cobbled footways from behind prim grass-plots. It looked like a place which had seen better days and was proud in its poverty, for very few "Apartments" cards were displayed in the old-fashioned bay windows. No. 41 was half-way up the street on the right-hand side, and was distinguished from its fellows by a magnolia in the centre of the grass-plot, and two parallel close-clipped ivy screens which had been trained to grow in panel fashion on both sides of the front door.

Crewe walked up the gravel path and rang the bell. After a considerable pause, he rang again. His second ring brought a grim-faced servant to the door, who, when he asked if her mistress was in, opened the door and invited him to enter. She took him into a small sitting-room, and vanished with a gruff intimation that she would tell Mrs. Penfield.

Five minutes elapsed before a woman entered the room noiselessly and stood before him. She was a woman of attractive appearance, about thirty, with clear grey eyes and well kept brown hair, and her graceful and ladylike demeanour suggested that she was of superior class to the type of womanhood usually associated with seaside apartment houses.

"I understand that you are looking for apartments?" she said in a pleasant voice.

"No," said Crewe. "I came to see Mr. Brett."

"He is not in," was the reply. Her smile had gone and her voice had lost its ingratiating tone. She looked at Crewe steadily.

"When do you expect him in?"

"He is away."

"When do you expect him back?"

"I cannot say definitely when he will be back."

"Do you expect him in the course of the next few days?"

"He may come any time." Her suspicions were fully aroused, and with the object of dismissing him and also extracting some information from him she said, "And who shall I tell him called?"

Crewe handed her a card and watched her as she read the name.

"Mr. Crewe!" she exclaimed with a note of surprise and alarm in her voice. "Not Mr. Crewe of—of London?"

"I live in London," he replied.

"Not Mr. Crewe, the—famous detective?"

"That is my occupation," was the modest rejoinder.

"Oh, I am pleased to see you," was her unexpected exclamation. She smiled as she looked him over. He was much younger and much better-looking than the Mr. Crewe of her imagination, and these things lessened her fear of him. "Inspector Murchison came down to see Mr. Brett on Saturday last, but he had gone away two days before," she said. "I promised the inspector I would send him word when Mr. Brett returned." She seemed to have changed completely since learning Crewe's name, and to be anxious to supply information.

"I have seen Inspector Murchison," he said.

"If I knew Mr. Brett's present address I would telegraph to him," she continued. "I don't think he can have heard of the murder of poor Mr. Lumsden, or he would have come back at once."

"I have no doubt of that," said Crewe.

"As of course you know, from the inspector, Mr. Brett is engaged from time to time on very important business of a confidential nature for the Government. He has often been away for three weeks at a time without sending me as much as a postcard."

"On what day did he go away?" asked Crewe.

"On Thursday last—Thursday morning. It was on Friday night that Mr. Lumsden was killed, was it not?"

"It was on Friday night that his body was discovered," said Crewe.

"A dreadful crime," she continued.

"Did Mr. Brett leave by train?" he asked.

"Yes—that is, as far as I know. Oh, of course he must have gone by train. He only took a light suitcase with him, so I do not expect he will be away very long."

There was a pause during which she did some earnest thinking.

"Perhaps you would like to look at Mr. Brett's rooms?"

"If it is not too much trouble." He was suspicious

of the change in her attitude after learning his name.

She led the way upstairs and opened a door on the first landing.

"This is his sitting-room," she said.

It was a large, comfortably furnished room, with a window looking onto the front garden. Crewe's keen eye took in the details of the interior. The manner in which the room had been left suggested that its owner intended to return. Several pipes and a box of cigars, nearly full, stood on a table near the fireplace. Beside them was a folded newspaper, and on top of it was a novel.

An arm-chair was drawn up close to the fire-place, and beside it was a pair of slippers. Near the window was another table, on which there was an open writing-desk containing notepaper, envelopes and pens. The room looked neat and tidy, as if for an occupant of regular habits who liked his comfort to be studied. It was this impression which gave Crewe the clue to the landlady's invitation to inspect the apartments. If Brett had anything to hide he could depend on the loyal support of Mrs. Penfield.

Among the photographs which decorated the room, the one that claimed Crewe's attention was that which occupied the place of honour in the centre of the mantelpiece. It was enclosed in a silver frame. He took it in his hands to examine it closely, and glancing at Mrs. Penfield as he lifted it down he saw her give a slight disdainful toss of her head.

"A very pretty girl," said Crewe, looking critically at the photograph.

"It is very flattering," was the cold comment of his companion.

"But even allowing for that"—he left the sentence unfinished, as if unable to find words for his admiration of the subject of the photograph. His real interest in the photograph was that he had recently seen the sitter, and was astonished to find that she had some connection with Brett. "Do you know her?"

"I have seen her. She came here several times to see Mr. Brett. She came to-day about an hour ago."

"She didn't know that Mr. Brett had gone away?"

It occurred to Mrs. Penfield that she had made a mistake in volunteering this information—a mistake due to the feminine desire to convey the impression that the subject of the photograph was in the habit of running after Mr. Brett.

"She wanted to know when he would be back," she answered hastily.

"What is her name?" asked Crewe.

"Miss Maynard."

"Is she Mr. Brett's fiancée?"

"I have heard some people say that they are engaged, but I never heard Mr. Brett say so. At any rate, she doesn't wear an engagement ring."

"That seems to settle it," said Crewe, who knew the value of sympathy in a jealous nature. "And this photograph, I presume, is one of Mr. Brett," he added, pointing to a photograph of a young man which stood at the other end of the mantelpiece.

Mrs. Penfield nodded without speaking.

"Would you like to look at Mr. Brett's bedroom?" she asked after a pause.

"I may as well, now that I am here."

She led the way to the door of another room and

Crewe entered it. Here, again, there were many indications that the occupant of the room did not ex-
.pect to be absent for any great length of time. It was
smaller than the sitting-room, but it looked very cheerful and cosy. Behind the door a dressing-gown
was hanging.

Crewe's rapid inspection of the room showed him
that there was no shaving tackle visible, and that
there were no hair-brushes or clothes-brushes on the
dressing-table. It was to be assumed from these facts
that Mr. Brett had taken his brushes and shaving
things with him. As far as appearances went, his
departure had not been hurried.

"A very nice set of rooms," said Crewe. "I think
you said you promised to let Inspector Murchison
know when Mr. Brett returns. I shall get the inspector to ring me up when he hears from you. There
are one or two questions I should like to ask Mr.
Brett. When he comes back, will you please tell him
I called?"

Crewe's next act was to get his car and visit the
garage kept by Gosford in High Street. Inside the
building he saw the proprietor standing by a large
grey motor-car in the centre of the garage, watching
a workman in blue overalls who was doing something
to one of the wheels.

"Not much the worse," said Crewe, nodding his
head in the direction of the grey car, and addressing
himself to the proprietor of the garage.

Gosford, a short stout man, looked hard at him as
he approached. He was clean-shaven, and his puffed-
out cheeks made his large face look like a ball.

Gosford again looked at Crewe out of his little

black eyes, but said nothing. His business caution
acted as a curb on his natural geniality, for he had
learnt by experience of the folly of giving information to strangers until he knew what business brought
them into the garage.

"Not much the worse for its accident," said Crewe.
"You were not long in getting it into repair."

The proprietor's glance wandered backwards and
forwards from the car to his visitor.

"As good as ever," he said, "Do you want to buy
it?"

"No," said Crewe. "I have one already." He
nodded in the direction of his car outside.

"She's a beauty," said Gosford. "But those Bod-
esly touring cars run into a lot of money. You paid
a big price for her, I'll be bound."

"Oh, yes. You motor-car people are never reasonable—manufacturers, garage proprietors, repairers,
you are all alike."

"No, no, sir, we are very reasonable here. That
is what I pride myself on."

"In that case I'll know where to bring my repairs.
But to-day all I want is some petrol. That is what
I came for, but when I saw this car I thought I'd
like to see what sort of job you had made of it. The
last time I saw it was when it was lying in the ditch
about six miles from here on the road to Ashlingsea."

"Oh, you saw her there?" said Mr. Gosford genially.
"But there wasn't much the matter with her, beyond
a bent axle."

"I hope that is what you told the gentleman who
left it there—Mr. ——?"

"Mr. Brett," said Mr. Gosford, coming to the relief of his visitor's obvious effort to recall a name.

"Ah, yes; Mr. Brett," said Crewe. "Was it Thursday or Friday that I met him on the Ashlingsea road in this car?"

"Friday, sir. This car wasn't out on Thursday. Friday was the night of the big storm. She was out in it all night. I didn't know where she was until Mr. Brett rang me up on Saturday morning."

"So he was in Staveley on Saturday morning?"

"No, no, sir. He said he was speaking from Lewes. He must have caught an early train out from Staveley or Ashlingsea before we were open. That is why he didn't ring up before."

Crewe, on leaving the garage, drove through the western outskirts of the town, and kept on till he passed the sand dunes, and the cliff road stretched to Ashlingsea like a strip of white ribbon between the green downs and grey sea. About a mile past the sand dunes he saw a small stone cottage with a thatched roof, standing back on the downs about fifty yards from the road.

Crewe stopped his car, and walked up the slope to the little cottage. The gate was open, and he walked through the tiny garden, which was crowded with sweet-scented wallflowers and late roses, and knocked at the door.

His knock brought a woman to the door—an infirm and bent old woman, with scattered grey locks falling over her withered face. She peered up at him with rheumy eyes.

Crewe looked at the old woman in some doubt whether she was not past answering any questions.

K

Before he could put the point to the proof she solved it for him by turning her head and crying in a shrill cracked voice:

"Harry, lad, come here and see to the gentleman."

A man approached from the back in reply to the call. He was short and stout, and his perspiring face and bare arms showed that he had been hard at work. He looked at Crewe, made a movement of his knuckle towards his forehead, and waited for him to speak.

"I am trying to get in touch with a friend of mine who I believe motored along this road on Friday last," said Crewe. "It was on Friday night that we had the big storm. He must have driven along here on Friday afternoon; he was driving a big grey car. Did you see him?"

"Friday afternoon?" the man repeated. "I'm just trying to get my bearings a bit. Yes, Friday was the night we had the storm, and Friday was the day I seen this gentleman I'm thinking of."

"In a grey car?" suggested Crewe.

"In a grey car, as you say, sir. There ain't so many cars pass along this road this time of year."

"Then you saw a grey car go past in the direction of Ashlingsea on Friday afternoon?" said Crewe. He put a hand in his trousers pocket and jingled the silver there.

"I did," exclaimed the other, with the positiveness of a man who had awakened to the fact that he possessed valuable information for which he was to be paid. "I was standing here at this very door after selling two bushels of apples to Mr. Hope, and was just thinking about going back to dig some more taters, when I happened to hear a motor-car coming along. It was the grey car, sure enough, sir. No doubt about that."

"And was there anyone with my friend—or was he alone in the car?"

This was a puzzling question, because it contained no indication of the answer wanted.

"I can't say I noticed anybody at the time, cos I was thinking more about my taters—it's a bit late to be getting up taters, as you know, sir. I'd left 'em over late through having so much thatching to do, there being so few about as can thatch now that the war is on, and not many at the best o' times—thatching being a job as takes time to learn. My father he was best thatcher they ever did have hereabouts, and it was him taught me."

"And there was no one but my friend in the car?"

"I couldn't say that I did see any one, my mind being more on taters, but, mind you, sir, there might have been. Your friend he went past so quickly I didn't rightly see into the car—not from here. It ain't reasonable to expect it, is it, sir?"

"No, of course not," said Crewe. "I'm very much obliged to you." He produced half a crown and handed it to the man.

"Thank you, sir." The unexpected amount of his reward had a stimulating effect. "I'll tell you a strange thing about your friend, sir, now that I've had time to think about it. I hadn't dug moren a row, or perhaps a row and a half of my taters, when I seen him coming back again."

"Coming back again?" exclaimed Crewe. "Surely not."

"Yes, sir; the same grey car."

"Driving back in the direction of Staveley?"

"Driving back along the road he'd come."

"And this would be less than an hour after you saw him pass the first time?"

"Not more'n half-hour. I reckon it don't take me full twenty minutes to dig a row o' taters."

"But the grey car I mean didn't go back past here to Staveley." said Crewe. "It was wrecked on Friday night about four miles from here in the direction of Ashlingsea."

"That's right," exclaimed the man, with childish delight. "Didn't I see it go past here noon Saturday—another car drawing it because it wouldn't work. I said to myself, something's gone wrong with it."

"But, according to your story, it was driven back to Staveley that afternoon. The car you saw going back to Staveley could not have been the car that was wrecked on Friday, unless the driver turned round again and went back towards Ashlingsea—but that seems impossible."

"That's what he did, sir. That's what I was going to tell you, only I hadn't come to it. What I said was, I hadn't dug moren a row and half of taters after dinner afore I see this car coming back Staveley way, and when I'd got to end of second row I happened to look up the road and there was this car coming back again. I didn't know what to think—that is, at first. I stood there with the fork in my hand thinking and thinking and saying to myself I'd not give it up—I'm a rare one, sir, when I make up my mind. I don't wonder it's puzzled you, sir, just as it puzzled me. What has he been driving up and down for—backwards and forwards? That's how it puzzled me. Then it came to me quite sudden like—he'd lost something and had drove back along the road until he found it."

CHAPTER XII

It was not Elsie Maynard's first visit to London, but her visits had been so few that London had presented itself to her as a vast labyrinth of streets, shops and houses. The prevailing impression of all previous visits was that, since it was a simple matter to get lost involuntarily in the labyrinth, it would be a simple matter for any one to disappear voluntarily and remain hidden from search. But on this occasion, when there was need for secrecy as to her visit and its object, she fancied the vast city to be full of prying eyes.

It seemed improbable that among the thousands of people she met in the streets there would not be some one who knew her. There might be some one watching her—some one who had received a telephone message regarding her journey by train from Ashlingsea. To disappear from some one who was watching her seemed to be impossible, for among the throng of people it was impossible to single out the watcher.

From Victoria Station she took a tube ticket to Earl's Court, so as to give the impression to any one who was following her that her destination was in the west of London. She inspected closely all the people who followed her into the carriage. She alighted at South Kensington and changed to the Piccadilly tube. She got out at Holborn and then took a bus to Aldgate. She walked along to the junction of Whitechapel Road and Commercial Road, where she took a tram. After a short journey by tram along Commercial Road she got out and walked along the south side of the street, keeping a look out for the names of the side streets.

When she reached Quilter Street she turned down it, and eventually stopped at the door of No. 23. It was a short street with a monotonous row of houses on each side. At one side of the corner where it joined Commercial Road was a steam laundry, and at the other side a grocer's which was also a post office. The faded wrappings of the tinned goods which had been displayed for many months in the windows were indicative of the comparative poverty of the locality. In the ground-floor windows of most of the houses were cardboard notices showing that tailoring was the craft by which the inhabitants earned their bread. It was here that a great deal of the work sent out by tailors' shops in the City was done, and the placards in the windows proclaimed a desire for work from chance customers whose clothes needed repairs and pressing.

There were dirty ragged children playing in the gutters, and dirty slatternly women, with black shawls over their heads and shoulders and jugs in their hands, were to be seen hurrying along the pavement for milk and beer. Although Miss Maynard had taken care not to dress herself elaborately for her journey to London, she was aware that her appearance before the door of No. 23 was attracting some attention among the women standing at their doors and gossiping across area railings. When the door

was opened by a girl in her early teens who had her
sleeves rolled up and was wearing a piece of sacking
as an apron, Miss Maynard entered hurriedly and
closed the door after her.

"Does Mr. Miller live here?" she asked.

"Yes," replied the girl.

"Is he in now?"

"Yes, he told me was expecting a lady to call. Are
you her?"

"Yes."

"First floor—front," said the girl, jerking a dirty
thumb in the direction of the stairs as an indication
to her visitor that she could find her way up unaided.

But before she had reached the top of the stairs
the door of the front room on the first floor was
opened, and the man she had come to see appeared
on the stairs to welcome her. He clasped her hands
eagerly and led her to his room, closing the door
carefully behind him. For a moment he hesitated
and then placed his arms round her. Her head fell
back on his shoulder and he pressed his lips to hers
in a long lingering kiss.

Arnold Brett was a young man of spare build whose
military training had taught him to keep his shoulders
well back. He had a slight black moustache, and his
hair, which was carefully brushed down on his head,
was raven black in colour. His aquiline nose seemed
to emphasize the sharpness of his features; the glance
from his dark eyes was restless and crafty.

"Darling, I knew you would come," he said. He
released her, but only for the purpose of taking her
again in his arms and kissing her.

"But why are you here?" she asked, giving a glance

at the impoverished furniture—the narrow bed with its faded counterpane, the cheap chest of drawers, the dressing-table with a cracked mirror, the dirty window curtains and the single wooden chair.

"Before God, I swear I had nothing to do with it, Elsie," he exclaimed passionately.

It was a relief to hear him declare his innocence. Even if he had spoken without emphasis she would not have doubted his word. It was because her belief in his innocence deepened the mystery of his reason for hiding that she repeated:

"But why are you here?"

"Do you believe me?" he asked. Between lovers faith counts for much more than reason.

"Of course I do."

"I knew you would," he said. "It is because I know you were true that I asked you to come. I am beginning to think that perhaps I made a great mistake in running away. But I was unnerved by the accident. I was thrown out of the car and I must have been unconscious in the road for more than an hour. And, recalling how poor Frank had met his death, it seemed to me that there was a diabolical scheme on foot to murder me as well. Perhaps I was wrong. Tell me everything. Do the police suspect me? Have they a warrant out for me? Did you go to the farm that night? I have sent out for a newspaper each day, but the London newspapers have said very little about the murder. All I have seen is a couple of small paragraphs."

She was more immediately concerned in the discovery that he had been thrown out of a motor-car and injured than in his thirst for information about

the murder at Cliff Farm. She was solicitous as to
the extent of the injury he had suffered, the length
of time he had been unconscious, and his movements
after he came to his senses on the lonely road. Not
only were her feminine sympathies stirred by the
thought of the sufferings of the man she loved, but
by the fear that the accident must have affected his
mind temporarily and prompted him to hide himself.

He was too impatient for her news to spare time
for more than a vague disconnected account of the
accident. He assured her that he was all right again,
except for a cut on the head which he showed her.
It was on her news more than on anything else that
the question of his return to Staveley depended.

She told him in response to his questions that the
murder had created a sensation. Every one was talking about it. The *Staveley Courier* had published a
two column account of the tragedy with details about
the victim and the eccentricities of his grandfather in
later years. Stress was laid, in the newspaper account
of the story, on the rumour that old Joseph Lumsden
had buried his money after the war broke out, and
on the disappointment of the legatees whose legacies
could not be paid at his death because the money
could not be found. The police, it was stated, had
questioned these legatees as to their movements on
the night of the murder. The theory of the police
seemed to be that the murder had been committed by
some one who had heard about the buried money and
believed it was hidden in the house, or thought the
victim had known where it was hidden.

She told him that Scotland Yard had sent down a
detective to investigate the crime, and that Mr. Crewe,

the famous private detective, was also working on it. "Crewe!" he exclaimed in dismay. "Who has brought him into it?"

"He happened to be staying at Staveley with Sir George Granville on the night of the murder, and when Mr. Marsland rang up his uncle, Sir George Granville, from the Ashlingsea police station to say he was all right, and to tell Sir George about the murder, Mr Crewe was naturally interested in it. He took up the case on his own initiative because his host's nephew discovered the body."

"I can't follow you," he said. "Who is Mr. Marsland?" He started back with a look of terror in his eyes. "My God, you don't mean Captain Marsland? That is who it is; that is who it is! I knew I was right."

"Arnold, what is the matter?" she exclaimed, raising to her feet and putting a hand on his shoulder. "You look dreadful."

"Captain Marsland," he muttered. "Captain Marsland come to life again." He raised his clenched hand and shook it slowly as if to give impressive emphasis to his words. "That is the man who shot poor Frank. I knew I was right."

"Impossible."

He turned on her fiercely.

"Impossible," he echoed. "Who are you to say it is impossible? What do you know about it or about him? Perhaps you are in love with him?"

"Don't be foolish, Arnold," she said sternly. "The Mr. Marsland I am speaking of is not a captain—at least, he does not wear uniform, and I have not heard any one call him 'captain.' At any rate, it is impossible for him to have killed Frank Lumsden. I was at the farm before he was, and poor Frank's dead body was upstairs all the time I was there, though I did not know it."

"All the time you were there? When did you get there?"

"About six o'clock—just as the storm came on."

"Six o'clock? And was there no one at the house when you got there?"

"No one."

"You saw no trace of anyone having been there?"

"No. I found the key of the door in the lock and naturally I thought that Frank had left it there—that you and he were inside. You remember that you told me to be there about six o'clock, and that you and Frank would be there before then."

"Yes. That was the arrangement, but—well, never mind that, Elsie, now; tell me your story."

"I opened the door and walked in," she said. "I called out 'Is there anybody in?' but I got no answer. I thought then that you and Frank were in one of the sheds, and I sat down in the sitting-room, expecting you would be back in a moment. I took the key out of the door so as to make you knock in order to get in. The rain was just commencing then, but it had been blowing hard for half an hour. About ten minutes after I had been in the sitting-room there was a knock at the front door. Naturally I thought it was you. I rushed to open it and as I flung it back I asked what had kept you so long. But the man on the door step was a stranger—this Mr. Marsland."

"What is he like?" asked Brett quickly.

"He is rather good-looking; fair-haired and fair-skinned and blue-eyed—the Saxon type. He is about medium height—not quite so tall as you."

"How old is he?"

"Quite young—about 26 or 27, I should say."

"Does he wear glasses—gold-rimmed eyeglasses?"

"He was not wearing them then, but he does wear them as a rule. I think he told me subsequently that he had lost a pair while he was riding along—blown off by the wind."

"What explanation did he give of his visit?"

"He had been riding across the downs from Staveley and had lost his way in the storm. His horse was lame and when he saw the house he decided to seek shelter."

"Did you believe him?"

"Of course I did—then."

"Do you believe him now?"

"I don't know, Arnold, after what you have said. He may have been there before I was—it may have been he who left the key in the door."

"I am sure of it."

"He came in and sat down—he certainly acted as if he had never been in the house before. I do not know how long we were in the sitting-room—perhaps twenty minutes. We did not talk very much. I was busy trying to think what had become of you and Frank. I thought it best to tell him as little as possible, so I made up a story that I had found the door open and had walked in with the intention of taking shelter until the storm was over. I said nothing about the key. I began to get a little nervous as we sat there listening to the storm. I was upset about you,"

"Go on," he said impatiently, as she paused.

"Presently we heard a crash upstairs—it was like breaking glass or china. Mr. Marsland said he would go upstairs and see what it was. I determined to go with him, as I was too frightened by that time to stay alone. On one of the stairs he picked up Grandfather Lumsden's cryptogram. I felt then that Frank had been there, and that something dreadful had happened. We went upstairs, and there we found Frank's dead body in the arm-chair. I thought at first that he had been taken ill after you and he got there that afternoon, and that he had died alone while you were away trying to get a doctor. But Mr. Marsland said he had been shot. Poor Frank! What a dreadful end."

"What time did you leave?"

"We left almost at once. That would be about a quarter to seven. He went to Ashlingsea police station to report the discovery of the body. I asked him not to drag me into it—not to tell the police that I had been at the farm. I thought that was the best thing to do until I saw you—until I found where you had been."

"Quite right, Elsie—everything you do is right, my dear girl. And while you and this Marsland were at the farm I was just recovering consciousness on the Staveley road after a bad smash. It was after five o'clock before I left Staveley; I had told Frank I would leave about three o'clock, but I was delayed by several things. He told me he would come along the road to meet me. I was driving along the road fairly fast in order to reach the farm before the storm broke, and I must have been dazed by a flash of lightning. The next thing I remember was being awakened by the rain falling on my face as I lay unconscious beside the car, which had been overturned."

"Were you badly hurt, dear?"

"I was badly shaken and bruised, but the only cut was the one on my head. I didn't know what to do at first. I thought I would walk back to Staveley and tell them at the garage about the car. But finally I decided to go on to the Cliff Farm, as it was so much nearer than Staveley, and then go to Staveley by train in the morning. It must have been nearly eight o'clock when I reached the farm and found the front door open."

"We locked it," she interposed. "That is, Mr. Marsland did: he told me that he was sure he heard the lock click."

"It was open when I got there—wide open," he persisted.

"Then Mr. Marsland was right. The murderer was in the house while we were there. The crash we heard was made by him, and after we went away he bolted and left the hall door open."

"The murderer was in the house while you were there," he said. "There is nothing more certain than that. The murderer was Captain Marsland."

"I can't believe it," she said.

"Wasn't it he who put the idea into your head, after you had left the house, that the murderer might have been upstairs all the time?"

"Yes, it was."

"And he told you that he had slammed the hall door when he left? You didn't see him close it?"

"No, I was waiting for him down the path. After

seeing poor Frank I felt too frightened to stay in the house."

"Marsland left the door open, but told you he had closed it, his object being to give the police the impression that it had been left open by some one who left the house after he did. But I closed it when I left—I distinctly remember doing so."

"What makes you suspect Marsland? He had no grudge against Frank. Why should he kill him?"

"If Marsland didn't kill him, who did?"

"Any one may have done so. A tramp, for instance, who had broken into the house and was there when Frank came home."

"Do tramps in this country carry revolvers?"

"Not usually. But since the war many of the men discharged from the army do."

"There you've said it. Many of the officers who have been discharged carry revolvers, but not the men. They have got used to doing it. At the front only officers carry revolvers. And Marsland is an officer—a captain. He was a captain in the London Rifle Brigade, in the battalion to which Frank and I belonged."

"Oh!" There was a note of dismay in the exclamation of surprise. "Does he know you, Arnold?"

"I was not one of his company, but of course he knows me."

"Did he know Frank? Do you think he knew Frank when he saw his dead body in the room?"

"Of course he knew Frank. Frank was in his Company."

"He did not say anything to me about this as we

walked home," said Elsie thoughtfully. "And perhaps
he has not told the police. It is very strange."

"There is nothing strange about it. He had good
reasons for saying nothing."

"You think he shot Frank? Why should he commit such a crime?"

"My dear Elsie, strange things happen in war.
Frank told me something about Captain Marsland,
and as soon as you mentioned his name it all came
back to me. But we thought he was dead. Frank told
me he was killed at the front—a stray bullet or something."

"What was it that Frank told you about him? I
must know."

"Marsland sent a man to certain death to get him
out of the way. One night he sent Frank and another
man—Collingwood, I think Frank said his name was
—as a listening patrol. They had to crawl up near
the German trenches and, lying down with their ears
to the ground, listen for sounds in the German
trenches which might indicate that the Germans were
getting ready to make an attack. While they were
out this fellow Collingwood told Frank his history.
Collingwood had a sort of premonition that he would
not get back alive, and he took Frank into his confidence. He said he knew that Marsland had sent
him out in the hope that the Germans would get him.
It appears that Collingwood and Marsland were both
in love with the same girl, and she preferred Collingwood, though her parents didn't approve of him. Collingwood was a gentleman, like a great many more of
the rankers in Kitchener's Army. He gave Frank
a letter to this girl, and her photograph, and asked

Frank to see that she got them if he himself was killed. And killed he was that night—through the treachery of Marsland. While they were listening they heard the Germans getting ready for an attack. They crept back to warn their comrades, but there was no one to warn. The trench had been evacuated. When Marsland sent Frank and Collingwood out as a listening patrol he had an order in his pocket to vacate the trench, as it had been decided to fall back half a mile to a better position. He thought he was sending Collingwood and Frank to their death. Collingwood was killed. The Germans attacked before he and Frank could get away, but Frank, as you know, was taken prisoner. I was taken prisoner the same day, but at a different sector about a mile away. Subsequently Frank and I met as prisoners—and after being tortured by the Germans we got away."

"And did Frank deliver Collingwood's letter to the girl?"

"No, that is the sad part of it. The Germans took all his papers from him and he never saw them again. He did not know the address of the girl or even her name."

"It was a dreadful thing for Captain Marsland to do," she murmured.

"A great many dreadful things have been done out there," he said. "I'll tell you my idea of how this murder was committed. Marsland thought Frank had been killed by the Germans. After riding across the downs beyond Staveley he met Frank, who was walking along the road to meet me. He stopped Frank and pretended to be very friendly to him. They talked over old times at the front, Marsland being anxious to know how Collingwood had died and whether Collingwood had any idea that he had been sent to his death. As there was no sign of my car, Frank turned back with Marsland to the farm. While they were in the house Frank let slip the fact that Collingwood had confided in him before he died. Perhaps Marsland became aware of it through an effort on Frank's part to get from him the name of the girl to whom Collingwood had been practically engaged.

"No doubt there were angry words between them; and Marsland, in order to save himself from being exposed by Frank to the regimental authorities, and to the girl, shot him dead. That would be a few minutes before you reached the farm. When you reached the house Marsland had gone outside to re-move traces of the crime—perhaps to burn something or to wash blood-stains from his hands or clothing at the pump. He left the key in the door so that he could enter the house again. When he found the key gone he was confused: he was not certain whether he had placed the key in the lock. He did not believe that any one had entered the house, but to make sure on that point he knocked. He was surprised when you opened the door, but he played his part so well that you did not suspect he had been in the house before. As you had not discovered the body, he thought it best that you and he should discover it together. That would be less suspicious, as far as he was concerned, than for you to go away without discovering it. Had you betrayed any suspicion that you thought he was the murderer he would have shot you too, and then made off."

"But his horse was there," she said. "It was quite

lame. He could not have ridden away on it; and to leave it behind was to leave the police a convincing clue that he had been to Cliff Farm."

"I was forgetting about his horse," said Brett. "It was the fact that his horse was there which made him knock after he saw the key had been taken from the door. He had to brazen it out."

"The police have no suspicion of him, so far as I can ascertain," said the girl.

"We must direct their attention to him," was the reply.

"Will you come back to Staveley and tell Inspector Murchison?"

"No, that would be injudicious. My instinct was right in telling me to get out of sight when I saw Frank's dead body. It was after you left the house with Marsland that I got there. The door was open as I said—Marsland left it open purposely, and told you a lie about closing it. I went upstairs, as I couldn't see Frank about below, and when I saw him dead I felt immediately that his murder was but the continuation of some black deed in France. I knew instinctively that if I didn't disappear I should be the next victim. And so I should be if Marsland knew how much I know about him. The man is a cold-blooded villain, who thinks nothing of taking human life. If I went back to Staveley and accused him, he would take steps to put me out of the way. We must get him arrested for the murder, and when he is under lock and key I'll come back to Staveley and tell the police all I know about him."

"But how can we get the police to arrest him unless you first tell them all you know?" she asked.

"We must find a way," he said thoughtfully.

CHAPTER XIII

CREWE engaged a room in Whitethorn Gardens in order to watch Mrs. Penfield's movements, and took up his post of observation immediately. As he did not want Mrs. Penfield to know he was watching her house, he had chosen an attic bedroom on the opposite side and some distance higher up the steep street—an elevated vantage point, which not only commanded a view of all the houses in the street but of a great portion of Staveley and the surrounding country-side as well. From this eyrie the detective could see the front, the downs, and the distant cliff road to Ashlingsea; but the residence of Brett's landlady engrossed his attention.

There was very little sign of life in the street. One or two old ladies walked primly in the front gardens before dusk, but went inside as soon as the evening sea-mist began to rise. Sedate maidservants lit the gas and lowered blinds, and the street was left to darkness till a lamplighter came and lit a street-lamp which stood near No. 41. Crewe observed that the front rooms of No. 41 remained black and unlighted: apparently Mrs. Penfield lived in the back of the house and took her meals there.

As darkness was falling, Mrs. Penfield's elderly servant came from the back of the house, carrying a large basket. She went out of the front gate, turned up the street, and disappeared round the corner.

About half an hour later Crewe heard the front gate click, and saw Mrs. Penfield appear. Her face was plainly visible by the street light as she glanced anxiously up and down the street several times, as though she feared she was watched. Then she turned down the street and walked quickly away.

Crewe ran downstairs, let himself noiselessly out of the front door and followed quickly in her wake. As he neared the bottom of the street, he saw her a little distance in front of him. When she reached the end of Whitethorn Gardens she turned to the right along the sea front.

The night was mild, and a few drops of rain were falling. The front seemed deserted, and was shrouded in a mist which reduced the lamplights to a yellow glimmer. It was an easy matter for Crewe to follow closely behind the woman, conscious that the mist would shield him from observation if she turned.

Mrs. Penfield walked rapidly along the front till she came to High Street. Half-way along the front the mist seemed suddenly to grow thicker and Crewe crept closer in order to keep her in view. She walked swiftly with her head down, looking neither to the right nor the left. She passed under the faint light of a street lamp, and as Crewe came up behind he saw a uniformed figure in front of him. It was Police Constable Heather who had come over from Ashlingsea on official business. Heather was so pleased at this unexpected meeting with the great London detective that he called out in a loud voice:

"Good night, Mr. Crewe."

Crewe answered softly and passed on. He could only hope that Mrs. Penfield was so absorbed in her own thoughts that she had not heard Constable Heather's stentorian utterance of his name. Suddenly he heard her footsteps cease and he, too, came to a stop. Then he saw her confronting him.

"Why are you following me, Mr. Crewe?" she asked in quick excited tones. "It was you who telephoned to me to come up and see Inspector Murchison. I should have known it was a hoax. You wanted to get me out of the house."

"If I wanted to get you out of the house, Mrs. Penfield, why should I follow you?" asked Crewe.

"But you were following me," she persisted.

"It is not the sort of night I would choose for such work," he replied.

"When I heard that this man call out your name, I knew I had been hoaxed."

"By whom?" asked Crewe, who was puzzled at this example of feminine reasoning.

"I shall go back and see," she said. "I will ring up Inspector Murchison from there and find out if he sent a message to me to go up to the police station."

Crewe was keenly interested in knowing if she had been hoaxed, and by whom. Therefore he offered to accompany her home, as it was not a nice night for a lady to be in the street unattended.

When they reached 41 Whitethorn Gardens, she opened the gate, and walked up to the house rapidly. At the porch she stopped, touched Crewe lightly on the arm, and pointed to the front door. In the dim light a patch of blackness showed; the door was open.

"Come with me," she whispered, "and we will take him by surprise. Don't strike a match; give me your hand."

She walked noiselessly along the dark hall, and turning into a passage some distance down it led the way through an open doorway into a room—a small and stuffy storeroom, Crewe imagined it to be, as the air was suggestive of cheese and preserves.

"Go, Arnold, the police are here! Go at once!"

The words rang shrilly through the house. Crewe realized that he had been tricked by the woman and he sprang forward to the door. But the click of a lock told him he was too late. He struck a match and its light revealed to him Mrs. Penfield standing with her back against the door she had closed.

"There is a candle on the shelf behind you," she said composedly.

Crewe's glance followed the turn of her head; he lit the candle with his expiring match. The candle flickered, then burnt brightly, and the detective saw that he was in a small storeroom with shelves lining the walls. He turned again to Mrs. Penfield who was watching him closely.

"Why did you alarm him?" he asked. "You think it was Brett?"

Although his tone was one of curiosity rather than anger, the woman threw her arms out at full length as though she feared he would attempt to drag her away from the door.

"Do not be afraid," said Crewe. "You have nothing to fear from me. And, as for him, it is too late to pursue him."

"I must give him ample time to make his escape," she said. "You will go and tell the police he was here."

"What makes you think it was Brett?" asked

Crewe. "If he came back this way—if he hoaxed you with a telephone message in order to get you out of the house—he has shown a lamentable want of trust in you."

"He knows he can trust me," she said confidently. "He can never doubt it after to-night."

"I cannot conceive why he should take the great risk of coming back," he said meditatively.

"That means you would like to go up to his rooms and find out what he came for. But I forbid you. If you attempt to go upstairs, I will rouse the neighbourhood with the cry that there are burglars in the house."

"I think you have more reason to be afraid of the police than I," said Crewe. "However, I am in your hands. As far as I am concerned, you can have full credit for having saved him to-night."

She showed her faith in this assurance by unlocking the door. Taking the candle from the shelf, she led the way along the passage and the hall again. She opened the front door, and held the candle higher to light him out. She stood in the open doorway till Crewe reached the garden gate.

He walked back along the front. The mist was still rising from the sea in great white billows, which rolled across the beach and shrouded everything in an impenetrable veil. It penetrated unpleasantly into the eyes and throat, and Crewe was glad when he turned off the deserted parade and reached Sir George Granville's house.

The servant who admitted him told him the family were in the drawing-room, and thither he directed his steps. Lady Granville was seated at the piano, playing

softly. Marsland in an easy chair was listlessly turning over the pages of a bound volume of *Punch*. Sir
George was in another easy chair a little distance
away, nodding in placid slumber with his handsome
white beard on his breast, and an extinguished cigar
between his fingers.

Lady Granville smiled at Crewe as he entered, and
stopped playing. The cessation of the music awakened Sir George, and when he saw Crewe his eyes
wandered towards the chess-table.

"Do you feel inclined for a game of chess?" he exclaimed in his loud voice. "I want my revenge, you
know."

"I'll be pleased to give it to you," responded Crewe.

"A very unpleasant night outside," said Marsland.

"The mist seems to be thicker up this end of the
front," replied Crewe. "Have you been out in it?"

"I came in about five minutes ago. I went for a
walk."

Lady Granville took a book and seated herself not
far from the chess-table. Marsland came and stood
near the players, watching the game. He soon got
tired of it, however, and went back to *Punch*. Sir
George was a slow player at all times, and his anxiety
when pitted against a renowned player like Crewe
made him slower than usual. He studied each move
of Crewe's in all its bearings before replying, scruti-
nizing the board with set face, endeavouring to penetrate his opponent's intentions, and imagining subtle
traps where none existed. Meanwhile, his fingers hov-
ered nervously above the pieces with the irresolute-
ness of a chess-player weighed down by the heavy
responsibility of his next move, and, finally, when the

plunge had been taken Sir George sat back, stroking his long white beard doubtfully, and fixed his eyes on Crewe, as though mutely asking his opinion of the move. "Game" seemed an inappropriate word to apply to chess as played by Sir George Granville.

It was during one of these strategical pauses, after the game had been in progress for nearly an hour, that Crewe heard a frightened exclamation from Lady Granville. He looked up and saw Marsland standing near the fire-place with his hand over his heart, swaying as though about to fall. Crewe sprang forward and supported him to an easy chair.

"A little brandy," said Crewe quietly.

Sir George hurriedly brought a decanter of brandy and a glass, and Crewe poured a little down Marsland's throat. The colour came slowly back to the young man's cheeks, and he smiled feebly at the three faces looking down at him.

"I'm afraid I've been giving you a lot of trouble," he said, with an obvious effort to collect himself.

"I'll ring up for Dr. Harrison," Sir George spoke in a loud voice, as though to reassure himself.

"There is not the slightest need to send for Harrison," said Marsland. "I'm quite right again. I must expect these attacks occasionally for some time to come. They're nothing—just weakness. All I need is a good night's rest, and if you'll excuse me I'll retire now." He got up and walked resolutely out of the room with square shoulders, as though to demonstrate to those watching him that no trace of his weakness remained.

"Do you think it is safe to leave him alone?" said Sir George turning to Crewe, as the door closed on his nephew's retreating figure. "I feel very anxious about him. Anything might happen to him during the night."

"A good night's rest will do him more good than anything else. He has been under a rather severe nervous strain during the last few days. We will go to his room in a few minutes to see how he is."

They settled down to their game again and Lady Granville moved up her chair near the chess-table for the sake of their company and pretended to take an interest in the game. Only a few moves had been made when there was a loud report of an explosion. Lady Granville jumped up from her chair and screamed and then fell back into the chair in a faint.

"Look to her," said Crewe to his host, "while I go and see what's the matter."

As he ran along the hall to the staircase he met two of the maids, who with white faces and hands clasped in front of them seemed too frightened to move.

"Where was it?" asked Crewe. "Upstairs?"

"Yes, sir, upstairs," said one of them.

"It came from Mr. Marsland's room," added the other, in an awed whisper.

Crewe ran straight for Marsland's room, expecting to find there some evidence of a tragedy. As he burst into the room he saw to his great relief that Marsland was there, leaning out of the window.

"What is it?" asked Crewe. "Did you fire a revolver?"

Marsland, who was wearing a dressing-gown, came from the window. In his right hand he was holding a big revolver.

"I missed him," he said.

"Missed whom?"

"A burglar."

"It is very early in the night for a burglar to be out."

"He took advantage of the mist. He must have thought that there was no one in the room. I had turned out the light and was resting on the bed. I was half asleep, but he knocked a brush off the dressing-table as he was getting through the window and that woke me up. I caught a good glimpse of him and I fired. He dropped at once, and I thought I had hit him, but when I looked out of the window I saw him disappear in the mist. What an awful pity I didn't get him."

"How did you happen to be lying down with a revolver beside you?" asked Crewe.

"I often take it to bed with me. That is the result of the life at the front. And to-night I had a kind of presentiment that I should need it."

It occurred to Crewe that the young man had been subject to hallucinations during his illness. This habit of sleeping with a revolver under his pillow seemed to indicate that his cure was still far from complete. Was the burglar a phantom of a sick mind?

He went over to the window for the purpose of looking out but his attention was arrested by a stain on the outside sill.

"You did not miss him altogether," he said to Marsland. "Look here."

Marsland touched the stain and held a blood-stained finger up to the light for his own inspection.

CHAPTER XIV

CREWE steered to the stone landing-place and tied the little motor-boat to a rusty iron ring which dangled from a stout wooden stake, wedged between two of the seaweed covered stones. The tide was out, and the top of the landing-place stood well out of the water, but it was an easy matter for a young and vigorous man to spring up to the top, though three rough and slippery steps had been cut near the ring, perhaps for the original builder in his old and infirm days.

Looking down, he noticed that while his little boat floated easily enough alongside, a boat of slightly deeper draught would have scraped on the rocky bottom, which was visible through the clear water. The surface of the landing-place was moist, and the intersections between the rough stones were filled with seaweed and shells, indicating that the place was covered at high tide.

Crewe had come from Staveley by boat instead of motoring across, his object being to make a complete investigation of Cliff Farm without attracting chance attention or rural curiosity about his motor-car, which was too big to go into the stables. He wanted to be undisturbed and uninterrupted in his investigation of the house. As he entered the boat-house, he looked back to where he had left his boat, and saw that the landing-place was high enough out of the water to prevent passers-by on the cliff road seeing the boat before high tide. By that time he hoped to have completed his investigations and be on his way back to Staveley.

The boat-house was a small and rickety structure perched on a rough foundation of stones, which had been stacked to the same height as the landing-place. The inside was dismal and damp, and the woodwork was decaying. Part of the roof had fallen in, and the action of wind and sea and storm had partly destroyed the boarded sides. Many of the boards had parted from the joists, and hung loosely, or had fallen on the stones. An old boat lay on the oozing stones, with its name, *Polly*, barely decipherable on the stern, and a kedge anchor and rotting coil of rope inside it. Crewe had no doubt that it was the boat James Lumsden used to go fishing in many years ago. A few decayed boards in front of the boat-house indicated the remains of a wooden causeway for launching the boat. In a corner of the shed was a rusty iron windlass, which suggested the means whereby the eccentric old man had been able to house his boat without assistance when he returned with his catch.

Having finished his scrutiny of the boatshed and its contents, Crewe made his way up the cliff path, and walked across the strip of downs to the farm.

Cliff Farm looked the picture of desolation and loneliness in the chill, grey autumn afternoon. Its gaunt, closely-shuttered ugliness confronted Crewe uncompromisingly, as though defying him to wrest from it the secret of the tragic death of its owner. It already had that air of neglect and desertion which speedily overtakes the house which has lost its habitants. There was no sign of any kind of life; the meadows were empty of live-stock. Somewhere in the outbuildings at the side of the house an unfastened door flapped and banged drearily in the wind. Even the front door required main strength to force it open after it had been unlocked, as though it shared with the remainder of the house the determination to keep the secret of the place, and resented intrusion. The interior of the house was dark, close and musty. Through the closed and shuttered windows not a ray of light or a breath of air had been able to find an entrance.

Crewe's first act was to open the shutters and the windows on the ground floor; his next to fling open the front and back doors, and the doors of the rooms. He wanted all the light he could get for the task before him, and some fresh air to breathe. He soon had both: wholesale, pure strong air from the downs, blowing in through doors and windows, stirring up the accumulated dust on the floors, causing it to float and dance in the sunbeams that streamed in the front windows from the rays of an evening sun, which had succeeded in freeing himself in his last moments above the horizon from the mass of grey clouds that had made the day so chill and cheerless.

Crewe commenced to examine each room and its contents with the object of trying to discover something which would assist him in his investigation of the Cliff Farm murder. He worked carefully and minutely, but with the swiftness and method of a practised observer.

The front room that he first entered detained him

only a few minutes. Originally designed for the sitting-room, it had been dismantled and contained very little furniture, and had evidently not been used for a considerable time. A slight fissure in the out-side wall explained the reason: the fissure had made the room uninhabitable by admitting wind and weather, causing damp to appear on the walls, and loosening the wall-paper till it hung in festoons.

Crewe next examined the opposite front room in which Sergeant Westaway conducted his preliminary inquiries into the murder. This room was simply furnished with furniture of an antique pattern. Apparently it had been used at a more or less recent date as the sitting-room, for a few old books and a couple of modern cheaply bound novels were lying about; a needle with a piece of darning cotton which was stuck in the wall suggested a woman's occupation, or perhaps the murdered man or his grandson had done bachelor darning there in the winter evenings. The latter hypothesis seemed most probable to Crewe: only a very untidy member of the other sex would have left a darning needle sticking in the sitting-room wall.

Crewe then examined the room behind the front room in which Marsland and Miss Maynard had sat before discovering the murdered man. It was the front room of an English farm-house of a bygone age, kept for show and state occasions but not for use, crowded with big horse-hair chairs and a horse-hair sofa. There were two tables—a large round one with a mahogany top and a smaller one used as a stand for the lamp Marsland had lit—a glass case of stuffed birds; an old clock in a black case on the mantelpiece, which had been stopped so long that its works

M

were festooned with spiders' webs; a few dingy oil-paintings on the walls, alternately representing scenes from the Scriptures and the English chase, and a moth-eaten carpet on the floor. There was also a small glass bookcase in a corner containing some bound volumes of the *Leisure Hour* of the sixties, *Peter Parley's Annual, Johnson's Dictionary,* an ancient *Every Day Book,* and an old family Bible with brass clasps.

It was in the room next to the sitting-room that Crewe found the first article which suggested possibilities of a clue. It was a small room, which had evidently been used by a former occupant as an office, for it contained an oak case holding account books, some files of yellowing bills hanging from nails on the wall, and an old-fashioned writing bureau. It was this last article that attracted Crewe's attention. It was unlocked, and he examined closely the papers it contained. But they threw no light on the mystery of Cliff Farm, being for the most part business letters, receipted bills, and household accounts.

There was a bundle of faded letters in one of the pigeon-holes tied with black ribbon, which had been written to Mrs. James Lumsden from somebody who signed himself "Yours to command, Geoffrey La Touche." These letters were forty years old, and had been sent during a period of three years from "Her Majesty's sloop *Hyacinth*" at different foreign ports. They were stiff and formal, though withal courteous in tone, and various passages in them suggested that the writer had been an officer in the Royal Navy and a relative of Mrs. Lumsden. They ceased with a letter written to "James Lumsden, Esq.," expressing the writer's

"deep regret and sincere sorrow" on learning of his
"dear niece's sad and premature end."

There was another room opposite this office which
had doubtless been intended for a breakfast-room, but
was now stored with odds and ends: superfluous
articles of furniture, some trunks, a pile of bound
volumes of the *Illustrated London News*, and a few
boxes full of miscellaneous rubbish. The passage on
which these rooms opened terminated in two stone
steps leading into the kitchen, which was the full
width of the house. A notable piece of furniture in
this room was an oaken dresser with shelves reaching
to the ceiling. There were also a deal table, some
kitchen chairs, and an arm-chair.

From the blackened beams of its low sloping ceiling
some hams and strings of onions hung, and an open
tea-caddy stood on the table, with a leaden spoon in
it, as though somebody had recently been making tea.
An old brown earthenware teapot stood by the fire-
place with tea-leaves still in the pot, and Crewe noticed
on the mantelpiece a churchwarden pipe, with a spill
of paper alongside. He found a pair of horn spectacles and an old newspaper on the top of the press
beside the old-fashioned fire-place. Evidently the
kitchen had been the favourite room of Frank Lumsden's grandfather—the eccentric old man who had
built the landing-place.

Before examining the upper portion of the house
Crewe closed the doors and windows he had opened,
restoring things to the condition in which he had
found them. Then he went upstairs, and, after opening the windows and blinds as he had opened them

downstairs, entered the room in which the murdered man had been discovered.

It was while Crewe was thus engaged that his quick ears detected a slight crunch of footsteps on the ground outside, as though somebody was approaching the house. The room he was searching looked out on pasture land, but he was aware that there was a gravel path on the other side, running from the outbuildings at the side to the rear of the house. He crossed over to the corresponding room on that side of the house, and looked out of the open window, but could see no one.

He ran quietly downstairs and into the kitchen. His idea was to watch the intruder by looking through one of the kitchen windows, without revealing his own presence, but he found to his annoyance that the little diamond shaped kitchen window which looked out on the back was so placed as to command a view of only a small portion of the bricked yard at the back of the house.

He waited for a moment in the hope that the visitor would enter the house through the unlocked kitchen door, but as he heard no further sound he decided to go in search of the person whose footsteps he had heard. He opened the door and looked over the empty yard. Suddenly a woman's figure appeared in the doorway of the barn on the left. Immediately she saw Crewe she retreated into the shed in the hope that she had not been seen. In order to undeceive her on this point, Crewe walked down the yard to the barn, but before he reached it she came out to meet him. She was young and pretty and well dressed.

"You are Mr. Crewe." she said with composure.

"And you are Miss Maynard. We have not met before, but I have heard a great deal about you."

She read suspicion in his use of the conventional phrase and she decided to meet it.

"I came out to look at the old place—at the scene of this dreadful tragedy—before finally deciding what I ought to do."

He realized that having said so much she had more to say, and he gave her no assistance.

"Perhaps Mr. Marsland has not told you, Mr. Crewe, that I was with him in the house when he discovered the body."

"He has not," replied Crewe.

"That makes it all the more difficult for me. I do not mind telling you, for you are his friend, and you are such a clever man that I feel I will be right in taking your advice."

Crewe's mental reservation to be slow in offering her advice was an indication that his suspicions of her were not allayed.

"I also sought shelter here from the storm on that fateful night," she continued. "But because I was afraid of the gossip of Ashlingsea I asked Mr. Marsland if he would mind keeping my name out of it. And he very generously promised to do so."

"A grave error on both sides," said Crewe.

She was quick in seizing the first opening he gave her.

"That is the conclusion I have come to; that is why I think I ought to go to the police and tell them that I was here. They may be able to make something out of my story—they may be able to see more in it than I can. My simple statement of facts might fit in with

some other information in their possession of which
I know nothing, and in that way might lead to the
detection of the man who killed Frank Lumsden. But
how can I go to them and tell them I was here after
I begged Mr. Marsland to say nothing about me? He
would never forgive me for placing him in such an
embarrassing position. It would not be right."

"And it is not right to keep from the police any
information to which they are entitled."

"That is my difficulty," she said, with a smile of
gratitude to him for stating it so clearly.

"I have no hesitation in advising you to tell the
police the whole truth," said Crewe.

"And Mr. Marsland?"

"He must extract himself from the position in which
his promise to you has placed him. He knows that
the promise should never have been made, and doubtless in the end he will be glad to have been released
from it."

"I hope he will understand my motives," she said.

"Perhaps not. But he will begin to realize, what
all young men have to learn, that it is sometimes difficult to understand the motives which actuate young
ladies."

That reply seemed to indicate to her that their conversation had reached the level of polite banter.

"Will you plead for me?" she asked.

"That is outside my province," was the disappoint-
ing reply. "I understood you to say, Miss Maynard,
that you came here that night for shelter from the
storm. Did you arrive at the house before Marsland
or after him?"

There was a moment of hesitation before her reply was given.

"A few minutes before him."

"No doubt you will materially assist the police by giving them a full account of what you know," said Crewe.

CHAPTER XV

"Good morning, sergeant."

"Good morning, Miss Maynard. What can I do for you?"

It was seldom that Sergeant Westaway was so obliging as to make a voluntary offer of his services, but then it was still more seldom that a young lady of Miss Maynard's social standing came to seek his advice or assistance at the police station. As the daughter of a well-to-do lady, Miss Maynard was entitled to official respect.

The sergeant had known Miss Maynard since her mother had first come to live at Ashlingsea fifteen years ago. He had seen her grow up from a little girl to a young lady, but the years had increased the gulf between them. As a schoolgirl home from her holidays it was within the sergeant's official privilege to exchange a word or two when saluting her in the street. Her development into long dresses made anything more than a bare salutation savour of familiarity, and the sergeant knew his place too well to be guilty of familiarity with those above him.

With scrupulous care he had always uttered the name "Miss Maynard," when saluting her in those days, so that she might recognize that he was one of the first to admit the claims of adolescence to the honours of maturity. Then came a time with the further lapse of years when she reached the threshold of womanhood, and to utter her name in salutation would have savoured of familiarity. So the salute became a silent one as indicative of Sergeant Westaway's recognition that his voice could not carry across the increased gulf between them.

"I have something very important to tell you," said Miss Maynard, in reply to his intimation that the full extent of his official powers were at her disposal.

"Ah!"

The sergeant realized that a matter of great personal importance to Miss Maynard might readily prove to be of minor consequence to him when viewed through official glasses; but there was no hint of this in the combination of politeness and obsequiousness with which he opened the door leading from the main room of the little police station to his private room behind it.

He placed a chair for her at the office table and then went round to his own chair and stood beside it. There was a pause, due to the desire to be helped with questions, but Sergeant Westaway's social sense was greater than his sense of official importance, and he waited for her to begin.

"It is about the Cliff Farm murder," she said in a low voice.

"Oh!" It was an exclamation in which astonishment and anticipation of official delight were blended. "And do you—do you know anything about it?" he asked.

"I am not sure what you will think of my story—whether there is any clue in it. I must leave that for you to judge. But I feel that I ought to tell you all that I do know."

"Quite right," said the sergeant. His official manner, rising like a tide, was submerging his social sense of inequality. "There is nothing like telling the police the truth, the whole truth, and nothing but the truth. It is always the best way." His social sense made a last manifestation before it threw up its arms and sank. "Not that I suppose for one moment, Miss Maynard, that you had anything to do with it—that is to say, that you actually participated in the crime."

He looked at her inquiringly and she shook her head, smiling sadly as she did so.

"But there is no reason why, after all, you might not know who did it," said the sergeant in a coaxing voice which represented an appeal to her to do her best to justify his high hopes. "In some respects it is a mysterious crime, and although the police have their suspicions—and very strong suspicions too—they are always glad to get reliable information, especially when it supports their suspicions."

"And whom do you suspect?" she asked.

Sergeant Westaway was taken aback at such a question. It was such an outrageous attempt to penetrate the veil of official secrecy that he could refrain from rebuking her only by excusing it on the ground of her youth and inexperience.

"At present I can say nothing," was his reply.

She turned aside from his official manœuvring and took up her own story:

"What I came to tell you is that I was at Cliff Farm on the night that poor Mr. Lumsden was shot."

"You were there when he was shot?" exclaimed the sergeant.

"No; he was dead when I got there."

"Did you hear the shot?"

"No."

"But you saw some one?"

"I saw Mr Marsland."

"Ah!" The commonplace tone in which the word was uttered indicated that the sergeant was deeply disappointed with her story. "We know all about his visit there. He came and told us—it was through him that we discovered the body. He has been straightforwardness itself: he has told us everything."

"Did he tell you I was there?"

"No; he has not mentioned your name. Perhaps he didn't see you."

"We were in the house together, and I was with him when he went upstairs and discovered the body."

"He has said nothing about this," said the sergeant impressively. "His conduct is very strange in that respect."

"I am afraid I am to blame for that," she said. "As he walked home with me from the farm on his way to the police station I asked him if he would mind saying nothing about my presence at the house. I told him that I was anxious to avoid all the worry and unpleasantness I should have to put up with if it was publicly known that I had been there. He readily agreed not to mention my name. I thought at the time that it was very kind of him, but in thinking it all over since I am convinced that I did wrong. I have come to the conclusion that it was a very extra-ordinary thing for him to agree to as he did, not knowing me—we had never met before. I felt that the right thing to do was to come to you and tell you all I know so that you can compare it with what

Mr. Marsland has told you. In that way you will be able to make fuller inquiries, and to acquit him of any sinister motive in his kind offer to me to keep my name out of it."

The sergeant nodded his head slowly. There was much to take in, and he was not a rapid thinker.

"Any sinister motive?" he repeated after a long pause.

"Of course I don't wish to cast any suspicions on Mr. Marsland," she said looking at the police officer steadily. "But it has already occurred to you, Sergeant, that Mr. Marsland, in kindly keeping my name out of it, had to depart from the truth in the story he told you about his presence at Cliff Farm, and that he may have thought it advisable to depart from the truth in some other particulars as well."

The sergeant's mental process would not have carried him that far without assistance, but there was no conscious indication of assistance in the emphasis with which he said:

"I see that."

"Let me tell you exactly what happened so far as I am concerned," she went on.

"Yes, certainly." He sat down in his chair and vaguely seized his pen. "I'll write it down, Miss Maynard, and get you to sign it. Don't go too fast for me; and it will be better for you if you take time —you will be able to think it over as you go along. This promises to be most important. Detective Gillett of Scotland Yard will be anxious to see it. I am sorry he's not here now; he has been recalled to London, but I expect him down again to-morrow."

"On Friday, the night of the storm, I left my house

about dusk—that would be after five o'clock—with the intention of taking a walk," she began. "I walked along the downs in the direction of Cliff Farm, intending to return along the sands from the cliff pathway. I was on the downs when the storm began to gather. I thought of retracing my steps, but the storm gathered so swiftly and blew so fiercely that I was compelled to seek shelter in the only house for miles around—Cliff Farm.

"The wind was blowing hard and big drops of rain were falling when I reached the door. I knocked, but received no answer. Then I noticed that the key was in the door. Owing to the darkness, which had come on rapidly with the storm, I had not seen it at first. The door had a Yale lock and the key turned very easily. I was wearing light gloves, and when I turned the key in the lock I noticed it was sticky. I looked at my glove and saw a red stain—it was blood."

"Ah!" interrupted Sergeant Westaway. "A red stain—blood? Just wait a minute while I catch up to you."

"I was slightly alarmed at that," she continued, after a pause; "but I had no suspicion that a cruel murder had been committed. In my alarm I took the key out of the lock and closed the door. I felt safer with the door locked against any possible intruder. I went into the sitting-room and sat down, after lighting a candle that I found on the hallstand. Then it occurred to me that Mr Lumsden might have left the key in the door while he went to one of the outbuildings to do some work. The blood might have got on it from a small cut on his hand."

"What did you do with the key?" asked the Sergeant.

"I brought it with me here." She opened her bag and handed a key to the police officer.

Sergeant Westaway looked at it closely. Inside the hole made for the purpose of placing the key on a ring he saw a slight stain of dried blood. He nodded to Miss Maynard and she continued her story.

"I felt more at ease then, and when I heard a knock at the door I felt sure it was he—that he had seen the light of the candle through the window and knew that whoever had taken the key had entered the house. I opened the door, but it was not Mr. Lumsden I saw, but Mr. Marsland. He said something about wanting shelter from the storm—that his horse had gone lame. He came inside and sat down. I told him that I, too, had sought shelter from the storm and that I supposed Mr. Lumsden, the owner of the house, was in one of the outbuildings attending to the animals. I saw that he was watching me closely and I felt uneasy. Then I saw him put his hand to the upper pocket of his waistcoat."

"What was that for?" asked the sergeant.

"I think he must have lost a pair of glasses and temporarily forgotten that they were gone. He was not wearing glasses when I saw him but I have noticed since that he does wear them."

"I've noticed the same thing," said the sergeant. "He was not wearing glasses the night he came here to report the discovery of Mr. Lumsden's body—I am sure of that."

Miss Maynard, on resuming her narrative, told how Mr. Marsland and she, hearing a crash in one of the rooms overhead, went upstairs to investigate and found the dead body of the victim sitting in an armchair. When she realized that a dreadful crime had been committed she ran out of the house in terror. She waited in the path for Mr. Marsland and he was kind enough to escort her home. It was because she was so unnerved by the tragedy that she had asked Mr. Marsland to keep her name out of it not to tell any one that she had taken shelter at the farm. It was a dreadful experience and she wanted to try and forget all about it. But now she realized that she had done wrong and that she should have come to the police station with Mr. Marsland and told what she knew.

"That is quite right, Miss Maynard," said the sergeant, as he finished writing down her statement. "Does Mr. Marsland know that you have come here to-day with the intention of making a statement?"

"No; he does not, and for that reason I feel that I am not treating him fairly after he was so kind in consenting to keep my name out of it."

The sergeant had but a limited view of moral ethics where they conflicted with the interests of the police.

"He should not have kept your name from me," he said. "But, apart from what you have told me, have you any reason for suspecting that Mr. Marsland had anything to do with the murder of Frank Lumsden?"

"That it was he who left the key in the door?"

"Well—yes."

"If that is the case, his object in leaving the house for a few minutes might be to destroy traces of his guilt. But I saw nothing of a suspicious nature in his manner after I admitted him to the house."

The sergeant was impressed with the closeness of her reasoning—it seemed to shed more light. Clearly she had given the matter the fullest consideration before deciding to make a statement.

She added with a slight laugh:

"You cannot call his action in feeling for a missing pair of glasses suspicious?"

"No, no," said the sergeant generously. "We can scarcely call that suspicious."

"What I do regard as suspicious—or, at any rate, as wanting in straightforwardness—is the fact that Mr. Marsland did not tell me that he knew Mr. Lumsden in France. They were both in the London Rifle Brigade—Mr. Marsland was a captain and Mr. Lumsden a private."

"Where did you learn this, Miss Maynard?" was the excited question. "Are you sure?"

"Hasn't he told the police?" she asked in a tone of astonishment. "Then perhaps it is not true."

"Where did you hear it?"

"In Staveley. I was talking to a wounded officer there on the front—Mr. Blake. He knew Mr. Marsland as Captain Marsland and he knew Mr. Lumsden as well. I think he said poor Mr. Lumsden had been Captain Marsland's orderly for a time."

"I must look into this," said Sergeant Westaway.

"Unfortunately Mr. Blake has returned to the front. He left Staveley yesterday."

"No matter. There are other ways of getting at the truth, Miss Maynard. As I said, Detective Gillett will be down here to-morrow and I'll show him your statement. He will probably want to interview you himself and in that case I'll send for you. But don't you be alarmed—he's a nice gentlemanly young fellow and knows how to treat a lady."

He was about to bow her out of the station when he suddenly remembered that she had not signed her statement.

"Would you please read through this and sign it?" he asked. "A very important statement—clear and concise. I feel I must congratulate you about it, Miss Maynard."

She read through the sergeant's summary of her narrative, but was unable to congratulate him on the way in which he had done his work. She felt that the statement she and her lover had compiled, to guide her in her narrative to the police, was a far more comprehensive document.

CHAPTER XVI

Miss Maynard's statement made such an impression
on Sergeant Westaway that he determined to ride over
to Staveley that afternoon and lay it before Inspector
Murchison. He was so restless and excited at the new
phase of the Cliff Farm murder which had been
opened up by the young lady's revelations that he
decided the matter was too important to be allowed
to remain where it was until Detective Gillett returned
to Ashlingsea on the following day.

Besides, twenty-five years' rustication in Ashlingsea
had made him so much of an idealist that he actually
believed that any zealous activity he displayed in the
only great crime which had ever happened during his
long régime at Ashlingsea would be placed to his
credit in the official quarters.

After a midday dinner Sergeant Westaway wheeled
forth his bicycle and, having handed over to Constable
Heather the official responsibility of maintaining order
in Ashlingsea, pedalled away along the cliff road to
Staveley. The road was level for the greater part of
the way and he reached Staveley in a little more than
an hour of the time of his departure from Ashlingsea.

Several persons—mostly women—were in the front
office of the police station, waiting their turn to lay
their troubles before the recognized guide and confidant
of Staveley, but the constable in charge, who knew
Sergeant Westaway, deferred to his official position

by taking him straight into the presence of Inspector Murchison and closing the door behind him.

The inspector was seated in his office chair talking earnestly to a shabby young woman who carried a baby, and was crying bitterly. He looked up as Westaway entered, and then he rose from his chair, as an intimation to the young woman in front of him that he had given her as much of the Government's time as she had a right to expect. The young woman took the hint, rose to her feet and turned to go. On her way to the door she turned round and said in a pleading voice:

"You'll do the best you can to get him back, won't you, sir?"

"You can rely on me, Mrs. Richards," responded the inspector, adding cheerily: "Keep your heart up; things are bound to come right in the end."

The young woman received this philosophic remark with a sob as she closed the door behind her.

"A very sad case, that," said Inspector Murchison to Sergeant Westaway.

"Eh—yes?" responded the sergeant absently, for he was thinking of other things.

"She's Fanny Richards, the wife of Tom Richards, the saddler's son," continued the inspector. "I've known her since she was *that* high. Tom Richards was called up for service a little while ago, and his wife moved heaven and earth to get him exempted. She went to the right quarters too—she used to be housemaid there—but perhaps I'd better not mention names. At all events, the tribunal gave her husband total exemption. And what does her husband do? Is he grateful? Not a bit! Two days after the

tribunal had exempted him the scoundrel cleared out
—disappeared from the district with a chambermaid
from one of the hotels on the front. I tell you, Westaway, the ingratitude of some of our sex to the women
they have sworn to love and cherish makes me angry.
But, however, you haven't come from Ashlingsea to
discuss the failings of human nature with me. What
can I do for you?"

Before leaving Ashlingsea, Sergeant Westaway had
withdrawn Miss Maynard's statement from its official
repository, and placed it carefully in his pocket-book.
His hand wandered towards his breast pocket as he
replied that his visit to Staveley was connected with
the Cliff Farm case.

"And what is the latest news about that?" asked the
inspector with interest.

It was the moment for Sergeant Westaway's triumph, and he slowly drew his pocket-book from his
breast pocket and extracted the statement.

"I have made an important discovery," he an-
nounced, in a voice which he vainly strove to keep
officially calm. "It affects a—well-known and leading
gentleman of your district. This paper"—he flattened
it out on the table with a trembling hand—"is a statement made by Miss Maynard of Ashlingsea, which
implicates Mr. Marsland, the nephew of Sir George
Granville."

"In the Cliff Farm case?"

Sergeant Westaway nodded portentously, and wiped
the perspiration from his forehead—for the office fire
was hot and he had ridden fast.

Inspector Murchison took up the girl's statement,
and read it through. When he had finished it, he

turned to the front page, and read it through again. Then he glanced up at his colleague gravely.

"This is very important," he said. "It throws a new aspect on the case."

Sergeant Westaway nodded.

"This girl," pursued Inspector Murchison, "she is of fairly good position, is she not?"

Sergeant Westaway nodded again.

"Her mother is a lady of independent means."

"I've heard of them, and I've seen the young lady and her mother once or twice when they've visited Staveley. Do you think the young lady is telling the whole truth here?"

"Undoubtedly." Sergeant Westaway's tone indicated that when a member of the leading family of Ashlingsea set out to tell the truth nothing was kept back.

The inspector got up from his chair and took a few turns up and down the office in a meditative way.

"It's a most extraordinary disclosure that this young woman has made," he said at length. "Extraordinary —and awkward. I do not know what Sir George Granville will say when he learns that his nephew, instead of assisting the police, made a false and misleading statement. It is a very grave thing; a very dangerous thing in such a grave crime as this. It will give Sir George Granville a dreadful shock."

"It gave me a shock," said Sergeant Westaway.

"No doubt," replied the inspector. "But Sir George Granville—is a different matter. We must consider his feelings; we must try to spare them. I hardly know what is best to be done. Obviously, the matter cannot be allowed to remain where it is, yet it is difficult to see what is the proper course of action to pursue. I think the best thing will be to wait until Gillett returns from London and leave it to him. When do you expect him back?"

"I expect him back in the morning. I wired to him that I had obtained most important information."

"I'll be at the station when the London express comes in in the morning. If Gillett is on board I'll go on with him to Ashlingsea."

In accordance with this arrangement, Inspector Murchison arrived at Ashlingsea in the morning, in the company of Detective Gillett.

If Sergeant Westaway expected praise from the representative of Scotland Yard it was not forthcoming. Detective Gillett seemed in a peevish humour. His boyish face looked tired and careworn, and his blue eyes were clouded.

"Let me have a look at this statement that you are making such a fuss about," he said.

Long afterwards, when Sergeant Westaway had ample leisure to go over all the events in connection with the Cliff Farm case, he alighted on the conviction that the reason Detective Gillett was so offensive and abrupt in regard to Miss Maynard's statement was that he did not like important information to reach the police while he was absent.

"It is a voluntary and signed statement by Miss Maynard, a young lady of the district, who was at Cliff Farm the night of the murder," said the sergeant, with dignity.

"So much I know from Inspector Murchison, and also that the statement in some way implicates young what's his name—Marsland. Let me have the document itself, Westaway."

The sergeant took it from his desk, and placed it in Detective Gillett's hands.

"I have added on a separate sheet of paper a few notes I gathered in the course of conversation with Miss Maynard. The most important of them deals with the fact that young Marsland was a captain in the Army, and that Lumsden was under his command in France."

Gillett began with an air of official weariness to read the document Westaway had handed to him, but before he had read far the abstraction vanished from his face, and was replaced by keen professional interest. He read it closely and carefully, and then he produced his pocket-book and stowed it away.

"Westaway," he said, "this is a somewhat important contribution to the case." He paused for a moment and then turned sharply on Inspector Murchison. "I think you should have told me, Murchison, how damaging a piece of evidence this is against young Marsland."

"Not so damaging," said the inspector, in defence. "You see, young Marsland is Sir George Granville's nephew——"

"So you told me half a dozen times in the train," said Gillett, "and as I knew it before I wasn't much impressed with the information. What I say is that this statement places Marsland in a very awkward position. He has been deceiving us from first to last."

"I admit it is very thoughtless—very foolish of him," replied the inspector. "But surely, Gillett, you don't think this young gentleman had anything to do with the murder?"

"I am not going to be so foolish as to say that it could not possibly be him who did it. What does he mean by hiding from us the fact that Lumsden was under his command in France, and that on the night of the murder he met this girl Maynard at the farm. He seems to be a young gentleman who keeps back a great deal that the police ought to know. And I think you will admit, Murchison, that in that respect he is behaving like a very guilty man."

"But there may be other explanations which will place his conduct in a reasonable light—reasonable but foolish," said the inspector, with an earnest disregard for the way in which these words contradicted each other. "Sir George Granville himself told me his nephew was an officer in the Army, but on account of his nervous breakdown the Army was never mentioned in his presence. And as for keeping Miss Maynard's name out of his statement after she had asked him to do so—why it seems to me the sort of thing that any young man would do for a pretty girl."

"Especially if it played into his hands. If Marsland committed the crime, he must have jumped at the chance offered him by Miss Maynard to keep silence about her presence at the farm, because that left him a free hand in the statement he made to Westaway. He had no need to be careful about any part of his statement, because he had not to harmonize any of it with what she knew about his presence there."

"And what are you going to do about her statement?" asked the inspector. "You will confront Marsland with it?"

"Yes, but before I do that I am going to make a search of the farm for clues."

"But you have already done that. Westaway told me that he and Heather put in two days searching the buildings and the ground round the house."

"Inspector, you are not quite equal to the demands of the situation," said the Scotland Yard man patronizingly. "Westaway, myself and Heather searched the house, the out-buildings and the grounds for clues —for traces left behind unwittingly by the murderer. Our impression then was that the murderer had got away as soon as he could—everything pointed to that. But in the light of this girl's statement we must now search for clues purposely hidden by the murderer. What was Marsland doing when he went outside the house and left the key in the door so as to let himself in again? Hiding something, of course! And where would he hide it?

"There is only one place we haven't searched, and that is the well," continued Gillett. "The reason I didn't have it emptied before was because I was not looking for hidden traces—the circumstances of the crime suggested that the murderer had gone off with the weapon that ended Lumsden's life. But this girl's statement showed that Marsland went out of the house and came back. What was he doing while he was outside? This is what I am going to find out."

"I'll go up to the farm with you," said the inspector. "I want to see what comes of this. I want to know what I've got to say to Sir George Granville."

"You've got to say nothing; you leave it to me," said Detective Gillett. "How long will it take to get the well emptied, Westaway?"

"Four or five hours ought to be long enough, if I can get a couple of good men," said the sergeant.

"See about it at once. Send Heather up with the men to superintend. We will drive out there this afternoon. I have some inquiries to make in the village this morning, and I must also see Miss Maynard."

Gillett, after interviewing Miss Maynard and having his lunch with Inspector Murchison at *The Black-Horned Sheep,* got into an antiquated hooded vehicle, drawn by a venerable white horse, which Sergeant Westaway hired at the inn to take them to Cliff Farm. The innkeeper, who, like all the rest of the town, was bursting with curiosity to learn the latest developments in the case, had eagerly volunteered to drive the police officers up to the farm, but Sergeant Westaway, determined that village gossip should learn nothing through him, had resolutely declined the offer, and drove the equipage himself. They set off with half the village gaping at them from their doors.

Sergeant Westaway had intended to ask Detective Gillett for details concerning his interview with Miss Maynard, but he found that the sluggish and ancient quadruped between the shafts needed incessant urging and rein-jerking to keep him moving at all. This gave him no time for conversation with the detective, who was seated in the back of the vehicle with Inspector Murchison.

When they reached Cliff Farm Sergeant Westaway found another problem to engage his attention. A number of Ashlingsea people had been impelled by curiosity to take a hand in the pumping operations, until tiring of that mechanical labour, they had distributed themselves around the farm, strolling about, gazing vacantly at the farm buildings, or peering through the windows of the house. Constable Heather, who had been sent up with the fishermen in order that constituted authority might be represented in the pumping proceedings, frankly admitted to his superior officer that he had been unable to keep the curious spectators away from the scene.

On hearing this, Sergeant Westaway jumped from the vehicle, and strode into the farmyard with a stern authority which had never been weakened by convivial friendship at *The Black-Horned Sheep*. It says much for the inherent rural respect for law and order that he was able to turn out the intruders in less than five minutes, although the majority of them lingered reluctantly outside the front fence, and watched the proceedings from a distance.

The two fishermen whom Constable Heather had engaged for the task of emptying the well had, with the ingenuity which distinguishes those who make their living on the sea, reduced the undertaking to its simplest elements. A light trench had been dug on that side of the well where the ground had a gentle slope, and, following the lie of the land, had been continued until it connected with one of the main drains of the farm. Therefore, all that remained for the two fishermen to do was to man the pump in turns till the well was empty, the water pouring steadily into the improvised trench and so reaching the main drain, which was carrying the water away to the ditch beside the road. The originator of this plan was an elderly man with a round red face, a moist eye, and an argumentative manner. As the originator of the labour-saving device, he had exercised the right of superior intelligence to relegate to his companion most of the hard labour of carrying it out.

"You see," he said to Inspector Murchison, who happened to be nearest to him, "Tom here"—he indicated his assistant—"wanted to dig a long trench to yon hedge and carry the water out into the valley, but I says 'What's the use of going to all that trouble when it can be done a quicker way?' I says to Tom, 'Let's put a bit of gumption into it and empty it the easiest way. For once the water's out of the well, it don't matter a dump where it runs, for it's no good to nobody.'"

"Very true," said Inspector Murchison, who believed in being polite to everybody.

" 'Therefore,' says I to Tom, 'it stands to reason that the quickest way to empty the well, and the way with least trouble to ourselves, will be to cut from here to that there drain there.'"

"How much longer will you be emptying it?" demanded Detective Gillett, approaching the well and interrupting the flow of the old man's eloquence.

"That depends, sir, on what water there's in it."

This reply was too philosophical to appeal to the practical minded detective. He declared with some sharpness that the sooner it was emptied the better it would be for everybody.

"We are getting towards the bottom now, sir," said the man at the pump, who interpreted the detective's words as a promise that beer would make its appearance when the water had gone. "It ain't a very deep well, not more than fourteen feet at most, and I should say another half hour—maybe more—would see the end of this here job."

"Very well, then, be as quick as you can."

The three police officers remained beside the well, watching the pumping. In a little more than half an hour the flow of water from the mouth of the pump began to decrease. Then the pump began to gurgle and the water stopped. Suction had ceased and the well was practically empty.

Under Detective Gillett's instructions the men who had emptied the well removed the boards which covered the top, and one of them went to the barn and returned with a long ladder. Between them they lowered the ladder into the empty well. The ladder was more than long enough to reach the bottom, for the top was several feet above the mouth of the well.

"That will do, men," ordered the Scotland Yard detective. He climbed to the edge of the well as he spoke.

"Have you a light?" asked Sergeant Westaway in a moment of inspiration.

For reply Detective Gillett displayed a powerful electric torch, and placed one foot on the ladder.

"Better take the stable lantern, sir," urged the inventor of the well-emptying plan. "You'll find it better down there than them new-fangled lights. You'll be able to see further with a sensible lantern."

"And you'd better put on my boots," said the other fisherman. "The well's a bricked 'un, but it'll be main wet and muddy down there."

Detective Gillett pronounced both ideas excellent and acted on them. Sergeant Westaway procured the stable lantern, and lighted it while the detective drew on the fisherman's long sea boots. Thus equipped, and holding the lantern in his right hand, with an empty bag over his shoulder, the Scotland Yard man stepped on to the ladder, and disappeared from view.

Sergeant Westaway intimated to the fishermen who had emptied the tank that the work for which they had been engaged was finished; but it was some minutes before he could make it clear to their slow intellects that their presence was no longer required. When they did understand, they were very loath to withdraw, for they had looked forward with delight to seeing the emptied well yield up some ghastly secret—perhaps another murdered body—and it was only by the exercise of much sternness that Sergeant Westaway was able to get them away from the scene by personally escorting them off the farm and locking the gate after them.

He returned to the well to see Detective Gillett emerging from it. Gillett was carrying the bag and the lantern in one hand, and it was obvious that the bag contained something heavy. The triumphant face of the detective, as he emerged into the upper air, indicated that he had made some important discovery. He stepped off the ladder and emptied the contents of the bag on the ground. They consisted of a heavy pair of boots, hobnailed and iron-shod, such as are worn by country labourers and farmers, and a five-chambered revolver. The revolver was rusty through immersion in the water, and the boots were sodden and pulpy from the same cause.

Inspector Murchison and Sergeant Westaway inspected the articles in silence. At length the former said:

"This is a very important discovery."

"I would direct your attention to the fact that it is

a Webley revolver—one of the two patterns approved by the War Office for Army officers," said Dective Gillett. "Unless I am much mistaken it is a 4.5—that is the regulation calibre for the Army. And I have discovered more than that!"

The police officers ceased looking at the articles on the ground, and directed their eyes to the Scotland Yard detective in response to the note of exultation in his voice. In answer to their look he put his hand into a side pocket and withdrew a small article which he had wrapped in a handkerchief. Unrolling the latter carefully, he held up for their inspection a pair of gold-rimmed eyeglasses.

CHAPTER XVII

"WE have evidence, Captain Marsland, that the statement you made to Sergeant Westaway regarding your discovery of the dead body of Frank Lumsden at Cliff Farm on the night of Friday, 16th October, is untrue."

If Detective Gillett had expected the young man to display either alarm or resentment at this statement he was disappointed. Marsland made no outward sign of astonishment at being addressed by his military title by the detective, or at being accused of having made a false statement. With steady eyes he met the detective's searching gaze.

In response to a request telephoned by Detective Gillett to Sir George Granville's house at Staveley, Marsland and Crewe had motored over to Ashlingsea police station. They had been met on their arrival by the detective and Sergeant Westaway, and after a constrained welcome had been conducted to the Sergeant's inner room. The door had been carefully closed, and Constable Heather, who was in the outer room, had been told by his superior that on no account were they to be disturbed.

There was such a long pause after Detective Gillett had exploded his bomb, that the obligation of opening up the situation suggested itself to him.

"Do you deny that?" he asked.

"I do not." In a clear tone and without any indication of embarrassment the young man made his reply.

"You admit that your statement is false?"

"I do."

"What was your object in making a false statement to the police?"

"I am not prepared to tell you at present."

"Well, perhaps you know your own business best, Captain Marsland, but I warn you that you are in a very serious position. It is for you to decide whether the truth will help you or not."

"Do you intend to make a charge against me?"

Gillett was taken aback at this blunt question. He had arranged the interview because he believed he was in a position to embarrass the young man with a veiled threat of police action, but the young man, instead of waiting for the threats, wanted to know if the police were prepared to act. But Detective Gillett was too experienced an officer to display the weakness of his hand.

"I intend to detain you until I have made further inquiries," he said.

"How long will these inquiries take?" asked Crewe.

"No one knows better than you, Mr. Crewe, that it is impossible for me to answer such a question," said the Scotland Yard man. "One thing leads to another in these cases. As Captain Marsland shows no disposition to help us, they will take at least three or four days."

"But perhaps I can help you," suggested Crewe.

"Well, I don't know what evidence you have picked up in the course of your investigations, Mr. Crewe, but I can tell you that Westaway and I have some evidence that will startle you. Haven't we, Westaway?"

"Very startling evidence indeed," said the sergeant, in a proud official tone.

"I am glad of that," said Crewe. "Perhaps the addition of the little I have picked up—that is the addition of whatever part of it is new to you—will enable you to solve this puzzling crime."

"Very likely indeed," said Gillett. "There are not many links missing in our chain of evidence."

"I congratulate you," responded Crewe. "There are a good many missing in mine."

Gillett broke into a laugh in which there was a distinct note of self-satisfaction.

"That is a very candid admission, Mr. Crewe."

"As between you and me why shouldn't there be candour?" said Crewe. "But what about my young friend Marsland? As it is a case for candour between you and me, we can't have him present. For my part, I should prefer that he was present, but of course that is impossible from your point of view. You cannot go into your case against him in his presence."

"Certainly not," said Gillett decisively. "And before I produce my evidence to you, Mr. Crewe, I must have your word of honour not to tell a living soul, not to breathe a hint of it to any one, least of all to Captain Marsland. If you give me your word of honour I'll be satisfied. That is the sort of reputation you have at Scotland Yard—if you want to know."

"It is very good of you to talk that way," replied Crewe. "I give you my word of honour not to speak to any one of what happens here, until you give me permission to do so. Marsland will wait outside in charge of Constable Heather. He will give you his word of honour not to attempt to escape."

"Is that so?" asked Gillett of the young man.

Marsland nodded, and was handed over to Constable Heather's care by Sergeant Westaway. When the sergeant returned he closed the door carefully.

"Lock it," said Gillett. "And cover up the keyhole; we don't want any one peeping through at what we've got here."

"I like this," said Crewe with a smile. "I feel that I am behind the scenes."

"As regards Captain Marsland," said Gillett after a pause, "I may as well tell you, Mr. Crewe, that I don't want to deal more harshly with him than the situation demands—at this stage. Things may be very different a little later—it may be outside my power to show him any consideration. But I don't want to detain him here—I don't want to lock him up if it can be avoided. You know what talk there would be both here and in Staveley. I am thinking of his uncle, Sir George Granville. I'll tell you what I'll do. If he will give me his word of honour that he will not attempt to escape, and if you and his uncle will do the same, I'll let him go back to Staveley in charge of Heather. There will be no difficulty in explaining Heather's presence there to any friends of Sir George's. What do you think of it?"

"Excellent!" said Crewe.

What was most excellent about it, in the private opinion of Crewe, was the ingenious way in which it extricated Detective Gillett from an awkward situation. When he had arranged the interview for the purpose of frightening Marsland with a threat of detention, he had had this plan in his mind. He had not quite sufficient evidence against Marsland to justify him in arresting that young man without some damaging admissions on the part of the young man himself. And the plan to place him in charge of Heather was a technical escape from the difficulties that surrounded Marsland's actual arrest at that stage; but, on the other hand, it would appear in the young man's eyes as though he were under arrest and this was likely to have an important influence in getting some sort of confession from him.

"Bring out those things," said Detective Gillett to Sergeant Westaway, and pointing to the cupboard against the wall.

Westaway produced a hand-bag and placed it on the table. Gillett took a bunch of keys from his trousers pocket and unlocked the bag.

"First of all, here is the key of the house," he said, as he held out in the palm of his hand the key of a Yale lock. "As you must have noticed, Mr. Crewe, the front door of the farmhouse closes with a modern Yale lock; the old lock is broken and the bolt is tied back with a string. You will notice, inside the hole for the key to go on a ring, that there is a stain of blood. Next, we have a pair of heavy boots. These were worn by the man who murdered Frank Lumsden, for they correspond exactly with the plaster casts we took of the footprints outside the window."

Westaway, who had opened the door of the cupboard, placed on the table near Crewe two plaster casts.

Crewe, after returning the key he had been examining, compared the boots with the plaster casts.

"I believe you are right," he said, after a pause.

"Here we have the bullet that was fired. As you will remember, Mr. Crewe, it went clean through Lumsden's body, and through the window. But what you don't know is that it struck a man who was hiding in the garden near the window. It struck him in the left arm."

"Who was this man?" asked Crewe.

"His name is Tom Jauncey. He is the son of an old shepherd who worked for Lumsden's grandfather."

"One of the servants who was left a legacy in the old man's will?" said Crewe inquiringly.

"That is correct," replied Gillett. "From the bullet we go to the weapon that fired it. Here it is—an ordinary Webley revolver such as is issued to army officers, Mr. Crewe."

"Yes, I know a little about them," said Crewe, as he took it in his hands to look at it.

"And, last of all, here is a pair of glasses which we have ascertained came from the well-known optical firm of Baker & Co., who have branches all over London, and were made for Captain Marsland."

"Where did you find them?" asked Crewe.

"In the well at the farm."

"How did they get there?"

"I don't think it is an unnatural assumption that they were blown off when the wearer was stooping over the well to drop some articles into it. Remember that there was a big storm and a high wind on the night of the murder. The boots and the revolver we also found in the well. Our theory is that the murderer dropped these things into the well in order to get rid of them, and that while he was doing it his glasses were blown into the well. As you know, Marsland wears glasses—he is wearing them now. But Sergeant Westaway will swear that he was not wearing them when he came to the station to report the discovery of the body. We have other interesting evidence in the same direction, but let that go for the present."

"But the boots," said Crewe. "You don't pretend that they belong to Marsland?"

"They probably belonged to the murdered man—that is a point which we have not yet settled."

"And how does that fit in with your theory that the murderer broke into the house?"

"The murderer found these boots in the barn, the cowshed, or one of the other outbuildings. Lumsden did not wear such heavy boots habitually—remember that he had been a clerk, not a farmer. But he would want a heavy pair of boots like these for walking about the farm-yard in wet weather, and probably he kept them in one of the outbuildings, or at any rate left them there on the last occasion he wore them. The intending murderer, prowling about the outbuildings before breaking into the house, found these boots, and with the object of hiding his traces put them on. After he had finished with them he put on his own boots and threw these down the well."

"And your theory is that Marsland is the murderer?"

"I don't say that our case against him is quite complete yet, but the evidence against him is very strong."

"Can you suggest any motive?"

"Yes, Marsland was a captain in the London Rifle

Brigade; Lumsden was a private in the same battalion. They served together in France."

"But the motive?" asked Crewe.

"Our information is that Lumsden and a man against whom Captain Marsland had a personal grudge—a man whom it was his interest to get out of the way—were sent by Captain Marsland on a false mission towards the German lines. Marsland expected that both would fall victims to the Germans. Lumsden's companion was killed, but Lumsden was captured alive and subsequently escaped. What is more likely than that Marsland, riding across the downs, should call in at Cliff Farm when his horse fell lame. There, to his surprise, he found that Lumsden was the owner of the farm. They talked over old times, and Marsland learned that Lumsden was aware of his secret motive in sending them on such a dangerous mission. Marsland took his leave, but determined to put Lumsden out of the way. He stole back and hid in the outbuildings, broke into the house, and shot the man who could expose him."

"A very ingenious piece of work," said Crewe. "Everything dovetails in."

"I am glad you agree with it," said Gillett.

"But I don't," was the unexpected reply. "Lumsden was not murdered at the farm. He was shot in the open, somewhere between Staveley and Ashlingsea, and his dead body was brought into the house in a motor-car. It could not have been Marsland who brought the dead body there, because he was on horseback, and his lamed horse was in the stable at the farm when we were all there next day."

CHAPTER XVIII

"You are on the wrong track, Mr. Crewe," said Gillett, who was determined not to part with the theory he had built up round the evidence he had collected. "I was positive the murder took place in the house. This man Jauncey, whom I mentioned, can swear that he heard a shot fired. And more than that, he can swear that he was hit by the bullet. This is the bullet that was extracted from his wound in the left arm. It fits this revolver."

"My dear Gillett, I don't dispute any of these things," said Crewe. "They merely support my contention that the murder was not committed at the farm, but that the body was brought there, and that the man who took the body there took certain steps with the object of creating the impression that the tragedy took place in the room in which the body was found."

"What evidence have you of that?" asked Sergeant Westaway, coming to the aid of his official superior.

"The bullet that killed Lumsden went clear through his body—so much was decided at the post-mortem examination," Crewe said. "But that fact was also evident from a cursory examination of the body, as we saw it in the chair. You will remember that I drew attention to the fact when we were looking at the body. Your theory is that the shot was fired as Lumsden was standing at the window, with his back towards his murderer, that the bullet went through him, through the window, and lodged in the arm of this man Jauncey who stated he was outside in the garden. But the course of the bullet through Lumsden's body was slightly upward. How in that case could it strike downward and wound a man on the ground ten or twelve feet below the windows on the first story?"

"The bullet might have been deflected by the glass of the window," said Gillett.

"It might have been, but it is highly improbable that ordinary window-glass would deflect a bullet—even a spent one. In any case this bullet hit the cherry-tree outside the window before hitting Jauncey. You will find that it cut the bark of the cherry-tree—the mark is 4 ft. 4½ inches from the ground."

"Then it was the cherry-tree that deflected it?" said Sergeant Westaway.

"Yes and no," said Crewe. "Certainly its course was deflected downwards after hitting the cherry-tree—I assume that Jauncey was close to the tree. But if it had not been travelling downwards, it would have hit the tree much higher up—somewhere near the level of the window. The bullet that hit Jauncey was fired in the room in which we saw the body, but it was fired by the man who took the body to the farm, with the intention of giving the impression that the crime took place there. Knowing that the bullet which killed Lumsden had gone through his body, he placed the body in a chair near the window and then fired a shot through the window. He made the mistake of going close up to the window to fire, and as a result he fired downwards instead of on a level at the height of the wound in Lumsden's body."

"If that is all you have to support your theory——"
began Detective Gillett.

"It isn't all," said Crewe, with a slight indication
of impatience. "It is only my first point. You will
recall that on the stairs there were indications that
a wet rag had been used for wiping away some traces
or stains. Inspector Payne suggested that the rag
had been used to wipe away muddy boot-marks on the
stairs—the traces of these boots. These boots were
not worn by the man as he went upstairs; he put them
on afterwards. Presently I will tell you why he
did. But the marks on the stairs were not the marks
of muddy boots. They were stains of blood which
dropped from the dead man's wound, as his body was
carried upstairs. These marks are in the hall leading
to the stairs and on the landing leading to the room
in which the body was placed. In the room itself no
attempt to remove the blood-stains was made, because they were an indication that the shooting took
place there. If he had been aware that there was
a stain of blood on the latch-key which he took from
the dead man's pocket, he would have washed it
away."

"If he had possession of the key in order to get the
body into the house in the way you state, Mr. Crewe,
why did he break into the house? Remember one of
the downstairs windows was forced."

"It was forced by the man who took the body there.
But he forced it in breaking out of the house—not
in breaking into it. He wanted to give the impression that some one had broken into the house, but
he was pressed for time—he was anxious to get away.
In searching for a rag in the kitchen with which

to wipe out the bloodstains, he saw these boots. They belonged to Lumsden, as you have said, but it was more likely that Lumsden kept them in the kitchen than in the barn or cowshed. This man—let us call him the murderer—saw in the boots a means of averting suspicion from himself. He decided to leave clues that would suggest that the murderer broke into the house. But, instead of going out of the front door and breaking into the house, he forced the window from inside the room. Then, with these boots on, he climbed out of the window backwards, and when he reached the ground he walked backwards across the garden bed to the path in order to give the impression that some one had walked forwards across the bed to the window.

"You saw from the sash of the window that the catch had been forced back by a knife, but apparently you overlooked the fact that the marks of the knife are much broader at the top, where the catch is, than at the bottom, where the knife would enter if the catch had been forced by some one outside. It was at the top, near the catch, and not at the bottom below it, that the knife was inserted; that is to say, the knife was used by some one inside the room. The footprints outside the window showed that they were made by a person walking backwards; the impression from the toe to the ball of the foot being very distinct and the rest of the foot indistinct. A person in walking backwards puts down his toes first, and gradually brings the rest of his foot down; a person walking forwards puts his heel down first and then puts down the rest of his foot as he brings his weight forward. Our man, having made his way to the garden path from the window, walked along the path to the motor-car at the gate, probably carrying his own boots in his hand. As soon as he entered his car he drove off along the road in the direction of Staveley with the lights out. He took a risk in travelling in the dark, and in spite of the fact that he knew the road well he came to grief before he reached Staveley."

"How do you know all this?" asked Gillett. "How do you know he had a car?" He had not given up his own theory in favour of Crewe's, but he realized that Crewe's theory was the more striking one.

"In Marsland's statement he said that his horse swerved from something in the dark as he was coming down the Cliff road, and fell lame," said Crewe. "The horse shied at the motor-car as it passed. Marsland neither saw nor heard the car because of the darkness, intensified by the storm, and because of the roar of the wind and waves."

"You don't really expect us to regard the swerving of the horse as proof there was a motor-car there?" demanded Gillett, with a superior smile.

"Contributory proof," said Crewe. "If you went along the cliff road, as I did on leaving the farm after meeting you there, you would have noticed that the danger post nearest the farm was out of the perpendicular. That was not the case previous to the night of the storm. This motor-car without lights bumped into it. The mark of the wheels where the car had left the road was quite plain when I looked—it had not been obliterated by the rain. Four miles away the car was run into the ditch and overturned. I saw it as Sir George Granville and I drove along to Cliff

Farm on Saturday morning. If you want information concerning it and the person who drove it you can obtain it at Gosford's garage at Staveley. The car was hired from Gosford."

"By whom?" asked Gillett.

"By a man named Arnold Brett, who was a very close friend of the dead man."

"I know all about Brett from Inspector Murchison," said Gillett. "He rang me up about him and promised to let me know when he came back to his lodgings at Staveley. He said that Brett was a close friend of Lumsden's, and would probably be able to give us some useful information when he returns."

"When will he return?" asked Crewe.

"You think he has cleared out?" suggested Gillett.

"I'm sure of it," was the reply.

"Murchison gave the impression that he was sure to come back—that he had left Staveley the day before the murder. I understood from Murchison that Brett is doing some secret service work for the Government, and that it was quite a regular thing for him to disappear suddenly."

"No doubt it was," said Crewe. "But this time he is not coming back."

"I'll ring up Murchison," said Gillett.

"Don't waste your time," was Crewe's reply. "Murchison is an excellent fellow—an ideal police official for a quiet seaside place where nothing happens, but too genial and unsuspecting for an emergency of this kind. Go and see Brett's apartments at Staveley—No. 41 Whitethorn Gardens—and the landlady, Mrs. Penfield, will tell you as she told Murchison, and as she told me also, that Brett left Staveley on secret service work on Thursday morning, 15th October, and that she expects him back at any moment. But go to Gosford and he will show you the car that Brett hired on Friday.

"He will tell you that on Saturday about midday Brett rang him up—from Lewes, Gosford says, but it was more probably from Marlingsea, on his way to London—and told him that he had met with an accident with the car, and that it was lying in the ditch on the side of the road about six miles out from Staveley on the road to this place. It was there that Gosford's foreman found the car when he went for it. If Brett hired a car at Staveley on Friday he couldn't have left Staveley on Thursday, as his landlady says. She doesn't know what to think in regard to this murder, but she is ready to shield Brett all she can because she is in love with him."

CHAPTER XIX

"I MUST say that I feel very grateful to you, Mr. Crewe," said Detective Gillett after a pause. "You have certainly got hold of some facts of which I was not aware. And your deductions are most interesting. What do you say, Westaway?"

"Most interesting," said the sergeant. "I had heard a lot of Mr. Crewe before I met him, but I'd like to say that it's a great privilege to listen to his deductions."

"Oh, I don't go so far as to accept his theory and abandon my own," interposed Gillett hurriedly. "To my mind there is truth in both of them, and the whole truth will probably be found in a judicious combination of both."

Crewe could scarcely hide his impatience at Gillett's obstinacy, and his determination to claim at least an equal share in solving the mystery.

"My dear Gillett," he said, "let us abandon theories and keep to facts. The great danger in our work is in fitting facts to theories instead of letting the facts speak for themselves. If you still think you have a case against Marsland, let us go into it. It is no part of my work to prove Marsland innocent if he is guilty; I have no object in proving Brett guilty if he is innocent. But as the guest of Sir George Granville, I want to save him and his nephew unnecessary distress and anxiety. By a full and frank discussion we can decide as man to man whether there is any real case for Marsland to answer. I admit that you have justification for some suspicions in regard to him, but let us see if the fog of suspicion cannot be cleared away by a discussion of the facts."

"It will take a great deal to convince me that he doesn't know more about this tragedy than he has told us," said Gillett doggedly.

"But are we to find him guilty merely because he chooses to keep silence on certain points?"

"What is his object in keeping silence? What was his object in making a false statement? What is his object in putting obstacles in our way? Is that the conduct of an innocent man?"

"It is not the conduct of a man anxious to help the police to the utmost of his power without regard to consequences," said Crewe. "But there is a wide gulf between being guilty of keeping something back and being guilty of murder."

"When the thing kept back suggests a motive for getting the man who was murdered out of the way, it is natural to see a connection between the two," returned Gillett.

"And what was the thing that Marsland kept back?"

"He kept back that he was an officer in the army— Captain in the London Rifle Brigade. He kept back that this man Lumsden was a private in his company."

"But the discovery of these things did not present any great difficulty to a police official of your resources, Gillett."

"No, they did not," the detective admitted. "But we should have been told of them in the first place."

"True. But listen to the explanation why you were not told. Marsland has been an invalid for some months. He was invalided out of the army because of wounds and nervous shock. He broke down as many others have broken down, under a long experience of the awful horrors of the front. In order to assist in his recovery the doctors ordered that as far as possible his mind should be kept from dwelling on the war. For this reason the war is never mentioned in his presence by those who know of his nervous condition. He is never addressed by them as an army officer, but as a civilian."

"All that is very interesting, Mr. Crewe, but it does not dispose of the information in our possession. You see, the circumstances in which Captain Marsland came into this affair were so very extraordinary, that he might well have told Westaway the truth about the military connection between himself and Lumsden. It was an occasion when the whole truth should have been told. We could not have been long in learning from his relatives that he was suffering from nervous shock, and we would have shown him every consideration."

"That is an excellent piece of special pleading," said Crewe. "But you do not take into consideration the fact that the evasion of everything that dealt with the Army, and particularly with his old regiment, has become a habit with Marsland."

"Our information," said Gillett slowly and impressively, "is that he believed Lumsden was dead—that he had been killed in France. That in his capacity as

P

an officer he sent Lumsden and another man to their death. He had a grudge against this other man. Lumsden's companion was killed but Lumsden was taken prisoner and subsequently escaped. If that is correct, it supplies a strong motive for getting Lumsden out of the way when he discovered that Lumsden was alive and in England."

"When did Marsland make this discovery?"

"That I don't know. But he could easily have made it and obtained Lumsden's address from the headquarters of the London Rifle Brigade."

"Did he make such inquiries there?"

"I have not obtained positive proof that he did. But as a retired officer of the Brigade, who knows his way about their headquarters, he could do it for himself in a way that would leave no proof."

"Who was the man that Marsland sent out on a mission of death with Lumsden?"

"I haven't got the name."

"Can't you get it?"

"I am afraid not. It is not a thing one could get from the regimental records."

"But cannot you get it from your informant—from the person who is your authority for the story?"

"Not very well."

"What does that mean?"

"Our informant is anonymous. He sent me a letter."

"And since when have you begun to place implicit faith in anonymous letters, my dear Gillett?"

The detective flushed under this gentle irony. "I don't place implicit faith in it. But it fits in with other information in our possession. And you ought to know better than to despise anonymous information, Mr. Crewe. It is not difficult to conceive circumstances in which a man is willing to give the police very valuable information, but will not come into the open to do it."

"But it is even less difficult," replied Crewe, "to conceive circumstances in which a man tries to divert suspicion from himself by directing the attentions of the police to some one else by means of an anonymous letter."

"I haven't overlooked that," said Gillett confidently.

"And this anonymous communication fits in with other information in your possession—other information that you have received from Miss Maynard?" Crewe looked steadily at Gillett, and then turned his gaze on Westaway.

"So, you know about her?" was Gillett's comment.

"She did me the honour of asking my advice when I met her two days ago at Cliff Farm."

"What was she doing there?"

"Didn't she tell you?"

"She did not."

"I understood from her that it was her firm determination to tell you everything—to take you fully into her confidence, and throw all the light she could on the tragedy."

"She told us that she was at the farm the night Captain Marsland was there," said Gillett. "She sought shelter there from the storm and went upstairs with Captain Marsland when the body was discovered. He said nothing whatever about this in his statement to Westaway."

"Nothing whatever," said Westaway. "He led me to believe he was entirely and absolutely alone"

"But why didn't she come to the police station that night and make her own statement?" asked Crewe. "Why all this delay?"

"Her first impulse was to keep her name out of it because of the way people would talk," said Sergeant Westaway, who, as an old resident of Ashlingsea, felt better qualified than Detective Gillett to interpret the mental process of one of the inhabitants of the little town.

"And so she asked Marsland to say nothing about her presence at the farm?" asked Crewe.

"She admits that," was Westaway's reply.

"Of course she had to admit it in order to clear the way for a statement implicating Marsland in the crime," said Crewe.

"That was not her motive. After thinking over all that happened, she decided that by shielding herself from idle gossip she might be helping unconsciously to shield the murderer."

"And she told you everything," said Crewe.

"Everything," said Sergeant Westaway emphatically.

"She told you why she was waiting at the farm on the night that Lumsden's dead body was brought there?"

"She went there for shelter from the storm," explained the confident sergeant. "That would be after the body was brought there—if your theory is correct, Mr. Crewe; and after he was shot in the house—if our theory is correct. Our theory is that Captain Marsland, after committing the crime, went outside the house to hide the traces of it—probably to get rid of these boots and revolver, which he threw down the well."

"It hasn't occurred to you, sergeant, that these things may have been placed in the well within the last few days in order that you might find them there?" said Crewe.

"Who would place them there?" asked Gillett coming to the rescue of the sergeant with a poser.

"I think you asked me just now what Miss Maynard was doing at the farm two days ago," said Crewe.

"And you think that there may be some connection between her visit there and these things?"

"With all due deference to the sergeant as a judge of character, and particularly of the feminine character, I am quite convinced that she has not told you everything."

"Can you tell us anything she is keeping back?"

"She is keeping back the real reason why she went to Cliff Farm on the night the body was taken there."

"You do not think she went there to shelter from the storm?"

"She had an appointment there," said Crewe.

"With whom?" asked Gillett breathlessly.

"With Brett—the man to whom she is engaged."

"What!" exclaimed Gillett.

"Surely she explained to you the nature of her relations with Brett?" said Crewe maliciously. "Except in regard to Marsland she does not seem to have taken you into her confidence at all."

"She may be playing a deep game," said Gillett, in a tone which indicated that although an attempt

might be made to hoodwink them, it was not likely
to prove successful.

"I think you will find that she is a very clever
young woman," was Crewe's comment.

"What was the nature of her appointment at Cliff
Farm with Brett? Why not meet him at Ashlingsea
or at Staveley?" asked Gillett.

"As to the nature of the appointment, I will refer
you for full details to Mrs. Grange. You know her,
sergeant, of course?" Crewe said, turning to Westaway.

"The dwarf woman at Staveley?" asked the sergeant.

"Yes. If I am not much mistaken Grange and his
wife were in the vicinity of Cliff Farm when the dead
body of the owner was brought there. What part
they played in the tragedy I must leave you to find
out from them. I am not certain myself of their
part, but I have a fairly clear idea. You can let
me know what admission you get from them. Before they admit anything it may be necessary to
frighten them with arrest, Gillett. But I don't suppose you mind doing that?"

"Not in the least," replied Gillett with a smile that
was free from embarrassment. "But what evidence
can I produce to show that I know they know all
about Miss Maynard's presence at the farm? What
evidence is there that this man and his wife were anywhere in the neighbourhood of the place?"

"They went over in the afternoon of October 16th
in a motor-boat in charge of a boatman at Staveley,
who is called Pedro, and wears a scarlet cloak.
Murchison told me that Pedro is the father of Mrs.

Grange, the dwarf woman—they are Italians. But
Grange, the husband, is an Englishman. He keeps a
second-hand bookshop in Curzon Street, at Staveley,
and lives over the shop with his wife. Is that not so,
Westaway?"

"Yes, sir. That is quite correct."

"They reached the landing-place at the foot of the
cliffs, near the farm, before there was any appearance of the storm. The next morning, as I was descending the cliff by the secret path, I found an
old felt hat on the rocks just before Pedro, who had
come over in his boat to look for it, reached the place.
My impression is that the hat belonged to Grange, and
was blown off as he was descending the cliff by the path
when the storm was abating. If it had been blown off
in the afternoon, while he was ascending the cliff in
daylight, he could have recovered it without much difficulty. The fact that he left it behind indicates that it
was blown off in the dark and that he was too excited
and upset to hunt for it. But on reaching Staveley in
Pedro's boat, after the storm had abated, he began
to think that his old hat was a dangerous object
to leave about in the vicinity of a house where there
was the body of a murdered man awaiting discovery by
the police, so he sent Pedro back to the landing-place
to recover the hat."

"But, hang it all, Crewe! Some of your reasoning about the hat is merely surmise. You say it was
blown off while Grange was descending the cliff path.
How do you arrive at that conclusion? It might
have been blown off at any time—while he was cross-
ing to the farm, or standing on the cliffs."

"No," replied Crewe. "The gale was blowing in from the sea, and if Grange's hat had blown off while he was on the cliffs it would have blown inward—that is, across the downs."

Detective Gillett nodded.

"I overlooked that point," he said. "Have you possession of the hat now?"

"Yes. You can have it if you call for it at Sir George Granville's, on your way to interview Grange this afternoon or to-morrow. But the Granges know that I have the hat. I went there with it just to convince myself that Grange did own it."

"Did he admit that it was his?"

"He denied it. But he is not a good hand at dissimulation. I offered to hand over the hat to him in exchange for a truthful account of all he and his wife knew about the tragedy, but the offer was not entertained. They denied that they were there at all."

"I'll soon get them to alter that tune!" exclaimed the resourceful Gillett. "I will put the screw on this man in the scarlet cloak until I squeeze something out of him."

"I am afraid you will have a slight difficulty in making Pedro reveal anything," said Crewe. "He is deaf and dumb."

Gillett looked somewhat confused at finding that his impetuous confidence had carried him beyond his resources.

"That is unfortunate," he said.

"It is of no consequence," returned Crewe, "for you have evidence in your possession that Mrs. Grange was inside the farmhouse. The comb you found in the sitting-room downstairs belongs to her. When I went to see her she was wearing one exactly similar to it. Apparently she had two of them. And she does not know where she lost the one the police have, or she would not wear its fellow."

CHAPTER XX

DINNER was just over at Sir George Granville's house, and Crewe, on hearing that Detective Gillett and Sergeant Westaway had called to see him, took them into the library at his host's suggestion.

"I have seen Grange and his wife, and also Mrs. Penfield," said Gillett.

"And what did you get from them?" asked Crewe.

"A great deal of interesting information—and most of it bearing out your theory, Mr. Crewe. I must say that this crime has more twists and turns than any I have ever had anything to do with."

"I formed the impression some time ago that it was a complicated and interesting case," said Crewe.

"And I want to say, Mr. Crewe, that you have been a great help to us. If it wasn't for you we shouldn't have got on the right track so soon, should we, sergeant?"

Sergeant Westaway, who was not very quick at arriving at conclusions, had discovered that Detective Gillett was generally ready to call him to official comradeship in the mistakes that had been made, but less disposed to give him an equal share in any success achieved. He nodded in silent acquiescence with the admission that they owed something to Crewe.

"And whom did you see first?" asked Crewe.

"I went to the garage first to learn about the motor-car Brett hired," said Gillett. "I had a look at their books, and found that he had the car on Friday afternoon. Gosford will not only swear by his books, but he remembers quite distinctly that it was on Friday that Brett had the car. As he told you, the next thing he heard of it was that it was lying in the ditch about six miles away. He says Brett, when telephoning, said he was speaking from Lewes—but that is probably a lie. As Brett was making his escape he would not be likely to say where he was. But I can easily find out from the telephone exchange where the call came from. It was a trunk call, and the only trunk call Gosford received that day, so there will be no difficulty in getting it from the records of the exchange. Then I went to Brett's lodgings in Whitethorn Gardens. This woman, Mrs. Penfield, tried to bluff me—she said she was certain that Brett had left on Thursday, and that Gosford was mistaken in thinking Brett had the car on Friday. But, when I threatened to arrest her for being an accessory, she broke down and admitted that Brett left her place after lunch on Friday to drive to Cliff Farm, and that she has not seen or heard of him since."

"Not seen or heard of him?" echoed Crewe meditatively.

"By this time I felt that I was getting on," continued Detective Gillett.

Sergeant Westaway nodded to himself in sour depression at the deliberate exclusion of himself from the story of progress.

"I next called at Grange's shop. Westaway showed me the place."

"Ah!" exclaimed the sergeant, as if he were in pain.

"I explained to Grange who I was, and he nearly fell through the floor with fright. I saw there would not be much difficulty in dealing with him. But the ugly little dwarf upstairs was a different proposition. She protested that she and her husband knew nothing about Cliff Farm, or what had happened there. Even when I produced the hat you gave me she would not give in. But when I produced the comb —it is exactly similar to the one she was wearing— it made an impression, and then when I followed that up with a threat to arrest them both——"

"Ah," interrupted Crewe with a smile, "that is where you Scotland Yard men have the advantage. And I must say that you don't neglect to use it on every occasion. If I could only threaten people with arrest I should be able to surmount many of the difficulties which confront me from time to time."

"It is a good card," admitted Detective Gillett, with the pride of a man who holds a strong hand which he has dealt himself. "It enabled me to get their story out of them, and a most interesting story it is."

"I thought it would be," said Crewe.

"The body was brought to the farm by Brett. Grange and his wife were in the house when he carried it upstairs."

"But did Brett know they were there?" asked Crewe.

"He did not; he never suspected there was anybody in the house. They hid on the top floor."

"And they were there when Miss Maynard came after Brett had gone," said Crewe, pursuing a train of thought. "They were there when Marsland and she went up to the first floor and discovered the body. It was Grange who knocked over the picture at the top of the staircase, and caused the noise which alarmed Marsland and Miss Maynard."

"Right," said Gillett. "You seem to know the whole story: it is not worth while for me to go over it."

"Oh, yes it is. If you got the whole truth out of that little dwarf and her husband, you will be able to fill in for me some blanks in my reconstruction of the crime."

Detective Gillett was mollified by the assurance that he had in his possession some information which was new to Crewe, and he resumed his story with interest:

"What do you think took the Granges over to the farm? It was to hold a séance there with the object of finding where old grandfather Lumsden had hidden his money. Young Lumsden had heard from Murchison something about the dwarf's psychic powers, and in company with Brett he went to see her. First of all they produced the cryptogram old Lumsden had left behind, and asked Grange if he knew anything about cryptograms or could get them a book on how to solve them. Grange couldn't help them there, and from that the conversation turned to spiritualism, and one of them—probably Brett—suggested that Mrs. Grange should try to solve the cryptogram by getting into communication with the spirit of old Lumsden and asking him where he had hidden the money. A splendid idea, don't you think, Mr. Crewe?"

"Excellent!"

"There is nothing in this spiritualistic business."

said Sergeant Westaway, with official certainty. "No good ever comes of those who dabble in it—I've seen cases of the kind at Ashlingsea. We had a sort of medium there once, but I managed to clear her out, after a lot of trouble."

"Once spiritualism gets into good working order there will be no work for police or detectives, sergeant," said Crewe. "The mediums will save all the trouble of collecting evidence."

"I don't believe in it at all; it is nothing but fraud and deception," returned Sergeant Westaway.

"Here is the cryptogram," said Detective Gillett.

He held out to Crewe a sheet of paper which he took from his pocket-book.

"A curious document!" said Crewe, examining it intently.

"I got it from the dwarf woman," said Gillett. "She had it hidden away in her sitting-room."

"I suppose she didn't want to part with it?"

"She did not. But when I threatened to arrest——"

"Well, I can honestly congratulate you on getting it," said Crewe. "I have been very anxious to see it. This is the cryptogram that Marsland found on the stairs, and subsequently disappeared from the house. Mrs. Grange secured it before she left the house, after the departure of Marsland and Miss Maynard."

"That is what I thought; but the dwarf says, 'No.' She says that this is the original cryptogram, and that she got it from young Lumsden in order to study it before holding a séance. Lumsden would not part with it until he had made a copy, in case anything happened to the original. Mrs. Grange took the original with her over to Cliff Farm, but it has never

ƆY X X U R J J X S X

Take heed and be quiet; fear not, neither be fainthearted for the two tails of those smoking firebrands, for the fierce anger of Rezin with Syria, and of the son of Remaliah.

Because Syria, Ephraim, and the son of Remaliah, have taken evil counsel against thee, saying,

Let us go up against Judah, and vex it, and let us make a breach therein for us, and set a king in the midst of it, even the son of Tabeal:

Thus saith the Lord God, It shall not stand, neither shall it come to pass.

And all the kings of the north, far and near, one with another, and all the kingdoms of the world, which are upon the face of the earth: and the king of Sheshach shall drink after them.

Therefore thou shalt say unto them, Thus saith the Lord of Hosts, the God of Israel; Drink ye, and be drunken, and spue, and fall, and rise no more, because of the sword which I will send among you.

been out of her possession since Lumsden gave it to her. She did not see the copy Lumsden made; she did not see it at the house, and does not know what became of it. However, the copy is of no consequence."

"Oh, isn't it?" said Crewe. "I would like to know where it went. The cryptogram can be solved just as well from the copy as the original."

"It probably got blown away and destroyed," said Detective Gillett. "There was a high wind that night."

"You might leave this with me for a day or two," said Crewe, looking at the cryptogram earnestly. "I take an interest in cryptograms."

"You must take great care of it," Detective Gillett replied. "I shall want to produce it as evidence at the trial."

"When you get Brett?"

"Yes. And now let us get back to my story. It was arranged that a séance should be held at the farm on Friday, October 16th."

"Who was to be there?" asked Crewe.

"Grange and his wife, Lumsden, Brett and Miss Maynard. This young lady has been playing a deep game, as you suggested. I will settle with her tomorrow."

"And this man, Tom Jauncey, who was shot in the arm, wasn't he one of the party?"

"No."

"I thought he might be there to represent the unpaid legatees," said Crewe.

"I have no doubt that he knew about the séance—that he had heard Brett and Miss Maynard talking about it. Brett was in the habit of visiting the young lady at her home. No doubt Jauncey went out to the farm in order to learn what happened, and see if the money was found."

"That is much more likely than that he went there to dig in the garden."

"Let me reconstruct the crime for you, Mr. Crewe. I have got all the threads," said Detective Gillett eagerly. "The séance was to take place at 6 p. m. on Friday. The dwarf and her husband went over to the place in the afternoon in the motor-boat belonging to old Pedro. They climbed the cliff, and on reaching the farm found that there was no one about, but that the front door was not locked. Lumsden had gone for a walk along the Staveley road to meet Brett, who was to motor over, and he had left the door unlocked, so that, if any of his guests arrived during his absence, they could enter the house and make themselves at home. He was not afraid of thieves going there, for very few people travel along that road on foot. That was the arrangement he had made with the Granges.

"They entered the house, and had a look round the old place. No doubt it occurred to them that if they were thoroughly acquainted with the rooms, and all the nooks and crannies, they would be able to give a more impressive séance. And perhaps they had an idea that in searching round they might find the money without the assistance of the former owner's spirit, in which case, I have no doubt, they would have helped themselves. They had reached the house about 5 o'clock, and they had not been there half an hour before the storm began to burst, and it got dark.

"It was probably the noise of the rising wind which prevented them hearing Brett's motor-car, and the

Q

first intimation they had that any one had arrived was hearing the front door open. They had closed it when they entered the house, their object being to examine the rooms undisturbed. Brett, thinking there was no one in the house, opened the door with Lumsden's key. The Granges who were on the top floor did not call out to him, as they had no satisfactory explanation to offer for exploring the house. They saw Brett staggering up the stairs carrying something on his left shoulder. At first they could not make out what it was, as it was dark inside the house. Half-way up the stairs Brett came to a halt to shift his burden, and he turned on an electric torch in order to see where he was. By the light of the torch the Granges saw that Brett was carrying the body of a man. They thought at first that Lumsden had been injured in an accident to the motor-car, but the fact that they heard no voices subsequently—that Brett did not speak aloud—convinces me that you were right, and that Lumsden was dead.

"Brett entered the room on the left of the stairs on the first floor, and was there some minutes—probably getting Lumsden's pocket-book, and disarranging the papers it contained in the way we saw. Then he went downstairs, and a few moments later the little dwarf, who was leaning over the staircase, saw him moving about below, with the torch in one hand and a bucket in the other. He began washing away the stains of blood in the hall, and on the staircase. He came up the stairs one by one with his bucket and torch, searching for blood-stains, and swabbing them with the cloth whenever he found them. After cleaning the stairs and landing in this way, he went downstairs with the bucket. A minute later he came back to the room which he had first entered, and immediately afterwards they heard a shot. This was the shot fired through the window. No doubt the bullet hit the cherry-tree, and then struck Jauncey in the arm. It seems a strange thing that Jauncey knew nothing about the motor-car at the gate. But of course it had no lights, and Jauncey, intent on spying, did not go up to the front gate to enter the garden. He must have got through the hedge lower down, and made his way across the home field. I must see him about this and ask him.

"After firing the shot Brett went downstairs again, and the Granges saw no more of him," continued Detective Gillett. "No doubt Brett found Lumsden's boots in the kitchen, as you said, and after putting them on forced the window downstairs and climbed out. He got into his car and drove off without lights, being very thankful to get away without any one seeing him—as he thought.

"The Granges did not know he had gone, and while they were quaking upstairs, wondering what to do, the front door was opened again and there was a light step in the hall. This was Miss Maynard. She had found the key in the lock which Brett had left there. By this time the storm had reached the farm. There was a high wind with heavy drops of rain. Miss Maynard, unconscious that there was a dead man upstairs, and Grange and his wife on the floor above, lighted the candle on the hallstand, and then took it into the sitting-room, where Brett had got out of the house. She sat down to wait for the appearance of Brett and Lumsden. No doubt the fact that she had found the key in the door convinced her that they were in the outbuildings. According to the Granges' story, Miss Maynard arrived less than ten minutes after Brett's final trip downstairs, and about a quarter of an hour after her arrival there came a knock at the front door. This was Captain Marsland.

"The rest of the story we know, from Captain Marsland's statement to Westaway, the only thing that is wrong with it being his omission of all mention of Miss Maynard. Grange, bending over the stairs to watch, knocked down the picture that made such a crash. When Captain Marsland and Miss Maynard found the body, she knew immediately that Brett must have had something to do with the tragedy, and therefore she asked Captain Marsland to say nothing about her presence there. If he had done so she would have had to give us an account of her movements, and the object of her visit there, and all this would have directed suspicion to Brett.

"Not till half an hour after Grange and his wife heard the door close, when Captain Marsland and Miss Maynard departed, did they venture downstairs. They looked in at the room in which the body had been taken, and by the light of matches they saw the dead man in the chair. They got away from the house as fast as they could. They found the path down the cliff, and while Grange was helping his wife down it his hat blew off. He thought nothing of this at the time. In the old boat-house at the foot of the cliff they found Pedro, who had been sheltering there from the storm. They waited in the boat-house until the storm abated, and about nine o'clock they pushed off in the boat for Staveley, which they were unable to reach until nearly midnight, owing to the rough sea running.

"They decided to say nothing about what they knew, their intention being to keep out of the whole affair. They were afraid that they would be worried a great deal by the police if they said anything, and they were still more afraid that the fact that they had been connected with a murder would ruin their business. In the morning old Pedro was sent over to the landing-place to find the hat Grange had lost."

"A very interesting story," said Crewe.

"It is," said Gillett with pride in his success as a narrator. "And it won't lose much in dramatic interest when it is unfolded in evidence at the trial. In fact, I think it will gain in interest. What a shock it will be to Brett when he finds that he was seen carrying the body of Lumsden upstairs!"

"You are convinced that Brett was the murderer?" asked Crewe.

"Absolutely certain. Aren't you?"

"No."

Detective Gillett stared in surprise at the inscrutable face of the man whose powers of deduction he had learned to look on with admiring awe. Sergeant Westaway, whose legs had become cramped owing to his uncomfortable attitude in a low chair, shifted his position uneasily, and also looked intently at Crewe.

"Then whom do you suspect?" exclaimed Gillett in astonishment.

"Suspect?" said Crewe with a slight note of protest in his voice. "I suspect no one. Suspicions in regard to this, that and the other merely cloud the view. Let us look at the facts and see what they prove."

"I don't think you want better proof of murder than that the man who was seen carrying the body of the murdered man subsequently disappears, in order to escape being questioned by the police."

"It looks what you call suspicious," said Crewe, "but it is not proof. You assume that Brett is the murderer, but you do not know any of the circumstances under which the crime was committed."

"Lumsden was walking along the road to meet Brett. They did meet, and in discussing this séance they quarrelled about the division of the money."

"But why quarrel about dividing the money before the money was found? They already had had some disappointments about finding the money."

"They may have quarrelled about something else. But why did Brett disappear, and why did he take the body to the farm and endeavour to manufacture misleading clues?"

"I admit that his conduct is suspicious—that it is difficult to account for. But if he is guilty—if he shot Lumsden on the road or when they were driving along the road—why did he take the body to the farm where it was sure to be discovered, as he knew the Granges were to get there by 6 p. m? Wouldn't it have been better for him to hide the body in a field or a ditch? That would have given him more time to escape."

"He took the body to the farm for the purpose of making us believe that the murder was committed there," rejoined Gillett slowly and positively.

"And then disappeared in order to direct the police suspicions to himself," said Crewe.

"No doubt he was inconsistent," Gillett admitted. "But a murderer manufacturing false clues would scarcely be in the frame of mind to think out everything beforehand. The object of leaving false clues was to get sufficient time to escape. Surely, Mr. Crewe, you are not going to say that you believe Brett had nothing to do with the murder—that he is an innocent man?"

"I believe that he knows more about the crime than you or I, and that he disappeared in order to escape being placed in a position in which he would have to tell most of what he knows."

"And another person who knows a great deal about the crime is Miss Maynard," said Gillett.

"Yes. I think you have some awkward questions to ask her."

"I have," replied the Scotland Yard representative emphatically.

"You might ask her where she got Marsland's eyeglasses that she dropped down the well. The boots and revolver she got from Brett—or perhaps Brett dropped them there himself on the night of the murder. But the eyeglasses are a different thing."

"She may have picked them up in the house, or along the garden path. I understand that Captain Marsland lost a pair of glasses that night."

"He did, but not the pair that were found in the well. The pair that he lost that night he has not found, but the pair you found in the well were in his possession for nearly a week after the murder. He is quite sure on that point, but does not know where he lost them."

"Of course, he knows that it was Miss Maynard who tried to direct our suspicions to him?" asked Gillett.

"I told him very little, and what I did tell him was for the purpose of satisfying him on a few minor points. That was implied in my promise to you. But he asked about her before I had mentioned her name. He asked if you had seen her."

"And I suppose he was very indignant with her?"

"No. He took it all very calmly. His calmness, his indifference, struck me as remarkable in one who has suffered from nervous shock."

"I would like to apologize to him if he is anywhere about—if it is not too much trouble to send for him."

"Not at all," said Crewe. He touched the bell, and when the parlour maid appeared, he sent her in search of Captain Marsland.

The young man entered the room a few minutes later in evening dress, and nodded cheerfully to the two police officials. He listened with a forgiving smile to Detective Gillett's halting apology for having believed that he had endeavoured to mislead the police in the statement made to Sergeant Westaway on the night of the murder.

"Miss Maynard will find that she has over-reached herself," said Gillett to the young man in conclusion. "I will look her up in the morning and frighten the truth out of her. She knows more about the crime than any one—except Brett. As far as I can see she will be lucky if she escapes arrest as an accomplice."

"Have you ever considered, Gillett, the possibility of her having been the principal?" asked Crewe.

"No," said the detective, who obviously was surprised at the suggestion. "Do you think that she fired the shot; that she and Brett are both in it?"

"She fits into the tragedy in a remarkable way—she fits into the story told by the Granges."

"Yes," said the detective doubtfully. "She does."

"Let us attempt to reconstruct the crime with her as the person who fired the shot," continued Crewe. "Mrs. Grange was to hold a séance at the farmhouse about 6 p. m. Lumsden, Brett and this girl were to be present. Lumsden walked along the road to Staveley in the expectation of meeting Brett, who was to drive over in a motor car. Miss Maynard, who was a good walker, set out from Ashlingsea. She left early in the afternoon, in the expectation that Brett would be at the farmhouse early. She found no one there and then set out along the Staveley road to meet Brett. He was late in starting from Staveley, and she met Lumsden, who, perhaps, was returning along the road. They decided to sit down for a little while and wait for Brett. Lumsden, who was in love with her, was overcome by passion, and seized her in his arms. There was a struggle in which the revolver that Lumsden carried fell out of his belt. She picked it up and in desperation shot him. A few minutes later Brett arrived in his car. He was horrified at what had occurred but his first thought was to save the girl he loved from the consequences of her act. He lifted the body of Lumsden into the car, and with Miss

Maynard beside him on the front seat, drove to the farmhouse. She waited in the car while he carried the body into the house, and took steps for giving the impression that Lumsden was shot by some one who broke into the house. Then he went back to the car, and after giving the girl his final directions bade her a tender farewell. She entered the house and waited in accordance with the plan Brett had thought out. She expected the Granges to arrive at any moment; she did not know they were hiding upstairs. Brett's plan was that she and the Granges should discover the body. That would clear her of suspicion of complicity in the tragedy. Marsland came to the house, and for Miss Maynard's purpose he suited her better than the Granges because he took on himself the discovery of the body and, at her request, kept her name out of it to the police. Brett disappeared that night, ostensibly on secret service work. His object was to shield his fiancée by directing suspicion to himself."

"I don't think Brett is capable of such chivalry," said Marsland.

"It is a very ingenious theory, very ingenious, indeed," said Gillett. "I don't say that it is absolutely correct, Mr. Crewe, but the reconstruction is very clever. What do you say, Westaway?"

"Very ingenious—very clever," said the Sergeant. "Only it is no good asking me to believe that Miss Maynard did it; I could never bring myself to believe that she was capable of it. I have known her since she was a litle girl. She is the daughter of a highly respected——"

"We know all about that," said Gillett impatiently.

"But lots of highly respectable people commit murder, Westaway. Even among the criminal classes there are no professional murderers. I'll see this young lady in the morning, Mr. Crewe, and let you know the result. I think I can promise that I'll shake the truth out of her."

CHAPTER XXI

Detective Gillett cycled across to Ashlingsea the following morning, after spending the night in Staveley as the guest of Inspector Murchison. The morning was clear, the downs were fresh and green beneath a blue sky, and the sea lapped gently at the foot of the cliffs. In the bay the white sails of several small boats stood out against the misty horizon. But Detective Gillett saw none of these things. His mind was too busily engaged in turning over the latest aspects of the Cliff Farm case to be susceptible to the influences of nature.

He reached Ashlingsea after an hour's ride and decided to call on Miss Maynard before going to the police station. The old stone house and its grounds lay still and clear in the morning sun. The carriage gates were open and Gillett cycled up the winding gravel drive. The house looked silent and deserted, but the shutters which protected the front windows were unclosed, and a large white peacock strutting on the lawn in front of the house uttered harsh cries at the sight of the man on a bicycle.

The bird's cries brought a rosy-cheeked maidservant to the front door, who stared curiously at Gillett as he jumped off his bicycle and approached her. A request for Miss Maynard brought a doubtful shake of the head from the girl, so Gillett produced his card and asked her to take it to her mistress. The girl

236

took the card, and shortly returned with the announcement that Mrs. Maynard would see him. She ushered him into a large, handsomely furnished room and left him.

A few minutes afterwards Gillett heard the sound of tapping in the hall outside the door. Then the door was opened by the maid who had admitted Gillett, and he saw an elderly lady, with refined features and grey hair, looking at him with haughty dark eyes. She was leaning on an ebony stick, and as she advanced into the room the detective saw that she was lame.

"I wanted to see Miss Maynard," said Gillett, making the best bow of which he was capable.

"You cannot see my daughter." She uttered the words in such a manner as to give Gillett the impression that she was speaking to somebody some distance away.

"Why not?"

"She is not at home."

"Where is she?"

"That I cannot tell you."

"When will she return?"

"I do not know."

"But, madam, I must know," replied Gillett. "Your daughter has placed herself in a very serious position by the statement she made to the police concerning the Cliff Farm murder, and it is important that I should see her at once. Where is she?"

"I decline to tell you."

"You are behaving very foolishly, madam, in taking this course. Surely you do not think she can evade me by hiding from me. If that is her attitude I will deal with it by taking out a warrant for her arrest."

"I must decline to discuss the matter any further with you."

Mrs. Maynard moved towards the bell as she spoke, as though she would ring for a servant to show the detective out of the house. Gillett, seeing that further argument was useless, did not wait for the servant to be summoned, but left the room without another word.

He rode down to the Ashlingsea police station, with an uneasy feeling that his plans for the capture of Brett were not destined to work out as smoothly as he had hoped. It had seemed to him a simple matter then to see Miss Maynard in the morning, "frighten the truth out of her," ascertain from her where her lover was hiding, and have him arrested as quickly as the telegraph wires could apprise the police in the particular locality he had chosen for his retreat. But he had overlooked the possibility of the hitch he had just encountered. Obviously the girl, in finding that Marsland had not been arrested, had begun to think that her plans had miscarried and had therefore decided to evade making any further statement to the police as long as she could.

Gillett was hopeful that Sergeant Westaway, with his local knowledge, would be able to tell him where she was likely to seek seclusion in order to escape being questioned.

He had not conceived the possibility of Miss Maynard having taken fright and disappeared from the town, because he deemed it impossible that she could have known that he was aware how she had tried to hoodwink the police. Yet that was the news that

Sergeant Westaway conveyed to him when he mentioned the young lady's name.

"She left Ashlingsea by the last train from here last night—the 9.30 to Staveley, which connects with the last train to London."

"What!" exclaimed the detective. "Do you mean to tell me you've let the girl slip out of your hands? Why the blazes didn't you stop her from going?"

"How was I to stop her?" replied the sergeant, in resentment at the imperative tone in which the detective spoke. "I didn't get home from Staveley last night until nearly ten o'clock and after looking in here I went straight to bed. The station-master told me about an hour ago that she had gone. She came along just before the train started, and he put her in a carriage himself. He thought it a bit strange, so he mentioned it to me when I was down on the station this morning. I rang up Inspector Murchison in order to let you know, but he told me you'd left for here."

"She's gone to warn Brett—she's in London by now," said Gillett. "The question is how did she get to know that I was coming over to see her this morning and expose the tissue of lies in her statement to you. How did she get to know that the game was up? You've said nothing to anybody, Westaway, about the conversation that took place last night at Sir George Granville's house?"

"Of course I've said nothing," replied Sergeant Westaway. "She had gone almost before I got back here last night."

"It beats me," said Gillett. "Who could have warned her?"

He picked up the telephone book off the office table,

and turned its leaves hurriedly. When he had found the number he wanted he took up the telephone and spoke into the receiver.

"Double one eight Staveley, and be quick. Is that Sir George Granville's? Is Mr. Crewe in? Yes, at once please. Is that you, Mr. Crewe? It's Gillett speaking. The girl has gone—cleared out. I cannot say: I've no idea. What's that you say? Oh, yes, I'll telephone to Scotland Yard and tell them to keep a look out for her, but I am afraid it won't be of much use—she's had too long a start. But it's now more necessary than ever that we should act quickly if we hope to lay our hands on the man. I think the first thing to be done is to make a thorough search of the cliff road for the actual spot where the job was done. Oh, you have? By Jove, that's good! I'd be glad if you'd come with me then, because it's on your theory that it was done away from the house that I'm working——"

Police Constable Heather entered the office at this point with a message for his superior officer. Sergeant Westaway, divided by anxiety to hear the telephone conversation and a determination that his subordinate should not hear it, imperiously motioned Constable Heather away. But as Constable Heather misunderstood the motion and showed no inclination to depart, Sergeant Westaway hurriedly led him out of the office into the front garden, heard what he had to say, and dismissed him with the mandate that he was on no account to be interrupted again. He then returned to the office, but the telephone conversation was finished, and Detective Gillett was seated in the sergeant's office chair, looking over a document which

Sergeant Westaway recognized as Miss Maynard's statement.

"Crewe's going to drive us along the cliff road this afternoon to see if we can locate the spot where Lumsden was shot," said the detective, restoring Miss Maynard's statement to his pocket-book and looking up. "I've arranged to meet him the other side of the cutting at the top of the farm, and we will drive back along the road in his car."

"Did Mr. Crewe express any opinion as to who—who had warned Miss Maynard to take to flight?" asked Sergeant Westaway eagerly.

"That was not a matter for discussion through the telephone," responded Gillett curtly. "I'll talk it over with him this afternoon. I'll call for you here, at two o'clock. I've several things to do in the meantime."

They met again at the appointed hour and cycled along as far as Cliff Farm, where they put up their bicycles. Then they walked up the hill from the farm. At the end of the cutting, they saw Crewe's big white car, stationary, and Crewe and Marsland standing on the greensward smoking cigars. The two police officers advanced to meet them.

"It's a bit of very bad luck about this girl disappearing, Mr. Crewe," said Gillett. "What do you make of it? Westaway thinks she may have gone to stay with friends at Staveley, and that her departure at this juncture is merely a coincidence."

"Miss Maynard would not pay a visit to friends by the last train at night," said Crewe.

"Then somebody warned her that the game was up and that safety lay in flight."

"I'm afraid that's the only reasonable explanation

R

for her disappearance," replied Crewe. "But who warned her?"

"That's the point!" exclaimed Gillett. "I have been thinking it over ever since I discovered she had gone, and I've come to the conclusion that it must have been that infernal little dwarf or her husband, though what is their object is by no means clear. Who else could it have been? The only other people who know that I intended to unmask her are yourself, Westaway and Mr. Marsland. By a process of elimination suspicion points to the Granges."

Crewe did not reply. While Gillett was speaking a flash of that inspiration which occasionally came to him when he was groping in the dark for light revealed to him the key by which the jigsaw of clues, incidents, hints, suspicions, and evidence in the Cliff Farm murder could be pieced together. But the problem was one of extraordinary intricacy, and he needed time to see if all the pieces would fit into the pattern.

It was at Detective Gillett's suggestion that they walked up to the top of the hill, to the headland where Marsland's horse had taken fright on the night of the storm.

He took Crewe's arm and walked ahead with him, leaving the sergeant to follow with Marsland. As they went along, he unconsciously revealed the extent of his dependence on Crewe's stronger intelligence by laying before him the remaining difficulties regarding the case. His chief concern was lest Miss Maynard should warn Brett in time to enable him to slip through the net which had been woven for him. To Crewe's inquiry whether the London police had come across any trace of him he shook his head.

"No, he is lying low, wherever he is. My own belief is that he has not gone to London, but that he is hidden somewhere in the Staveley district. I shall look for him here, and Scotland Yard is watching his London haunts. He's a pretty bad egg, you know. We've a record of him at Scotland Yard."

"What has he done?"

"He's identical with a fashionable rogue and swindler who, under the name of Delancey, kept a night club and a gambling hell in Piccadilly, during the first year of the war. We had reasons for closing the place without a prosecution, and Delancey, instead of being sent to gaol, was allowed to enlist. He returned to England a few months ago, invalided out of the army, where he was known under the name of Powell. Since then he has been employed by the Government in secret service work: mixing with the Germans who are still at large in this country, and getting information about German spies. He was given this work to do because he speaks German so fluently that he can pass as a German amongst Germans.

"I suppose this girl Maynard will try to join him wherever he is," resumed Gillett, after a pause. "It's a queer thing, don't you think, for a well-brought-up English girl of good family to make such a fool of herself over an unmitigated scoundrel like Delancey or Brett, or Powell, or whatever he calls himself? From what I have learnt up at Staveley this girl first met Brett about three months ago. I do not know how they came to know each other, but from her visit to Cliff Farm on the night of the murder I think that Lumsden must have introduced them. There was some bond between Brett and Lumsden which I have been unable to

244 THE MYSTERY OF THE DOWNS

fathom. It is true they knew each other through being
in the army together, but that fact doesn't account for
their continued association afterwards, because there
was nothing in common between the two men: Brett
was a double-dyed scoundrel, and Lumsden was a
simple, quiet sort of chap.

"It may have been the attraction of opposites, or,
it is more likely that Lumsden knew nothing about
Brett's past," continued Gillett. "Brett was certainly
not likely to reveal it, more especially after he met the
girl, because then he would keep up his friendship with
Lumsden in order to have opportunities of meeting her
at Cliff Farm. She also used to visit Brett at Staveley;
they've been seen together there several times. Apparently it was Brett's idea to keep his meetings with
this girl as secret as possible, and for that reason he
used to see her at Cliff Farm with Lumsden's con-
nivance. Nevertheless, he was not altogether successful in keeping his love affair dark. On two occasions
he was seen walking with the girl on Ashlingsea downs,
not far from her mother's house, and there's been
some local gossip in consequence—you know what
these small country places are for gossip."

"You've put this part of the case together very
well," said Crewe.

"Oh, it's not so bad," Gillett laughed complacently.
"Of course it was Scotland Yard that fished up all
that about Brett's antecedents. I flatter myself that
we do that kind of thing better in London than anywhere: it's difficult for a man to get rid of a shady
past in England. However, I'd be more satisfied with
my work if I had Brett under lock and key. What a
fool I was not to go straight across to that girl's house

last night after I saw you, instead of waiting till the morning!"

"It wouldn't have made much difference: I think she was warned by telephone, and probably the person who warned her knew you did not intend to look her up until the morning. If you had altered your plans she would have altered hers."

"I could have telephoned to have her stopped at Victoria or London Bridge."

"Not much use," responded Crewe, with a shake of the head. "She wouldn't have revealed Brett's hiding-place."

"I'd have kept her under lock and key to prevent her warning him," said Gillett viciously.

"Quite useless. Her detention would have been notified in the press. Brett would have taken warning and disappeared. By the way, Gillett, I'll be glad if you will refrain from referring to the doubt I formerly expressed about Brett's guilt. And I must ask Westaway to do the same."

"I thought you'd come round to my way of thinking," said Gillett. "It was plain to me that it couldn't be anyone but Brett. However, you can rest assured I won't try to rub it in. We all make mistakes at this game, but some don't care to acknowledge a mistake as candidly as you have done, Mr. Crewe."

The cliffs rose to a height of three hundred feet at this part of the road, and a piece of headland jutted out a hundred yards or so into the sea—a narrow strip of crumbling sandstone rock, running almost to a point, with sea-worn sides, dropping perpendicularly to the deep water below. Just past the headland, on the Staveley side, the road ran along the edge of the cliffs

for some distance, the side nearest to the sea being protected by a low fence, and flanked by "Danger" notices
at each end. Crewe pointed out the danger post which
had been knocked out of the perpendicular—it was the
one nearest to the headland.

Detective Gillett examined it very closely, and when
Marsland and the Sergeant joined them he asked Marsland if he could point out to him the exact spot where
his horse had taken fright on the night of the storm.

"I think it was somewhere about here, Crewe?
It was about here we saw the hoofmarks, wasn't it?"

Crewe measured the distance with a rule he had
brought with him from the motor-car.

"A trifle more to this way—about here," he said at
length.

Gillett glanced over the edge of the cliff, and at the
white water breaking over the jagged tooth-pointed
rocks nearly three hundred feet below.

"By Jove, you can congratulate yourself that you
happened to be on the right side of the road," he
said, addressing himself to Marsland. "If you'd gone
over there, you wouldn't have stood much chance."

"It was purely good fortune, or my horse's instinct,"
laughed Marsland. "The road was so dark that I
didn't know where I was myself. I couldn't see a
hand's turn in front of me."

"The marks of the car wheels ran off the road at
this point, bumped into the post, and then ran on to the
road again." Crewe traced the course with his stick.
"Brett had a narrower escape than Marsland. It's a
wonder that the impact didn't knock away that crazy
bit of fencing."

"When Brett is on his trial it will be necessary for

the jury to visit this spot," said Sergeant Westaway
solemnly.

"We've got to catch the beggar first," grumbled Gillett. "But let's get along and see if we can hit upon
the spot where the murder was actually committed.
How far along is it, Mr. Crewe, to where the country-
man you talked to saw him pass?"

"A little more than five miles from here."

"Then somewhere between the two places the murder must have been committed, I should say."

"I know the place—approximately," replied Crewe,
"I've been over the ground several times, and I've been
able to fix on it more or less definitely."

"How did you fix it?" asked Gillett curiously.

"I had several clues to help me," replied Crewe, in a
non-committal voice. "Let us get back to the car and
I will drive you to the place."

They walked back to the car and drove slowly along
the winding cliff road. About two miles from the
danger post the road turned slightly inland, and ran
for a quarter of a mile or more about two hundred
yards distant from the edge of the cliff. At this point
the downs began to rise above the level of the road, and
continued to do so until they were above the heads of
the party in the car. It was not a cutting; merely a
steep natural inclination of the land, and the road
skirted the foot of it for some distance. A ragged
fringe of beech-trees grew along the top of the bank;
doubtless they had been planted in this bare exposed
position of the downs to act as a wind screen for the
sheep which could be seen grazing higher up the slope.

Crewe pulled up the car and looked about him, then
turned his head and spoke to Gillett:

"This part of the road is worth examining. There are several features about it which fit in with my conception of the scene of the crime."

The four men got out of the car and walked forward, looking about them. Crewe walked a little ahead, with his eyes roving over the rising bank and the trees at the top. Several times he tried to clamber up the bank, but the incline was too steep.

"What are you trying to do?" said Gillett, who was watching his proceedings curiously.

"I am trying to fit in my theory of the crime by actual experiments. If I can satisfy myself that Lumsden was able to climb this bank at some point I believe we shall have reached the scene of the murder."

"But why is it necessary to prove that?" asked Gillett, in a puzzled voice. "Brett might have met him on the road, shot him from the car which had been pulled up, and then carried the body to Cliff Farm."

"My dear Gillett, have you forgotten that the bullet which killed Lumsden took an upward course after entering the body? If he had been shot from the car it would have gone downwards."

"Damn it! I forgot all about that point," exclaimed Gillett, reddening with vexation.

"Lumsden couldn't have been shot on the road, either, because in that case the bullet would have gone straight through him—unless the man who fired the shot knelt down in the road and fired upwards at him, which is not at all likely. Furthermore, Lumsden was shot in the back low down, and the bullet travelled upwards and came out above the heart. Therefore we've got to try and visualize a scene which fits in with these circumstances. That's why I have been looking at this bank so carefully. Let us suppose that Lumsden was walking along the road and encountered his would-be slayer. Lumsden saw the revolver, and turned to run. He thought his best chance of escape was across the downs, so he dashed towards the bank and sprang up it. He had almost reached the top when the shot was fired. That seems to me the most possible way of accounting for the upward course of the bullet."

"I see," said Gillett, nodding his head. "Brett might have fired from his seat in his car, in that case."

"Precisely," returned Crewe. "But the weak point in my argument is that so far we have not reached a point in the bank which is capable of being scaled."

"A little further along it narrows and is less steep," said Marsland, who had been listening intently to Crewe's remarks. "Come, and I will show you."

He led the way round the next bend of the road, and pointed out a spot where the branches of the trees which formed the wind screen hung down over the slope, which was much less steep. It was a comparatively easy matter to scramble up the bank at this point, and pull oneself up on to the downs by the aid of the overhanging branches.

Crewe made the experiment, and reached the top, without difficulty; so did Gillett. Marsland and Sergeant Westaway remained standing in the road below, watching the proceedings.

The downs from the top of the bank swept gradually upwards to the highest point of that part of the coast: a landmark known as the Giants' Knoll, a lofty hill surrounded by a ring of dark fir-trees, which gave the bald summit the appearance of a monk's tonsure.

This hill commanded an extensive view of the Channel and the surrounding country-side on a clear day. But Detective Gillett was not interested in the Giant's Knoll. He was busily engaged examining the brushwood and dwarf trees forming the wind screen at the point where they had scrambled up. Suddenly he turned and beckoned to Crewe with an air of some excitement.

"Look here!" he said, as Crewe approached. "This seems to bear out your theory." He pointed to the branch of a stunted beech-tree, which had been torn away from the parent trunk, but still hung to it, withered and lifeless, attached by a strip of bark.

"If Brett shot Lumsden as he was scrambling up the bank, Lumsden might easily have torn this branch off in his dying struggle—the instinct to clutch at something—as he fell back into the road."

"It's possible, but it's not a very convincing clue by itself," returned Crewe. "It might just as easily have been torn off by the violence of the storm. The thing is to follow it up. If Lumsden was shot at this point the bullet which went through him may have lodged in one of the trees."

Gillett had begun to search among the scattered trees at the top of the bank very much like an intelligent pointer hunting for game. He examined each tree closely from the bole upwards. Suddenly he gave a shout of triumph.

"Look here, Crewe."

He had come to a standstill at a tree which stood a few yards on the downs away from the wind screen—a small stunted oak with low and twisted branches. Fair in the centre of its gnarled trunk was a small hole, which Gillett was hacking at with a small penknife. As Crewe reached his side, he triumphantly extracted a bullet which had been partly flattened by contact with the tree.

"By Jove!" he exclaimed. "What a piece of luck! What a piece of luck!"

He held the bullet in the palm of his left hand, turning it over and over with the penknife which he held in his right. He was so absorbed in his discovery, that he did not notice Crewe stoop and pick up some small object which lay in the grass a few yards from the tree.

CHAPTER XXII

CREWE and Marsland sat at a table in Sir George Granville's library with the cryptogram before them. The detective was absorbed in examining it through a magnifying glass, but Marsland kept glancing from the paper to his companion's face, as though he expected to see there some indication of an immediate solution. Finally he remarked in a tone which suggested he was unable to control his impatience any longer:

"Well, what do you make of it?"

"Not very much as yet," replied Crewe, putting down the magnifying glass, "but there are one or two points of interest. In the first place, the paper has been cut with a pair of scissors from the fly-leaf or title-page of an old book—an expensive book of its period, of the late fifties, I should say—but the writing is of much later date. These facts are obvious, and do not help us much towards a solution of the contents."

"They may be obvious to you, but they are not so obvious to me," said Marsland, taking the paper into his hands and looking at it thoughtfully. "I suppose you judge the sheet to have been taken from an old book, because it is yellow with age, but why an expensive one of the fifties? And how do you know it was cut out with a pair of scissors? Again, how do you know the writing is of a much later date than the book? The ink is completely faded."

"The smooth yellow, and glossy surface of the blank
side of the paper indicates conclusively that it is the
title-page or fly-leaf of a good class book of the fifties.
You will not find that peculiar yellow colour—which
is not the effect of age—and velvety 'feel' in books
of a much later date. The unevenness of the cut
proves that the sheet was taken from the book
with a pair of scissors; haven't you ever noticed
that nobody—except, perhaps, a paperhanger—can cut
straight with a pair of scissors? If it had been cut
with a knife it might have slanted a little, but it would
have been straighter: a knife cut is always straighter
than the wavering cut of a pair of scissors directed by
the eye. The faded ink proves nothing: inferior ink
such as is sold in small village shops—from where the
ink at Cliff Farm was probably procured—will fade in
a few days; it is only the best ink that retains its
original colour for any length of time. But the character of this writing indicates to me that it was written
with a particular kind of fine nib, which was not in-
vented till after 1900."

"Can you make anything of the figures and letters on
the paper?" asked Marsland.

"That is where our difficulties commence. We have
to ascertain the connection between the figures and the
letters and the circle; to find out whether the former
explain the latter or whether the circle explains the
figures and the letters. If the figures and the letters
are a cryptogram we ought to be able to find the solution without much difficulty. The circle, however, is
a remarkable device, and it is difficult to fathom its
meaning without something to guide us. I thought at

first it might have been capable of some masonic interpretation, but now I doubt it. The most likely assumption is that the circle and the lines in some way indicate the hiding place of the money."

"By geometry?" suggested Marsland, closely examining the circle on the paper.

"I think not. It is hardly likely that the old farmer who concealed the treasure would be versed in the science of geometry. He may have drawn the circle to indicate a certain place where he had concealed the money, and added the two lines to indicate the radius or point where it was to be found."

"Local gossip declares that the old man hid his money somewhere in the landing-place or old boathouse, where it is covered at high tide, and that his ghost watches over it at low tide to prevent anybody stealing it. There are stories of treasure-seekers having been chased along the sands almost to Ashlingsea by the old man's ghost. The villagers give the landing-place and that part of the coast road a wide berth at night in consequence."

"I do not think the old man hid his money in the boat-house or landing-place," said Crewe. "He would have known that the action of weather and tide would make such a hiding-place unsafe. He would look for a safer place. He has almost certainly hidden it somewhere about the farm, and the circle and the letters and figures will tell us where, when we discover their meaning."

Crewe opened his notebook and commenced to make some calculations in figures. Marsland meantime occupied himself by looking at the circle through the magnifying glass, and in counting the figures in its circumference.

"Perhaps these marks in the circle represent paces," he said, struck by a new thought. "Suppose, for instance, that the old man measured off a piece of ground with a tape measure fastened to some point which would represent the pivot or centre of his circle. He may have fastened the end of his tape measure to the well pump in the bricked yard, and walked round in a circle holding the other end in his hand, sticking in pegs as he walked. The top figure inside the circle—150—may mean that the circle is 150 yards in circumference. Within the radius of the circle he buries his money, makes a drawing of the circle of figures and the remaining figures to indicate its whereabouts, and then removes the cord and pegs."

"Ingenious, but unlikely," commented Crewe. "For one thing, such a plan would need compass points to enable the searchers to take their bearings."

"North or south may be indicated in the cryptogram—when we discover it," said Marsland.

"No, no," said Crewe, shaking his head. "Your idea is based on treasure-hunt charts in novels. My experience is that in real life people do not go to much trouble in hiding money or valuables; they put them away in some chance place or odd receptacle which happens to appeal to them, and where I think they really have a better chance of remaining undiscovered for years than in a more elaborately contrived hiding-place. In the Farndon missing will case, involving one of the largest estates in England, the will was found after the lapse of ten years concealed in the back of a book, where the deceased Lord Farndon had placed it in his latter days, when he imagined himself surrounded by thieves. If you open a large book about the middle it discloses an aperture at the back sufficiently large to conceal a paper, and when the book is closed there will be no sign. Lord Farndon concealed his will in one of the estate ledgers which was in constant use for some time after his death, and yet the will would probably have never been discovered if a mouse had not eaten through the leather back long afterwards, disclosing the hidden parchment.

"In the case of the stolen Trimarden diamond, the thief—a servant in the house—escaped detection by hiding the jewel in a common wooden match-box in a candlestick in his bedroom. The police searched his room, but never thought of looking into the match-box, and he got away with the diamond. If he had not bragged of the trick in a tavern he would never have been caught. As regards hidden money, people of miserly proclivities who are frightened to put their money into banks prefer a hiding-place under cover to one in the open. A hiding-place in the house seems safer to them, and, moreover, it enables them to look at their money whenever they feel inclined. I knew one miser who used to hide sovereigns in a bar of yellow soap—thrusting them in till they were hidden from view. The treasure of Cliff Farm is hidden somewhere in the farm, and the circle and the cryptogram are the keys. The explanation is hidden in the cryptogram, and I have no doubt that there is a very simple explanation of the circle—when we discover the cryptogram."

"I remember as a boy at school that we used to have endless fun solving cryptograms which appeared in a boys' magazine," said Marsland. "Figures were substituted for letters, and the interpretation of the cryptogram depended largely on hitting on the book from which the figures had been taken. The system was to put down the number of the page, then the number of the line, then the number of letters in the line which would form a word. The key book happened to be a bound volume of the magazine in question: I guessed that, and won a prize. Another form of cryptogram for competition in the same journal was a transposition of the letters of the alphabet. But that was easily guessed, from the repeated occurrence of certain letters used to represent the vowels."

"I remember those boyish devices," said Crewe, with a smile. "But true cryptography is more scientifically based than that. Systems of secret writing are practically unlimited in number and variety—and so are solutions. Human nature hates being baffled, and the human brain has performed some really wonderful achievements—at the expense of much effort and patience—in solving systems of cryptography which the inventors deemed to be insoluble. I have a weakness for cryptograms myself, and at one time collected quite a small library on secret writing, from the earlier works by Bacon and Trithemius, to the more modern works by German cryptographists, who have devised some remarkably complicated systems which, no doubt, were largely used by the Germans before and during the war for secret service work. It is astonishing the number of books which have been written on the subject by men who believed they had discovered insoluble systems of secret writing, and by

S

men who have set out to prove that no system of secret writing is insoluble. Even the ancient Hebraic prophets used cryptography at times to veil their attacks on the wicked kings of Israel."

"How long do cryptograms—the more scientific, I mean—usually take to solve?"

"Some cryptograms can be solved in an hour; others may take months."

"Do you think that this one will prove very difficult?" asked Marsland, pointing to the Cliff Farm plan as he spoke.

"I cannot say until I have studied it more closely. The solution of any cryptogram depends first on whether you have any knowledge of the particular system used, and then on finding the key. It is quite possible, and frequently happens, that one is able to reconstruct the particular system of secret writing from which a cryptogram has been constructed, and then fail to find the key. A really scientific cryptogram never leaves the key to guesswork, but gives a carefully hidden clue for the finder to work upon; because most cryptograms are intended to be solved, and if the composer of the message left its discovery to guesswork he would be defeating his own ends. This particular cryptogram looks to me to be scientifically constructed; I cannot say yet whether it is possible to reconstruct it and solve it."

Crewe resumed his scrutiny of the plan, making occasional entries in his notebook as he did so.

Marsland leaned back in an easy chair, lit a cigar, and watched him in silence. The detective's remark convinced him that there was a wide difference between serious cryptography and the puzzle diversions of his schoolboy days, and he felt that he would be more of a hindrance than a help if he attempted to assist Crewe in his task of unravelling the secret of the hidden wealth whose hiding-place had been indicated by its deceased owner in the symbols and hieroglyphics on the faded sheet of paper. He reclined comfortably in his chair, watching languidly through half-closed eyes and a mist of cigar smoke the detective's intellectual face bent over the plan in intense concentration. After a while Crewe's face seemed to grow shadowy and indistinct, and finally it disappeared behind the tobacco smoke. Marsland had fallen fast asleep in his chair.

He was awakened by a hand on his shoulder, and struggled back to consciousness to find Crewe standing beside him, his dark eyes smiling down at him.

"I am afraid I fell into a doze," Marsland murmured apologetically, as the room and its surroundings came back to him.

"You've been sleeping soundly for nearly two hours," said Crewe, with a smile.

"Impossible!" exclaimed Marsland. He took out his watch and looked at it in astonishment. "By Jove, it's actually six o'clock. Why didn't you wake me?"

"What for? I became so absorbed in the old man's secret that I had no idea of the flight of time till I looked at my watch a few minutes ago. He has evolved a very neat cryptogram—very neat and workmanlike. It was quite a pleasure to try and decipher it."

"Have you found out anything about it?"

"I believe I have solved it."

"And what is the solution?" asked Marsland, now thoroughly awake. "Where is the money hidden?"

"Now you are going too fast," said Crewe. "I said I believed I have solved the secret. In other words, I believe I have hit on the old man's cryptogram, and the key which solves it, but I have deferred applying the key till I awakened you, as I thought you would like to share in it."

CHAPTER XXIII

CREWE went to the table and picked up the plan.

"My first impression was that the circle of figures represented some form of letters of the alphabet arranged on what is called the cardboard or trellis cipher, in which a message is concealed by altering the places of the letters without changing their powers. Such messages are generally written after the Chinese fashion—upwards and downwards—but there is no reason why a circle should not be used to conceal the message. In this case I did not expect to find a message hidden in the circle, but rather, the key to the solution of the letters above the circle, which, I was convinced, formed the real cryptogram.

"The recurring T's and M's in the top line seemed to indicate that it was some form of changed letter cipher, complicated by having to be read in connection with the figures in the circle, which represented other letters of the alphabet. The numbers, representing an ascending series from 6 to 89, with one recurring 6, suggested the possibility of this form of cryptogram having been used. The numbers in the centre suggested a sum, which, when done, would throw some light on the arithmetical puzzle in the centre of the circle by division, subtraction, or multiplication.

"I worked for a solution on these lines for some time, but ultimately came to the conclusion that the solution did not lie within them. I am not an arithmetician, but my calculations told me enough to make me realize that I was on the wrong track.

"I next attempted to ascertain if the two mysterious messages—the lines on the top and the circle of figures—were two separate messages read independently of one another. I did not think they were, but I determined to put it to the test. Obviously, if they were, the top line was merely a changed letter cipher, and nothing more. These are usually easy to decipher because of the frequency with which certain letters recur. In English the letter that occurs oftenest is E, then T, then A, O, N, I, then R, S, H; the others in lessening frequency down to J and Z, which are the least used letters in the English alphabet. The recurring letters in our cryptogram are T's and M's. Using these as a basis to give me the key, I tried all likely combinations on the changed letter basis, but without success.

"I came back to my original idea that the figures in the circle were the solvent of the line of letters above, and concentrated my efforts in attempting to discover their meaning. I finally came to the conclusion that the figures represented the pages or lines of some book."

"Like the cryptograms I used to solve when I was at school," suggested Marsland, with a smile.

"Rather more difficult than that. In that form of cryptogram rows of figures are turned into words once you hit on the right book. This cryptogram is much more ingenious, for it consists of three parts—a line

of meaningless letters and a circle of equally meaningless figures, with other figures within it, and some plain
English verses of Scripture, the whole probably inter-
dependent. If the circle of figures represented some
book necessary to the solution of the whole cryptogram, the first thing to find out was the book from
which the figures had been taken. I had not much
difficulty in arriving at the conclusion that this book
was a large brass-bound family Bible I saw at Cliff
Farm."

"I suppose the texts on the bottom of the sheet suggested that idea to you?" said Marsland.

Crewe shook his head.

"I've learnt to mistrust guesswork," he said. "It
would be a jump at random to come to the conclusion
that the cryptogram had been drawn on the fly-leaf of
a Bible because it contained some Scripture texts.
There is no connection between the facts. In fact, it
seemed unlikely to me at first that a religious man like
the old farmer would have mutilated his family Bible
for such a purpose. I was inclined to the view that
he had taken a fly-leaf from one of his *Leisure Hour*
bound volumes, which at the farm range from 1860
to the early seventies—a period of years when this
kind of glossy thick paper was much used for fly-leaves
by English printers. But while I was examining the
sheet through the magnifying glass I detected this
mark on the edge, which proved conclusively to me
that the cryptogram had been drawn on the fly-leaf of
the family Bible. Have a look at it through the glass
—you cannot detect it with the naked eye."

Crewe held the sheet edgeways as he spoke, and
pointed to one of the outer corners. Marsland gazed

intently through the glass, and was able to detect a minute glittering spot not much larger than a pin's point.

"I see it," he said, relinquishing the glass. "But I do not understand what it means."

"It is Dutch metal or gold-leaf. The book from which this sheet was cut was gilt-edged. That disposes of the volumes of *Leisure Hour* and other bound periodicals, none of which is gilt-edged. When I was looking at the books at the farm I noticed only two with gilt-edged leaves. One was the big family Bible, and the other was a large, old fashioned *Language of Flowers*. But this sheet could not have been cut from *The Language of Flowers*."

"Why not?"

"Because it has two rounded corners. As a rule, only sacred books and poetry are bound with rounded corners. In any case, I remember that *The Language of Flowers* at the farm is square-edged. Therefore the sheet on which the cryptogram has been drawn was cut from the Bible.

"The next question that faced me was how the numbers had been used: they did not represent the numbers of the pages, I was sure of that. The Bible is a book in which figures are used freely in the arrangement of the contents. The pages are numbered, the chapters are divided into verses which are numbered, and there is a numbered table of contents at the beginning of each chapter. Obviously, the Bible is an excellent book from which to devise a cryptogram of numbers owing to the multiplicity of figures used in it and the variety of ways in which they are arranged. I found both a Bible and Prayer Book in the bookshelves, here, and set to work to study the numerical arrangement of the chapters, the divisions of the verses, and the arrangement of figures at the head of the chapters."

"It was while I was thus engaged that I remembered that at the beginning of the authorised version of the Bible is inserted a table of the books of the Old and New Testaments, the pages on which they begin, and the number of chapters in each. Here was the possibility of a starting-point, sufficiently unusual to make a good concealment, yet not too remote. I turned to the table, and, on running my eye down it, I saw that the Psalms, and the Psalms alone, contain 150 chapters. Now, the first line of central figures in the cryptogram is 150. I was really fortunate in starting off with this discovery, because otherwise I might have been led off the track by the doubling and trebling of the 3 in the second line of central figures, and have wasted time trying to fathom some mystic interpretation of the 9—a numeral which has always had a special significance for humanity: the Nine Muses, the Nine Worthies, 'dressed up to the nines,' and so on. But with 150 as the indication that the cryptogram had been composed from the Book of Psalms, it was obvious that the next line of numerals in the centre directed attention to some particular portion of them. As there are not 396 verses in any chapter of the Psalms——"

"Just what I was going to point out," broke in Marsland.

"Quite so. But it was possible that 396 meant Psalm 39, 6. Therefore I turned to the thirty-ninth Psalm. Verse six of that Psalm reads:

" 'Surely every man walketh in a vain shew: surely they are disquieted in vain: he heapeth up riches, and knoweth not who shall gather.' "

"Appropriate enough," commented Marsland.

"There remained the final 6, under the 396, to be explained, before I was able to start on the table which had been used to build up the cryptogram. The fact that the figures in the outside circle start at 6 indicated that there was some connection between it and the inner 6. I came to the conclusion that the inner 6 meant one of two things: either the designer preferred to start from the number 6 because he thought the figure 1 was too clear an indication of the commencement of his cryptogram, or else he made his start from the sixth letter of the text. I thought the former the likelier solution, but I tried them both, to make sure. The first five figures on the latter solution gave me a recurring Y, which indicated that I was on the wrong track because it was essential there should be no recurring letters. There are no recurring letters in the other key, as the table shows:

6	7	8	9	10	11		12	13	14	15	16		17	18	19
S	u	r	e	l	y		e	v	e	r	y		m	a	n
1	2	3	4	5	6		7	8	9	10	11		12	13	14

20	21	22	23	24	25	26		27	28		29		30	31	32	33
w	a	l	k	e	t	h		i	n		a		v	a	i	n
15	16	17	18	19	20	21		22	23		24		25	26	27	28

34	35	36	37		38	39	40	41	42	43		44	45	46	47
s	h	e	w:		s	u	r	e	l	y		t	h	e	y
29	30	31	32		33	34	35	36	37	38		39	40	41	42

48	49	50		51	52	53	54	55	56	57	58	59	60		61	62
a	r	e		d	i	s	q	u	i	e	t	e	d		i	n
43	44	45		46	47	48	49	50	51	52	53	54	55		56	57

63	64	65	66		67	68		69	70	71	72	73	74	75
v	a	i	n:		h	e		h	e	a	p	e	t	h
58	59	60	61		62	63		64	65	66	67	68	69	70

76	77		78	79	80	81	82	83		84	85	86
u	p		r	i	c	h	e	s		a	n	d
71	72		73	74	75	76	77	78		79	80	81

87	88	89	90	91	92	93		94	95	96		97	98	99
k	n	o	w	e	t	h		n	o	t		w	h	o
82	83	84	85	86	87	88		89	90	91		92	93	94

100	101	102	103	104		105	106	107	108	109	110
s	h	a	l	l		g	a	t	h	e	r
95	96	97	98	99		100	101	102	103	104	105

"The circle of figures taken in their ascending order and starting with the second six, run thus:

6, 8, 9, 10, 11, 13, 17, 19, 20, 21, 23, 25, 26, 27, 39, 51, 54, 72, 80, 89.

Now, assuming that my interpretation of the solitary six in the circle is correct—that the old man started from six because he thought the use of the figure one gave away too much—we will substitute for these figures the letters which appear underneath them in the table. The substitution gives us the following row of letters:

S R E L Y V M N W A K T H I U D Q P C O S

"This is the line of letters from which we will endeavour to reconstruct the old man's cryptogram. We can, I think, go forward with the assurance that they are the actual letters represented by the cryptogram, for several reasons. There are no recurring letters, and they represent every letter in the text in consecutive order, with three exceptions which are capable of a simple explanation. The U has been taken from the second 'surely' instead of the first, to mislead the solver. Otherwise you would have surely

for the first five numbers, which would be too clear
an indication. The same reason exists for making A
the tenth letter instead of the eighth; which would
reveal the word 'man.' The final letter—the 'G' in
'gather'—has been excluded, for a reason which I will
presently explain."

"What about the second S—the final letter? Do you
not call that a recurring letter?" asked Marsland, who
was closely examining the table the detective had prepared.

"Not in the cryptographic sense. It is the first letter
of the text repeated after the line had been completed
without recurring letters. There is a special reason for
its use. The old man has worked on what is called the
keyword cipher, which is the most difficult of all ciphers
to discover. This system consists of various arrange-
ments, more or less elaborate, of tables of letters, set
down in the form of the multiplication table, and from
the table agreed upon messages are constructed whose
solution depends on the use of some preconcerted keyword. The most scientific adaptation of this principle
was constructed by Admiral Sir Francis Beaufort. In
his system the letters of the alphabet are set down one
under another from A to Z, then A is added to the line.
The next line starts with B and runs to another B at
the bottom. You continue till you have the whole
alphabet set down in this fashion. From this table
and an agreed keyword, which may consist of a proper
name or a sentence of several words, you construct
a cipher message."

"How?" asked Marsland, in a tone of keen interest.

"That is what I now propose to demonstrate to you,
if, as I think, the old man constructed his cryptogram

in accordance with this principle. I have come to the conclusion that he modified and adapted this system to his own ends, using the letters of the text from the Bible to conceal it better, and then made it more difficult still by turning the letters into figures after the manner I have described. He has also made a slight but not uncommon variation from the Beaufort principle by striking out the 'G' in 'gather,' which would follow the 'O' if every letter in the text was used once, and substituting the final S, instead of placing the 'S' after 'G.' But the clue that suggested to my mind that he had worked on this principle are the two figures 6 coming together at the top of the circle. In the substituted letters they form two S's. Now, why does he have two S's when he carefully avoids recurring letters in the rest of the table? And why did he insert the first S again, as represented by the figure 6, instead of taking the next S in this table?

"In pondering over these points I discovered, as I believe, the system of cryptogram he used to construct his secret. He wanted to make the cryptogram difficult of solution, but at the same time he wanted to give some indication of the form of cryptogram he was using when his heirs came to search for the money. The recurring S indicates that he was working on a modification of the system I have explained, in which you add the first letter of your first column to the bottom, and continue on that system throughout the table. It is not much of a hint, because we have got to find the keyword before we can use the table, but by its help we will start with the assumption that the old man worked on the following table:

```
S R E L Y V M N W A K T H I U D Q P C O S
R E L Y V M N W A K T H I U D Q P C O S R
E L Y V M N W A K T H I U D Q P C O S R E
L Y V M N W A K T H I U D Q P C O S R E L
Y V M N W A K T H I U D Q P C O S R E L Y
V M N W A K T H I U D Q P C O S R E L Y V
M N W A K T H I U D Q P C O S R E L Y V M
N W A K T H I U D Q P C O S R E L Y V M N
W A K T H I U D Q P C O S R E L Y V M N W
A K T H I U D Q P C O S R E L Y V M N W A
K T H I U D Q P C O S R E L Y V M N W A K
T H I U D Q P C O S R E L Y V M N W A K T
H I U D Q P C O S R E L Y V M N W A K T H
I U D Q P C O S R E L Y V M N W A K T H I
U D Q P C O S R E L Y V M N W A K T H I U
D Q P C O S R E L Y V M N W A K T H I U D
Q P C O S R E L Y V M N W A K T H I U D Q
P C O S R E L Y V M N W A K T H I U D Q P
C O S R E L Y V M N W A K T H I U D Q P C
O S R E L Y V M N W A K T H I U D Q P C O
S R E L Y V M N W A K T H I U D Q P C O S
```

"It is from this table, unless I am very much mistaken, that he constructed the cipher at the top of the sheet," said Crewe.

Marsland examined the curious table of letters, with close scrutiny, from various points of view, finally reversing it and examining it upside-down. He returned it to Crewe with a disappointed shake of his head.

"I can make nothing of it," he said.

"It is necessary for us to discover the keyword he worked on before we can make use of it," said Crewe. "Once we get the keyword, we will have no trouble in deciphering the mysterious message. The keyword is the real difficulty in ciphers of this kind. It is like the keyword of a combination lock. Without it, you cannot unlock the cipher. It is absolutely insoluble. Suppose, for example, he had picked a word at random out of the dictionary, and died without divulging it to anybody, we should have to go through the dictionary word for word, working the table on each word, till we came to the right one."

"But that would take years," exclaimed Marsland blankly.

"Unless we hit on it by a lucky accident. That is why the keyword cipher is practically insoluble without knowledge of the keyword. It is not even necessary to have a word. A prearranged code of letters will do, known only to the composer of the cryptogram. If he wanted anybody else to decipher his cryptogram, he would have to divulge to him not only the form of table he worked on but the code of letters forming the keyword."

"Well, I do not see we are much further forward," said Marsland despondently. "Of course, it's very clever of you to have found out what you have, but we are helpless without the keyword. The old man is not likely to have divulged it to anybody."

"You are wrong," said Crewe. "He has divulged it."

"To whom?"

"To this paper. As I said before, he did not want his cryptogram to be insoluble; he wanted his heirs to have his money, but he did not want it found very easily. You have forgotten the texts at the bottom of the paper. They have not been placed there for nothing. The keyboard is hidden in them."

"I forgot all about the texts—I was so interested in your reconstruction of the cryptogram," said Marsland. "As you say, he didn't put the texts there for nothing, so it seems likely that he has hidden the keyword in them. But even now we may have some difficulty in finding it. Do you propose to take the texts word for word, testing each with the table, till you find the right one?"

"That would take a long while," said Crewe. "I hope to simplify the process considerably. In fact, I think I have already discovered the keyword."

"You have!" exclaimed Marsland, in astonishment. "How have you managed that?"

"By deduction from the facts in front of us— or perhaps I should say by reflecting on the hints placed in the texts. Isn't there something about those texts that strikes you as peculiar?"

Marsland examined them attentively for some time, and shook his head.

"I'm afraid I'm not sufficiently well up in the Scriptures to notice anything peculiar about them. I should say they were from the Old Testament, but I couldn't tell you what part of it."

"The texts are from the Old Testament, from Jeremiah XXV and Isaiah VII. They are remarkable for the fact that they represent two passages—the only two instances in the whole Bible—where the writers used cryptograms to hide their actual meaning. In the first instance the prophet, Jeremiah, living in dangerous times, veils his attack on the King of Babylon by writing Sheshak for Babel—Babylon; that is, instead of using B B L, the second and twelfth letters of the Hebrew alphabet, from the beginning, he wrote Sh Sh K from the end—a simple form of cryptogram which is frequently used, even now. In the second instance the prophet Isaiah, working on a very similar form of cryptogram, writes 'Tabeal' for 'Remaliah.'

"Now, we are faced by two facts concerning the

presence of these two texts on the paper containing the cryptogram. In the first place, the cryptogram was complete without the texts: for what purpose, then, could they have been at the bottom of the sheet except to give a clue to the discovery of that keyword without which no recovery of the hidden treasure was possible, unless it was found by a lucky chance? In the second place, the selection by the old man of the only two cryptographic texts in the Bible was certainly not chance, but part of a deliberate harmonious design to guide the intelligent searcher to the right keyword. He was evidently versed in cryptography, constructed this one as carefully as a mechanic putting together a piece of mechanism, fitting all the parts carefully into one another. The figures in the centre of the circle give the key to the outside figures: the outside figures are the key to the cryptographic table of letters from which the cryptogram is to be solved; there remains the key to be found. It is not likely that the composer of such an ingenious cryptogram would leave the keyword to guesswork.

"The whole thing is a Bible cryptogram from first to last: figures, letters, words, and texts. It is even drawn on a sheet cut from the Bible. Why? Such an act might be deemed irreverent in a deeply religious man like the old man was, but when we piece the thing together we find that he was actuated by a re- ligious spirit throughout. Not the least skilful part of his cryptogram is his concealment of the keyword in the text at the bottom. The text would convey noth- ing to most people, for very few people know any- thing about cryptograms, still fewer people would know that these texts contain the only two cryptograms in the Bible. Therefore, in accordance with his harmonious design, it seems to me that the keyword should be found in the five alternatives of the cryptic texts: Babel, Babylon, Sheshak, Remaliah, or Tabeal.

"Babel and Babylon may be discarded because there is no letter B in the cryptographic table, and it is essential that the keyword shall contain no letter which doesn't also appear in the table. 'Sheshak' may also be discarded for the present as unlikely because of the awkwardness of the recurring 'Sh' in a keyword. There remain Tabeal and Remaliah. The tendency of the composer would be to use the longer word, because a long keyword is the better for the purpose. I think, therefore, we should first try whether Remaliah is the keyword we are in search of."

"By Jove, Crewe, that is cleverly reasoned out!" exclaimed Marsland, in some excitement. "Let's put it to the test. How do we apply this keyword to the table?"

"Easily enough. On this sheet of paper we will write down the cryptogram; and the keyword underneath it, letter for letter thus:

```
T Y N M V R T T H S M
R E M A L I A H R E M
```

"Now, the first word of the cryptogram is T. Look in the first column of the table for it, and then run your eye across the table for the first letter of the keyword. When you have found it, look at the top of the column and tell me the letter."

"K," said Marsland.

"Very well, then. We put down 'K' as the first word of the solution and proceed in like manner through the whole of the cipher. The second letter is Y—find it in the table, then look across for the second letter of the key E, and then to the top of the column. What letter have you?"

"C," said Marsland.

"KC, then, are the first two letters of our solution, and we go on to the third, always repeating the same process. N in the first column, M across, and the top gives you?"

"O," said Marsland.

"The next letter is M in the cryptogram and A in the keyword. What does the top of the column give you?"

"L," replied Marsland. "But I say, Crewe, do you think we are on the right track? K, C, O, L, is a queer start for a word isn't it? I know of no word commencing like that."

"I may be mistaken, but I do not think so," replied Crewe firmly. "Let us keep on till we've finished it, at all events."

They resumed their task, and ultimately brought out the letters: K, C, O, L, C, H, C, R, A, E, S. Marsland gazed at the result in dismay.

"By Jove, we're on the wrong track," he said ruefully. "It is the wrong word, Crewe. These letters mean nothing; you'll have to try again."

But Crewe did not reply. He was examining the result of his night's labours closely. Suddenly he put down the paper with an unusual light in his eye.

"No," he said. "I am right, the old man was thorough to the last detail. He has given another clue to his heirs in the circle and the two lines. They represent a clock face. But the figures round them run the reverse way to clock figures. The cryptogram reads backwards. Hold it up to that mirror, and see."

Marsland did so, and laid down the paper with a look of bewilderment.

"Search clock! The old grandfather clock at Cliff Farm!" he said,

CHAPTER XXIV

As the car swept round the deserted sea-front and through the scattered outskirts of the town, Crewe gradually increased the going, till by the time Staveley was left behind, and the Cliff road stretched in front of them, his powerful car was driving along at top speed. The night was not dark for the time of year; the windings of the road were visible some distance ahead: from the cliffs the rollers of the incoming tide could be seen breaking into white froth on the rocks below.

"It has occurred to me that, for a man who was afraid of a German invasion, old Lumsden selected a very bad hiding-place for his money," said Marsland. "He could not have known of the reputation the German soldiers made for themselves in stealing French clocks in the war of 1870."

"Perhaps not," replied Crewe. "But I do not think he intended to leave the money in the clock when the Germans came. If he fled from the farm he would have taken it with him. His object in hiding it in the clock was to have it constantly under his eye."

The car mounted the hill to the cutting through the cliff road near their destination, and as the road dipped downwards Crewe slackened the pace. Both of them were looking across towards the farm on the left. As it came into view Crewe exclaimed to his companion:

"Did you see that?"

"A light!" said Marsland excitedly.

"It is gone now; it was probably a match. There must be some one there. I wonder who it could be?"

"Perhaps it is Gillett. We will soon see."

"No, we will drive past. It may be some one who wants to escape being seen. We will run the car off the road a little way down past the farm, then extinguish the lights and make our way back."

He increased the pace of the car so that if there was any one at the farm it would appear that the car was going on to Ashlingsea. They both kept their eyes on the house as the car sped past, but there was no repetition of the flash of light they had seen. Less than half a mile away Crewe shut off the engine, and carefully ran the car off the road on to a grassy path. He extinguished the lights and jumped out of the car. He took an electric torch from his overcoat pocket and after turning it on to see if it was in order he set off in the direction of the farm.

"We will not keep to the road, as there may be some one on the watch," he said. "Follow me, I know my way across the fields."

He clambered over the gate of a field and set off at a run, with Marsland following him closely. He led the way over ditches and across hedges and fences until they reached the meadow at the side of the farm. Before climbing the low, brick wall Crewe waited for Marsland.

"You watch the front of the house while I go to the back. If you see any one challenge him in a loud voice so that I can hear you, and I'll come to your assistance. If I want you I'll call out."

They climbed the wall and dropped noiselessly on

to the grass.   Crewe waited until Marsland had taken
up his station behind a plum-tree in the garden, and
then crept towards the kitchen door.   He stood outside the door listening intently for a few minutes, but
as he heard no sound he selected the right key from
the bunch he had borrowed from Gillett, and turned
the lock.   He waited to see if the sound of the turning lock had alarmed any one inside the house.   Slowly
he turned the handle, opened the door and stepped
noiselessly into the kitchen.

A few minutes later Marsland heard him approaching him from the back of the house.

"Come quickly," he said.   "Some one has been before us and found the money, but he is coming back
again."

Marsland silently followed Crewe along the side of
the house to the kitchen, and into the room where the
great grandfather clock stood.   Crewe flashed the
torch on it, and Marsland started back with a cry of
astonishment.   The wooden case had been smashed beyond repair.   It had been hacked and splintered with
a heavy weapon, which had not only battered in the
front of the case, but smashed the back as well.   Pieces
of the wood had been pulled off and flung about the
room.   About the bottom of the broken case several
sovereigns were lying.

"The treasure!" he cried.   "It was here then.   Has
he got away with it?"

"Most of it, but not all of it," said Crewe.   "See
here!"   He knelt down by the case, plunged in his
hand, and drew forth a canvas bag which clinked as
he held it up.   "This is the sort of bag that banks
use for holding sovereigns—the banks put a thousand

sovereigns into each bag and seal it up so as to render it unnecessary to count the coins every time the bags are handled. There are four of these bags still here."

"But where are they hidden?" asked Marsland, in amazement. "Where did you find this one? Wasn't it lying on the floor when you came in?"

"The old man devised a skilful hiding-place," said Crewe. "He fitted the case with a false back, and stowed his treasure in between. Look here!"

He flashed the light around the interior of the case, and Marsland, looking closely, saw that the back of it, which had been smashed, was a false one, skilfully let in about three inches in front of the real back. In the space between the two backs the eccentric old owner of Cliff Farm had concealed his treasure as he had obtained it from the bank.

"It's an ingenious hiding-place," said Crewe. "He laid the clock on its face, took off the back, fitted his false slide into a groove, stacked in his money-bags, replaced the proper back, and then restored the clock to its original position. You see, he was careful to make the space between the false and the real backs so narrow that there was very little possibility of the hiding-place being discovered by chance or suspicion. Even the man who has forestalled us with the solution of the cryptogram was unable to discover the treasure until he had recourse to the clumsy method of smashing up the clock. This is what he used to do it." Crewe pointed to an axe lying near. "With that he smashed the case, found the treasure, and carried off what he could. He would be able to carry four of these bags at a time—two in each hand. He has left these four for another trip. How many trips he has already made I do not know, but probably more than one."

"He may be back again any moment," said Marsland, lowering his voice to a whisper. "Hadn't we better hide?"

"He won't be back just yet," said Crewe confidently.

"What makes you so certain of that?"

"He was here when we saw the flash of light. That is less than half an hour ago. To walk from here with four of these bags to the cliff, down the path in the dark to the boat he has waiting for him would take more than half an hour."

"But what makes you think he has a boat? Why do you feel sure he has come by sea?"

"Because that is the better way to come if he wanted to escape observation. If he came by road he would have brought a vehicle and would have taken the whole of the treasure away in a few minutes. But in a vehicle he might be met along the road by some one who knew him."

"Have you any idea who it is?" asked Marsland.

"Some one who has solved the cryptogram or got it solved for him," said Crewe. "By making a tour of the second-hand bookshops in London he probably got in touch with some one who has made a study of cryptograms, and in that way got it solved. There are some strange human types in these big second-hand bookshops in London—strange old men full of unexpected information in all sorts of subjects."

"But how did he get a copy of the cryptogram? Could he have got possession of the copy I found on the stairs?"

"I think so."

"How?"

"Miss Maynard gave it to him."

"Miss Maynard!" echoed the young man. "How could she have got it? She left the house with me and did not come back. In fact, she was very much opposed to coming back when I suggested that we should do so in order to get it."

"If she had it in her possession at the house her opposition to your proposal to go back for it is quite reasonable. I think you said that after you found the dead body upstairs she rushed downstairs and waited outside for you. She had ample time to go into the room and take the cryptogram from the table where you placed it. Doubtless her main thought was that its presence might implicate Brett in some way."

"Then it is Brett who has taken this money and is carrying down the cliff to the boat?" said Marsland excitedly.

"Yes. Probably Miss Maynard is down at the boat keeping guard over the bags as he brings them."

"And you think he will come back here for the rest?" asked Marsland.

Crewe noticed the eagerness in the young man's voice: it seemed as if Marsland was excited by the thought of meeting Brett.

"He is not likely to leave £4,000 behind unless he knows the place is being watched."

"Let us go towards the cliffs and meet him," declared Marsland impatiently. "To think that I am to meet him face to face, and here of all places."

"We might miss him in the dark, and he might get clean away."

"Where shall we hide?" asked the young man, again

sinking his voice to a whisper. "He may reach here any moment now."

"He came in by the front door. The lock has not been injured, so apparently he has a key. You hide in the room on the left—just inside, close to the door. I will hide in the cupboard underneath the staircase. When he reaches the clock he cannot escape without passing us. Give him time to get the money, and as soon as he has the bags in his hands ready to start off, we will both spring out at him."

Crewe watched Marsland enter the sitting-room on the left and then opened the door of the cupboard beneath the staircase and crouched down. The cupboard opened into the hall, and through the crack of the door Crewe was able to see into the room where the shattered clock was. The door of the room where Marsland was hidden also commanded a view of the interior of the room in which the clock stood. The stillness was so complete that Crewe could hear the watch in his pocket ticking off the ebbing moments. Once the distant yelp of a sheep-dog reached him, then there was another long period of stillness. Twice his keen ear caught a faint creaking in the old house, but he knew they were but the mysterious night noises which are so common in all old houses: the querulous creakings and complaints of beams and joists which have seen many human generations come and go.

But, as the time dragged on without a sound to indicate that the thief was returning, Crewe found to his vexation that he had increasing difficulty in keeping his senses alert in that dark and muffled silence. The close and confined atmosphere of the cupboard, the lack of air, his cramped position, compelled an unconquerable drowsiness.

Then he heard a sound which drove away his drowsiness—the sound of a key in a lock. He heard the door creak as it was pushed back and then came steps advancing along the hall, stumbling along noisily, as though their owner thought that the need for precautions ceased when the front door was passed: that once inside the house he was safe, and need not fear interruption.

There was a scrape and a splutter, and a flickering flame in the hall; the thief had struck a match. Through the crack of the cupboard door Crewe watched the tiny blue flame grow larger, turn yellow, and burn steadily, and he could see the dim outline of a man's back and a hand shielding the match showing transparent through the flame. The thief had struck his match with his face to the doorway. The outline of his other hand approached, and the light grew brighter—the intruder had lit a piece of candle. As it burnt up the man turned towards the clock, and Crewe saw the face of Brett for the first time. His impression was of a pair of hunted nervous eyes roving restlessly in a livid waxen mask, a tense sucked-in mouth.

He saw no more. Apparently Marsland had been too excited to wait until the thief had the bags in his hands, for Brett started as though he heard a movement, and quickly extinguished his candle. There was a moment of intense silence, and then Crewe heard Marsland's voice raised in a strange high-pitched scream that made it seem unfamiliar.

"Powell, you traitor and murderer! I am Marsland

—Captain Marsland. I will kill you without sending you to trial."

Crewe had thrown open the door of the cupboard at the first sound of the voice, but before he could get on to his feet there was the deafening sound of a revolver shot, followed by the rush of feet and the fall of a body.

The bullet had missed the thief, and Marsland, advancing on him after firing, had been knocked over by Brett's rush for the door. Before Crewe could reach him across Marsland's prostrate form Brett had thrown open the door and was outside the house.

Crewe dashed for the door in pursuit. He caught a glimpse of a fleeing figure, bent nearly double to shield himself from another shot, running down the gravel path at amazing speed. Then the figure was swallowed up in the night.

Crewe followed, without waiting to find out how Marsland had fared. He failed to catch another glimpse of Brett, but had no doubt he would make for the path down the cliff, about a quarter of a mile away, Crewe, who had been a long-distance runner at school, and was in excellent training, knew that he would last the distance better than Brett.

He caught sight of Brett again before half the distance between the downs and the cliffs had been covered—a fantastic flying figure bobbing into view against the sky-line for an instant as he ran across the crest of a little hill, and as suddenly disappeared again. But that brief glimpse of the fugitive revealed to Crewe that Brett had mistaken his course: he was running too much to the right.

Crewe ran on steadily in a straight line for the path.
When Brett discovered that he had run too wide he
would have to curve back, taking almost a semicir-
cular course before he reached the beginning of the
path.   Crewe's course was the shorter—the cord to
Brett's bow, and would bring him to the path before
Brett could possibly reach it.   The detective slackened
pace slightly, and cast a glance over his shoulder to
see if Marsland was following him; but he could not
see him.

Crewe reached the hidden path, and waited, listening, by the bushes which concealed the entrance.   Soon
his quick ear caught the pad of footsteps, and as they
drew nearer they were accompanied by the quick
breathing of a man running hard.   Then the form of
Brett loomed up, running straight for the path.

Crewe sprang at him as he came close, but the runner saw his danger in time to fling himself sideways.
He was on his feet again in an instant, and made away
along the edge of the cliff, bounding along with great
jumps among the rocks from point to point and rock to
rock.   Crewe drew so close that he could hear Brett's
panting breath as he ran, but each time Brett with
a desperate spurt put a few more yards between them
again.   Once he staggered and seemed about to fall,
but he sprang up again and ran with the speed of a
hare.

They had reached the rocky headland which jutted
into the sea a hundred yards or more by the dangerous turn of the cliff road.   Crewe slackened his pace
to call out a warning to the man he was pursuing.

"Look out or you will fall over the cliff!" he cried.

Brett paused, turned irresolutely, and then began

slowly to retrace his steps. But as he did so a figure appeared suddenly out of the gloom and dashed past Crewe towards him.

"You dog, I have you!" screamed Marsland. "You cannot get away from me again."

"Look out, Marsland!" cried Crewe, springing after him. "You will both go over."

Marsland ran on without heeding, cursing savagely at the hunted man. Brett had fled away again at the sound of his voice, and Crewe could hear his gasping breath as he stumbled over the slippery rocks. The two figures appeared clearly against the sky-line for a moment as they raced towards the end of the headland. Then the foremost disappeared over the cliff with a scream. Brett, endeavouring to double in his tracks at the edge of the headland, had slipped and gone over.

Marsland was standing on the edge of the cliff, peering down into the sea mist which veiled the water below, when Crewe reached his side. Crewe drew him back.

"Come away if you don't want to follow him," he said. "We shall have to get the police out to look for his body, but perhaps the sea will carry it away."

CHAPTER XXV.

THE search for the body began in the morning, at low tide. Inspector Murchison had come from Staveley to superintend, and from the landing-place he and Sergeant Westaway directed the operations of the Ashlingsea fishermen who had been engaged to make the search.

Some of the townspeople who had walked up from the town to witness the proceedings thought that the body would be swept out to sea and never recovered, but the fishermen, with a deeper knowledge of a treacherous piece of sea from which they wrested their living, shook their heads. If the gentleman had fallen in near the deep water of the landing-place the undercurrent might have carried him out into the Channel, but there were too many reefs and sand-banks running out from the headland, and too many cross-currents, to let a body be carried out to sea.

They gave it as their opinion that the body would be found before high tide, either in one of the shallows near the big sand-bank, a quarter of a mile out, or in one of the pools between the reefs whose jagged, pointed edges showed above the surface of the sea nearer the headland.

The sea lay grey and still under an October sky of dull silver. The boats, as they came from Ashlingsea, put in at the landing-place to receive the instructions of the police officers standing there, and then started to search. There were two rowers in each boat, and standing at the stern was a man holding the rope to which the grappling irons were attached. Slowly and mechanically the boats were rowed out some distance to sea, and then rowed back again. The men in the stern watched the ropes in their hands for the first sign of tautness which would indicate that the grappling irons had hooked in to something. Frequently one of the irons caught on a piece of rock, and when this happened the boat had to be eased back until the irons could be released. The boats searching further out, near the sand-bank, used nets instead of grappling irons.

Crewe, who had driven over in his car from Staveley, after watching this scene for some time, turned back to the road in order to put up his car at Cliff Farm. Marsland had not accompanied him. The young man had motored over with his uncle, who, after hearing from his nephew a full account of the events of the previous night, had insisted on participating in the search for the missing man. Sir George Granville, on arriving at the headland, had scrambled down the cliff with some idea of assisting in the search, and at the present moment was standing on the landing-place with Inspector Murchison, gesticulating to the rowers, and pointing out likely spots which he thought had escaped their attention.

Crewe, on regaining his car, found Marsland leaning against it, contemplating the scene before him with indifferent eyes. He nodded briefly to the detective, and then averted his eyes. Crewe explained his intention regarding the car, and Marsland said he might as

U

well go down with him. He got up into the front seat
with the same listlessness that had characterized his
previous actions, but did not speak again till they
reached the farm.

At the house Crewe and Marsland met Detective
Gillett, who had gone there to store his bicycle pre-
paratory to watching the operations of the fishermen
searching for the body.

"I have had a pretty busy time since you came along
to us last night," he said, referring to the visit of
Crewe and Marsland to Ashlingsea police station to
report the fall of Brett over the cliff. "We got the
money—£12,000 altogether. There was £8,000 in the
motor-boat and £4,000 here in the bottom of the old
clock case, as you said."

"What about the girl?" asked Crewe. "Was she
there?"

Detective Gillett looked in the direction of Marsland
before replying.

The young man, with the same air of detachment
that had marked his previous actions, had wandered
some distance down the gravel-walk, and was care-
lessly tossing pebbles from the path at some object
which was not apparent to the two men in the porch.

"I found her searching along the cliffs with a lantern," said Gillett, in a low voice. "She was looking
for Brett; she told me that she had heard a scream and
she thought he must have fallen over accidentally. I
didn't enlighten her. Poor thing, she is half-demented.
She has got it into her head that she is responsible for
some document or paper which Brett had given into
her safe-keeping, and which she handed back to him

last night at his request before he went to the farm to look for the money."

"Doesn't she know what is in the paper?" asked Crewe quickly.

"Her mind is in such a state that it is useless to question her. She keeps repeating that it was to be opened in the event of his death. It was only after great difficulty I ascertained from her that she had given the paper back to Brett last night. I am anxious that Brett's body should be recovered in order to ascertain what its contents are."

"I should think the girl would have a fair idea of the contents."

"I think so too, but she is not in a fit state to be questioned at present, and may not be for some time. The strain has been too much for her. In my opinion she is in for a severe illness."

"Where is she now?"

"At the station. Of course, I had to take her into custody on a charge of attempting to steal this money. Whether the public prosecutor will go on with the charge or whether he will bring any other charge of a more serious nature against her remains to be seen."

Marsland, who had abandoned his stone throwing, had strolled back to the porch in time to hear Gillett's last remarks.

"It is a strange thing to find a girl of her type in love with such a scoundrel," he said.

"Quite a common thing," said Detective Gillett, speaking from the experience of the seamy side of life which comes under the attention of Scotland Yard. "There are some women brought up in good surroundings who seem to be attracted irresistibly to scoundrels.

You never know what a woman will do. By the by, it is a good thing, Mr. Marsland, that you did not hit him when you fired at him last night. If you had killed him I should have had to arrest you, and the case would have had to go to a jury. Of course, there is no doubt how it would have ended, but it would have been an unpleasant experience for you."

"I shouldn't have minded that," was the young man's answer.

Gillett regarded this declaration as bravado, and merely continued:

"As it is, you are virtually responsible for his death in frightening him over the cliff, but the law takes no account of that."

"I should prefer to have shot him," said Marsland.

"Ah, well, I must get away and see what they are doing," said the Scotland Yard detective, who obviously disliked Marsland's attitude. "I suppose I'll see you again during the day?"

When he had gone off towards the cliffs Crewe turned to Marsland and said:

"I am going to have another look at the place—now that this case is concluded."

He entered the house and Marsland followed him. The interior looked more sombre and deserted than ever. The fortnight which had elapsed since the tragedy—during which time the place had been left untenanted—had intensified the air of desolation and neglect that brooded over the empty rooms, had thickened the dust on the moth-eaten carpets and heavy old furniture, and gave an uncanny air to the staring eyes of the stuffed animals which hung on the wall in glass cases—dead pets of dead occupants of Cliff Farm.

Crewe and Marsland looked through the house, entered the room where the grandfather clock stood, and Crewe pointed out the mark of the bullet which Marsland had fired at Brett the previous night. In his excitement he had fired too high, and the bullet had gone into the wall about eight feet from the floor, between two photographs which hung on the wall. One of these photographs was of James Lumsden, the eccentric old owner of Cliff Farm, who had broken his neck by falling downstairs. The other was Frank Lumsden, whose dead body had been found in the house by Marsland thirteen days before.

"That was the second time I missed Brett," said Marsland, staring at the bullet hole in the wall between the photographs.

"The second time?" echoed Crewe. "Do you mean that he was the burglar at whom you fired a week ago?"

"Yes. I came into the room just as he was getting out of the window. I caught only a glimpse of him but I knew him instantly. I had a presentiment that he was near and that is why I happened to be wearing my revolver."

"What was his object in breaking into the house?"

"He wanted to be sure that I was the man he had to fear just as I wanted to be sure that he was the man I wanted to kill. An hour before I had broken into his rooms at 41 Whitethorn Gardens, for the purpose of making sure about him. I saw his photograph there, and that is all I wanted."

"And it was you and not he who was in the house

when Mrs. Penfield called out that the police were in the house?"

"Yes, that was I. I didn't understand why she called out, but it served as a warning to me that she expected him. And so when I got back to my uncle's I got my revolver out of the drawer. The first I heard of him being in England was when Inspector Murchison told us, although I was prepared in a way after finding that Lumsden had been here. Murchison spoke of him as Brett, but I did not know him by that name. So to make sure I got Mrs. Penfield out of the house by a hoax on the telephone and broke into the place in her absence. I did not know that it was you who came back with her."

"But his object in breaking into your room was probably to get some article of yours which would help to bring suspicion against you with regard to Lumsden's death. No doubt it was he who took the glasses which were subsequently found in the well. As you lost a pair of glasses in the storm and arrived at the farm without them, Miss Maynard probably mentioned the fact to Brett. Did you tell her that you had lost your glasses that night?"

"I forget. Oh, yes, I did! I mentioned it when we were looking at the cryptogram on the stairs."

"He was certainly an enterprising scoundrel."

"Don't you wish to know why I wanted to kill him?" asked the young man after a pause.

"I do, very much."

"I feel that I must speak about it," he said. "And you are the only man to whom I can. You heard Murchison tell us that Lumsden and Brett, as he called himself, had been tortured by the Germans but that they gave away no information. That is their version; let me tell you the truth about them. Both of them belonged to my company in France. Lumsden had been under me for four or five months and I had nothing against him. He was a fairly good soldier and I thought I could depend upon him. Powell—or Brett—had come over with a recent draft. One night when I was holding a short advanced trench to the south of Armentières I sent Lumsden and Brett out on a listening patrol. The trench we were holding was reached through a sap: it was the first of four or five that were being dug as jumping off places for an attack on the German trenches.

"It was just about midnight that I sent Lumsden and Brett out and they ought to have been back by 2 a. m. It was the middle of summer and dawn commenced about 3 a. m. Either they had been captured or had lost their way and were waiting for dawn. When it was light enough to see the landscape, two figures appeared on the parapet of a German trench in front about three hundred yards away. They were calling and gesticulating to us. At that distance it was impossible to make out what they were saying, but from their gestures we gathered that the Germans had deserted the trench and it was ours if we liked to go over and occupy it.

"It came as such a surprise that none of us stopped to think; but if we had stopped no one would have thought of treachery. The men went over the parapet —every one of them. It was a race—they were laughing and joking as to who should be there first. And when we were within forty yards or so there was a volley from rifles and machine guns. The bullets seemed to come from every quarter. The men were taken by surprise and they dropped almost before they had time to realize what had happened. I was one of the first to go down but it was only a bullet in the leg. As I lay where I fell I was struck by another bullet in the shoulder. Then I crawled to a shell hole for shelter. I found seven of my men there, all of whom had been hit.

"We were not there long before the Germans commenced to lob hand grenades into the shell hole. How I escaped death I do not know: it was an awful experience to see those murderous bombs coming down and to be powerless to escape from them. I saw several of my poor men with limbs blown off dying in agony, and from what I learned subsequently much the same thing had happened in other shell holes where men had crawled for shelter. Out of my company of 82—we were not at full strength, and I had only three second lieutenants besides myself—I was the only one to come through alive. And I lay in a state of semi-collapse in the shell hole for two days before being rescued when our men drove the Germans out of their trenches."

"A dreadful experience," said Crewe sympathetically.

"These two miserable loathsome creatures, Brett and Lumsden, to save their own lives, had beckoned my company into the trap. They had been captured by the Germans, and no doubt were tortured in order to make them do what they did. But as British soldiers they should have died under torture rather than be guilty of treachery. The memory of how my poor men died without having a chance to defend themselves haunts me day and night. I hear their voices—their curses as they realized that they were the victims of a horrible act of treachery, their cries and moans in the agony of death."

He sat down on the upturned clock case and buried his face in his hands.

CHAPTER XXVI

"Am I the first man to whom you have told this story?" asked Crewe, in a gentle voice.

"Yes," said Marsland. "It is not a story that I would care to tell to many. It is not a story that reflects any credit on me—my company wiped out through treachery on the part of two of my men."

"But when you came back to England, wouldn't it have been better to have reported the matter to the military authorities and have had Brett and Lumsden tried by court martial?"

"I did not know they were in England until I came down here: I thought that if they were not dead they were prisoners in Germany. I have no witnesses for a court martial, and after being off my head in the hospital for a couple of months I doubt if a court martial would believe my story. Counsel for the defence would say I was suffering from delusions. And it would have driven me mad if such a scoundrel as Brett had been acquitted by a court martial for want of evidence. Besides, the satisfaction of having him shot was not to be compared with the satisfaction of shooting him down myself just as if he were a dog."

"But it is a terribly grave thing to take human life—to send a man to his death without trial."

"I have seen so many men die, Crewe, that death seems to me but a little thing. If a man deserves death, if he knows himself that he deserves it a hundredfold, why waste time in proving it to others? If I had shot Brett I should doubtless have had to stand my trial for murder. But if the police searched all over England could they have found a jury who would convict me if I saw fit to tell my story in the dock? Told by a man in the dock it would carry conviction; but told by a man in the witness-box at a court martial it might not."

"I believe there is some truth in that," said Crewe, in a firm, quiet voice. "But it is a matter which must be put to the test."

Marsland stood up and fixed on him an intent gaze.

"What do you mean?" he said. "If Brett is dead he died by accident—by a fall over the cliff. The law cannot touch me."

The detective did not speak, but his eyes held the young man's glance intently for a moment, and then traveled slowly to the portrait of Frank Lumsden on the wall.

"I mean that," he said slowly.

"Do you know all?" Marsland asked, in a voice which was little more than a whisper.

"I know that it was you who shot Frank Lumsden."

"Yes, I shot him!" The young man sprang to his feet and uttered the words in a loud, excited tone which rang through the empty house. "And so little do I regret what I have done, that if I had the chance to recall the past I would not falter—I would shoot him again."

"Sit down again," said Crewe kindly. "Do not excite yourself. You and I can discuss this thing quietly, whatever else is to happen afterwards."

"How long have you known that I did it?" asked Marsland, after a pause.

"It was not until yesterday that I felt quite certain. What annoys me—what offends my personal pride is that my impetuous young friend Gillett picked you out as the right man before I did. He was wrong in his facts, wrong in his deductions, wrong in his theories, and hopelessly wrong in his reconstruction of the crime. He had no more chance of proving a case against you than against the first man he might pick out 'blindfolded from a crowd, and yet he was right. True, he came to the conclusion that he was wrong when I put him right as to the circumstances under which the tragedy occurred, but that doesn't soothe my pride altogether. If there is one lesson I have learned from this case, it is that humility is a virtue that becomes us all.

"But, after all, I do not think I have been so very long in solving the problem," the detective continued. "It is only thirteen days since the tragedy took place, and from the first I saw it was a complicated case. I never ruled out the possibility of your being the right man after Brett and Miss Maynard tried to sheet home Lumsden's death to you. I do not think she was fully in Brett's confidence—in fact, it is fairly obvious that he would not tell her the story of his treachery. But he knew that you had shot Lumsden and she caught at his conviction without being fully convinced herself. Brett's conduct was inconsistent with guilt. But it was consistent with the knowledge that Lumsden had met his death at your hands and that he himself would share the same fate if you encountered him.

"I am under the impression that he reached Lumsden a few minutes after you rode away from the spot, and that Lumsden was then alive. Probably he was able to breathe out your name to Brett. The latter helped the dying man into the motor-car and started to drive back to Staveley for medical aid, and after passing the thatched cottage on the right he became aware that Lumsden had collapsed and was past human aid. So he decided to take the body to the farm, and in order to disappear, without drawing immediate suspicion on himself, he tried to indicate that Lumsden was shot in the house.

"Then he disappeared because he was afraid of you. If he had got you under lock and key he might have risked coming into the open and giving evidence against you. But I rather fancy that his intention was to get away to a foreign country with old Lumsden's money, and then put the police on your track by giving the true circumstances under which Lumsden was shot."

"Did he write to you?" asked Marsland.

"No."

"I was always afraid he would. What put you on my track?"

"The conviction that you had warned this girl to clear out as Gillett had obtained some awkward facts against her. You were the only person who had any object in warning her, though Gillett thinks you had even less reason to do so than Brett. I regarded you merely as an average human being and not actuated by Quixotic impulses. I remembered that she had tried to sheet home the crime to you and therefore you had little cause to be grateful to her—so far I am in accord with Gillett. But if you knew that she had nothing to do with the tragedy, and if you felt that

Gillett's close questioning might lead to information from Brett which would tell against you, it was common sense on your part to get her out of the way."

"It is wonderful how you have divined my mind and the line of thought I followed," said the young man. His even tones were an indication that he was regaining his composure.

"Next, there was your attempt to kill Brett instead of helping me to capture him. That told against you. True, it indicated that you had what you regarded as a just cause of deadly hatred. But if you were under the belief that Brett had killed Lumsden it would have suited you better to capture him than to shoot him. Your shot at Brett showed me that you knew it was not Brett who had killed Lumsden, and also that you feared if Brett were arrested he would charge you with shooting Lumsden."

"Go on," said the young man breathlessly.

"There is little more to tell," said Crewe. "I had to ask Gillett yesterday not to refer to the doubts I had expressed to him regarding Brett's guilt. I was afraid he might do so in your presence and that would have put you on your guard. The final proof came when Gillett discovered the bullet in the tree where Lumsden fell. At the moment Gillett found the bullet I picked up these in the grass."

Crewe produced from his waistcoat pocket a pair of eye-glasses.

"So that is where I lost them!" exclaimed Marsland. "It never occurred to me before. I have no recollection of their dropping off—I suppose I was too excited to notice they had gone."

"Your meeting with him was accidental?" said Crewe.

"Quite. I had been out riding on the downs and when I struck the road I wasn't sure which way I had to go to get home. I saw a man coming along the road and I rode up to him. It was Lumsden. I tell you, Crewe, he was terrified at the sight of me—no doubt he thought that I had been killed in France. As I was dismounting and tying up my horse he pleaded for his life. He grovelled at my feet in the dirt. But I didn't waste much time or pity. I told him that he had earned death a hundredfold, and that the only thing I was sorry for was that I could kill him only once. He sprang up the bank in the hope of getting away, but I brought him down with a single shot. I saw that he was done for and I left him gasping in the agony of death. I had no pity—I had seen so many men die, and I had seen my company of good men go to their deaths because of his treachery.

"I rode back over the downs, and caring little which way I went I lost my way and was overtaken by the storm. Eventually I saw the farm and went there for shelter. And upstairs I found the dead body of this man Lumsden. It was the strangest experience of my life. I did not know what to think—I could not make out how the body had got there. And when Miss Maynard asked me to say nothing to the police about her having been there I thought it was the least I could do for her. I knew that whatever errand had brought her there she had nothing to do with his death."

There was a long pause during which the two men looked at one another.

"You think that I had just cause for shooting him?" said Marsland.

"I think you had no right to take upon yourself the responsibility of saying 'The law will fail to punish these men and therefore I will punish them without invoking the aid of the law!'"

"I do not regret what I have done. As I said before, if I had to go through it again I would not hesitate to shoot him. Perhaps it is because I have lived so much with death while I was at the front that human life does not seem to me a sacred thing. These two men deserved death if ever men did."

"You believe that no jury would convict you?" said Crewe.

"I do not see how a jury of patriotic Englishmen could do so. But I do not care about that. I have finished with my life; I do not care what becomes of me. When I recall what I have been through over there in France, when I think of the thousands of brave men who have died agonized deaths, when I see again the shattered mutilated bodies of my men in the shell-hole with me—I want to forget that I have ever lived. All that remains to be done is that you should hand me over to the police."

"That is a responsibility which I should like to be spared," said Crewe gravely. "I think we may leave it to Brett."

"To Brett!" exclaimed Marsland, springing to his feet again in renewed excitement. "Do you think he has escaped death; do you think he has got away?"

"I feel sure he was killed. But if his body is recovered the police will learn from it that it was you who shot Lumsden."

"How will they find that out?"

"The girl Maynard has told them that he had an important paper in his possession when he was drowned and that is why they are so anxious to recover the body. They do not know the contents of the document but it is an easy matter to divine them. Let us look at this matter in the way in which Brett must have looked at it after thinking it over carefully. He knew that you had shot Lumsden; he knew that if he met you his life would not be worth a moment's purchase. The shot you fired at him when he was breaking into your room at Staveley was an emphatic warning on that point, if he needed any warning.

"Do you think that he would not take steps to bring his death and Lumsden's death home to you in the event of his being shot down? If he had got out of the country, as no doubt he had hoped to do, he would have put the police on your track for shooting Lumsden. If the police recover Brett's body, they will find on it a document setting forth Brett's account of how Lumsden met his death. No doubt his and Lumsden's treachery will be glossed over, but your share in the tragedy will be plainly put."

"I overlooked all this," said Marsland quietly. "Let us walk across to the cliffs and see what they are doing."

They left the farm and walked slowly towards the cliffs, each immersed in his own thoughts. There were a few groups of people on the road, and another group at the top of the hill. Suddenly there arose a shout, and the people on the road started running towards the cliffs.

"They've found it!" The cry of the people on the

X

beach below was carried up to the cliffs, and Crewe and Marsland, looking down, saw the fishermen in one of the boats close to the cliff lift from the water the dripping, stiffened figure of a man which had been brought to the surface by the grappling irons.

THE END

www.ingramcontent.com/pod-product-compliance
Lightning Source LLC
Chambersburg PA
CBHW020432030726
47495CB00006B/1768